Praise for *What Men Think About Sex*

'Mark Mason is one of those writers whose natural voice is that of "everybloke" – the Nick Hornby of *Fever Pitch* or the John O'Farrell of *The Best A Man Can Get' Heat* magazine

'Full of wit and male competitiveness' *OK!*

'A boy's *Sex And The City*, it will make men nod in agreement and women laugh out loud' *U* magazine

'Mason creates a thoroughly incorrigible protagonist that you just can't help but warm to' *Daily Record*

'An outrageous and entertaining romp . . . Men will identify with the ridiculous antics, while women will have a good laugh at their expense' *Vivid* magazine

'Lots of sex, plenty of pints and full of humour . . . Very entertaining' *Irish Tatler*

'Hilarious and outrageous' *Publishing News*

D1464540

Mark Mason was born in 1971. He lives in London. *The C Words* is his third novel. His first two, *What Men Think About Sex* and *The Catch*, are also published by Time Warner Books.

Also by Mark Mason

What Men Think About Sex

The Catch

The C Words

MARK MASON

TIME WARNER
BOOKS

TIME WARNER BOOKS

First published in Great Britain as a paperback original in July 2005
by Time Warner Books

A CIP catalogue record for this book
is available from the British Library.

ISBN 0 7515 3705 5

Typeset in Berkeley by M Rules
Printed and bound in Great Britain by
Clays Ltd, St Ives plc

Time Warner Books
An imprint of
Time Warner Book Group UK
Brettenham House
Lancaster Place
London WC2E 7EN

www.twbg.co.uk

For my parents

So there I am, in the middle of the bookshop, thinking, Come on, Alex, how hard can this be?

And do you know what, the answer was 'very'. Even though the book's cover (I hadn't picked it up yet – didn't dare do that) proudly announced 'Over three million copies sold worldwide!' Even though the chart on the wall next to the till told me it was number four in the bestseller list. Even though at least two other people had bought copies while I'd been in the shop (twenty minutes and counting, trying to summon up the nerve), and no, I had to be honest, they didn't look like complete losers. Or losers at all, come to that.

I gathered my courage and managed to pick the book up. 'There's no need to be such a wimp,' I told myself. 'Just buy the bloody thing. You're thirty-four years old, for crying out loud.' But that was the problem. Aren't you supposed to have this all sorted by your thirties? It's your teens when you're meant to have problems dealing with the opposite sex.

And it wasn't just the shame. It was the lack of romance. A *self-help* book. About finding a *partner*. Whatever happened to red roses? Then my inner voice chirped up again: 'Stop all that. You know it's not true. You went through it the other day. Now take the book to the till and *buy* it.'

1

I knew my inner voice was right.
But even so . . .
Even so.

Three days earlier. My flat (outskirts of a town in Kent). Rosie, a university mate, was round.

'That's it, keep an open mind. Find out about something before you dismiss it.'

'Rosie, it's not that I haven't got an open mind, it's that I've got a mind. Who'd read a book like this?'

'Me, for a start.'

Which was true. I couldn't understand it. In the thirteen years I'd known her, not once had Rosie shown the slightest interest in this sort of book. Everything from Jane Austen to *Bridget Jones* via *The Shipping News*, yes. But this? Never. Yet here she was, with her very own copy of *The Road To Commitment – Finding A Partner In Your Thirties*. By Susanna Grove. *Doctor* Susanna Grove, no less.

'Why are *you* reading *this*?'

'Clue's in the title, don't you think?'

'Yeah, but why do you need help from a quack author?'

Rosie laughed. Her teeth showed white against her bronzed skin (we'd had some good weather lately, and due to a Spanish mother Rosie's skin is dark enough to start with). 'She's not a "quack author".'

'She must be. Everyone who writes this sort of book's a quack. They're snake-oil salesmen for the soul.'

'If that's true, why do their books sell so many copies?'

'Because there's one born every minute, that's why. These books are for people who are desperate, not for people like us. They're skilfully packaged to take . . .' I turned the book over '. . . eight pounds ninety-nine off people who don't

2

know any better. Which is why I'm surprised you parted with your cash. I mean, I bet you Susanna Grove is a made-up name for a start. Designed to create the right impression. Like Laura Ashley. And she's probably not even a real doctor. Just says she is. Like . . .' I couldn't think of an example.

'Dr Hook?' suggested Rosie.

'Dr Hook wasn't a real doctor?!' I clasped a hand to my forehead. 'And there was I, for all those years, thinking his advice on being in love with a beautiful woman was backed by sound medical credentials.'

'Alex, this book is aimed at people *exactly* like us.'

'What, you're saying we're desperate? Speak for yourself.'

Rosie smiled. It was a smile that suggested she'd expected this sort of reaction from me. 'No, we're not desperate. But we are older than we used to be.'

'Meaning?'

'When you get to your mid-thirties, you start to hear a faint ticking sound, don't you?'

'Do you?'

'Well, I have. Time's running out. Things have changed.' She paused. 'I know what you're saying, Alex. You're right, we're in fairly similar positions. We've both got our own teeth, we're on the good-looking side of "adequate" . . .'

'Stop it with this flattery, Rosie, you're making me blush.'

'. . . we can attract people, maybe even charm them. But that's not enough any more. We're looking for more than just someone who fancies us. We're looking for someone we can spend the rest of our lives with.'

'Yeah, but why do you need Dr Susanna Grove to help you? You've done all right up to now when it comes to attracting people. You've got your own business, for God's sake.' It's called Big Day Out. One of those firms that organises 'experiences' you can buy as a treat for someone – hot-air ballooning, weekend at a health spa, that kind of thing.

'So?'

'So why would someone with their own business need a self-help book?'

'Just because I'm good at negotiating preferential deals with Silverstone race track it doesn't mean I'm going to be good at finding a boyfriend, does it? Not the right boyfriend, anyway. That's what I'm saying. Perhaps there's more to it than "keep trying until you find Mr Right". Perhaps you have to think it through before you even look for Mr Maybe.'

For the first time, I had to concede that Rosie might have a point. A book I certainly didn't need to read would be called *Temporarily Escaping Singledom: How To Casually Find Yourself In Relationships That Last For A Few Months, Or In The Odd Case A Couple Of Years, But Which Always Peter Out Sooner Or Later*. Granted, for some of my romantic career I hadn't been looking for anything permanent. But now I was. And though I thought I'd found it with Amy, it turned out I was wrong.

Perhaps Rosie sensed what I was thinking. 'You've got to remember that meeting people gets harder the older you are. More and more of them are getting married or settling down, so the pool of available talent gets smaller all the time. The older you get, the more important it is that your next choice is the right one. This isn't a game any more. It's your happiness we're talking about. It's not unromantic to put some thought into that. It's common sense.'

Perhaps. In the eight months since I'd split up with Amy, I'd been in potentially romantic situations with two women, both of them about my age. One was a friend-of-a-friend-of-an-acquaintance, who made a point of saying on our first and only date that she wasn't interested in casual flings any more. There was no Glenn Close menace in her tone, but the implication was clear enough. The other woman, who I met at a party, shared my keenness at the end of our second date to turn the romantic potential into reality, but after two weeks of enjoyably vigorous reality, we saw that the relationship's long-term chances were minimal. Both women said the same thing, though, when I suggested that we could still be friends. 'No thanks,' they said, 'I've got enough friends, I don't need any more friends, I need a partner.' No one had ever said that to me before. Often, in the past, I've stayed friends with a girlfriend after we split up. Still friends with Amy, for instance – the person I thought really was The One, except she kept pushing for us to settle down and have children. She'd tell you what she told me (more than a few times) before we parted, that I was 'scared of commitment'. But I don't think I am scared of commitment. It's just that I don't see why a couple have to express it by the woman getting pregnant right this minute. I think you should have some fun first, see a bit of the world together. That's all.

'As it says in the book . . .' continued Rosie.

'Stop! Stop right there! Already, Rosie, you are beginning to display the glint in the eye and the robotic voice normally seen in members of religious cults. You are a dear friend of mine. *Please* don't turn into one of those people who reads a book and then starts every sentence with "As it says in the book".'

She smiled. 'All right, point taken. Although to be fair to Dr Susanna, I haven't found any bits in the book where she asks for money or major organs.'

'You will. They always leave that stuff till the end. By

chapter twelve you'll be living in a cardboard box and down to your last kidney.'

With the aid of a cushion and a powerful throwing arm, Rosie signalled that the time for my flippancy was over. 'As I was about to say,' she continued, 'the book points out, and I, a free-thinking individual, *agree* with it, that our generation needs new guidance. People are waiting until they're in their thirties to settle down. That hardly ever happened in our parents' time. They were married and having families much younger than that. So we need advice on how to do it, what the pitfalls are, what's the best way of making it work.'

Again, I couldn't find anything there to disagree with. But still it depressed me. It all seemed so chilling. 'Why does it have to be Dr Susanna Grove who advises us, though?' I pronounced the name much as a High Court judge would pronounce the name of a pop star. 'I mean, who is she? I've never met the woman. She could be barking mad for all I know. Isn't it a bit sad getting advice on the most important decision in your life from a complete stranger?'

'I know what you mean,' said Rosie. 'But we need books like this because we haven't got Great-Aunt Ethels.'

'What's a Great-Aunt Ethel? Is that some new rhyming slang?'

'No, Alex, a Great-Aunt Ethel is, funnily enough, a Great-Aunt Ethel. Or that's what she was in my family, anyway. She sat in her front room, all day every day, dispensing tea and advice. Everyone used to go and see her. Not just people in our family, the whole neighbourhood. She knew everything that had happened since before the First World War, every marriage, every couple that had gone out together, or "courted" as I suppose she'd have said, every child that was born, every affair that had been covered up. You could go to her with anything that was on your mind, anything at all, because she'd seen it all before.'

'But the extended family's dead, so relationship experts are the new great-aunts?'

'You could say that. OK, they get their expertise from studying surveys and speaking to clients, but they're basically the same as Great-Aunt Ethel in her front room. There are patterns in human behaviour, things that tend to happen the same way for the same sort of people, and once you've spotted those you're pretty well placed to dish out the advice.'

'Mmm. Maybe.'

'And if you're going to take advice, you might as well take it from someone who's sold three million copies. Don't you think?'

'Mmm.'

She held up the book. 'You should get yourself a copy. You did mess up with Amy, after all.'

I didn't say anything.

Rosie looked at her watch. 'God, it's ten past five. I'd better be getting back into town. I'm going out for dinner.'

'Book paying dividends already, is it?'

Rosie laughed. 'With a couple of girlfriends. And before you ask, no, the book hasn't made me challenge my thinking quite *that* much.'

'OK, bring it off the page, make it travel. On a green.'

The Road To Commitment was on the floor beside me. Yes, bravery had finally won the day in Waterstone's. But I'd made sure the book was tightly wrapped in the bag, which I then sandwiched between two newspapers. Not the sort of book you want to be seen with, especially by your work colleagues.

The green light on the table in front of me lit up briefly.

I leaned into the microphone and said, quietly but authoritatively, as I had been instructed: 'Sinuchi – drive into the future.'

The producer (I think his name was Dom) looked back at me through the window that separated the control room from the studio. At least I think he was looking at me. Despite the fact we were inside, he was wearing sunglasses. Designer sunglasses. 'Great one, Alex. Beautiful. Bee. Yoo. Tee. FULL. You *am* de man.'

'Er, thank you.'

'I mean, you really got the *feel* of the ad, you know? When the car pulls away at the end, when it's taken that final curve on the mountain, *that's* the feel we wanted to get, and with that tag line *that's* the feel you have deeeee-livered. To the *max*.'

I smiled nervously. I would have said something as well, but over Dom's shoulder I could see Mick, the forty-something studio engineer, using his right hand to mime a guess about Dom's main leisure activity. I couldn't trust myself to speak without laughing.

'OK, that's a wrap, people. In the can.'

Yes, this is what I do for a living. I am a voice-over artist. Three or four times a week I go into small, expensively equipped studios in Soho and read out lines like 'Sinuchi – drive into the future.' Or perhaps, 'Coming soon on the Discovery Channel . . .' Or then again, I might even be recording the narration for that documentary on the Discovery Channel itself. They're the really long gigs. Sometimes they've been known to take an hour.

'What sort of a job is that for a grown man?' you ask. I'm really not sure how to answer you. It wasn't something I ever set out to do. In my previous life, when I had proper jobs, I worked for one of the big supermarket chains. We had to throw together an in-house video package for some of the bosses at head office and didn't have time to get a professional voice-over artist in. We all had a go at doing it ourselves and my effort was deemed the best. Somehow a copy found its way into the hands of the advertising agency we used, and one of the producers there said I wasn't half bad, maybe I should try and get into it properly. She put me in touch with an agent, who helped me put together a tape showing what I could do (a 'voice-reel') . . . And six years later here I am. Sitting in a studio saying, 'Sinuchi – drive into the future.'

I went through to the control room, said thanks and goodbye to Mick, politely declined Dom's offer of a "cino and breeze-shoot, man', and set off to my agent's office, which is just round the corner from Mick's studio, in a building that the Victorians used as a warehouse but which these days is peopled by media professionals of various types. Langley and Langley take up two whole floors of very well-appointed office space.

I got there to find this week's receptionist on the phone. Langley's get through work-experience volunteers like Stalin's gulags got through dissidents. No surprise they're kept so busy. The voice-over section's only one part of the agency. They represent actors and actresses as well. Film, TV, theatre, the lot. The whole place employs not far short of a hundred people. I sat down to wait, and picked up a copy of *Vanity Fair.* One of Langley's more famous clients was this month's cover star.

The rather fey-looking receptionist looked up. 'Can I help you?'

'Yeah – Alex Richards – hopefully Kathy's left some contracts for me to sign?' Kathy's my agent.

He began to search through a pile of papers on his desk. Before he got very far, though, the doors were flung open and a man in his late fifties appeared, about six foot three, with sandy, shoulder-length hair that was raffishly untidy, and a ruddy complexion. He wore a purple and turquoise Hawaiian shirt, khaki shorts whose fly-zip had lost a battle with his formidable belly by an inch and a half, and deck shoes with no socks. The sole of the right shoe had separated from its upper, and hung down like a thirsty dog's tongue.

One of Miles's more sober outfits.

In his right hand he held a magnum of Pol Roger champagne, which he thrust towards the receptionist. 'Be a good chap, would you? Get that round to Neville Saggers at SDZ.' A rival agency. 'Put this in with it.' He took a compliments slip from the desk and scribbled a message on it, chuckling to himself.

Turning round, he noticed me. 'Ah, if it isn't the man Richards!' he boomed. 'The finest voice-over artist in the land!' He strode over to shake my hand. The smell of booze on his breath reached me half a second before he did.

'Hello, Miles. Back early from lunch, aren't you? It's only twenty past four.'

He grinned. 'My dear Alex, the Good Lord did not create Château Haut-Brion 'sixty-four so that I could drink one piddling little glass of it and be back at my desk before my fucking secretary, now did He?'

'No, Miles.'

'No, Miles. He created that wonderful, heavenly, sensuous liquid to be savoured. To be lingered over. To be RELISHED!'

'Of course, Miles. By getting back here any earlier you'd have been mocking the Almighty.'

He started to reply, but a hiccup caught him unawares. Instead he just nodded.

Miles Langley was not, by all accounts, one of the better theatrical agents to enter the business at the end of the 1960s. What he was talented at, however, was spotting other agents who were good at the job, charming them, paying them well, and getting them to work for him. He hasn't got a feel for the job itself, but he has got a feel for people who've got a feel for it, and he's happy to let them bring the cash rolling in. Underneath the Good-Time Charlie exterior, and despite the fact that he's permanently half drunk, and often completely drunk, Miles knows exactly what he's doing when it comes to running a business. As proved by the six-bedroom house in Kensington, the yacht, the five grand a month he pays to his first wife, the five grand a month he pays to his second wife (the first was only on three until she found out), the Ferrari (inevitably it's red) . . . the list goes on. If you're wondering who the other Langley is, by the way, don't bother. There isn't one. Miles called his agency Langley and Langley out of sheer bragging confidence. 'So good I named it twice.' He's all right in small doses, but he can become a bit irritating if you get trapped with him at the Christmas party.

'What's with the champagne?' I asked.

Miles gave a sad shake of his head. 'Bet. I said my artists would win more awards than his lot at that ceremony the other night. Bloody judges. What do they know?' He paused for a subsidiary hiccup. 'And how does Alex find life at the moment? I trust you're getting plenty of work?'

'I'm doing all right, Miles, you know.'

He put an arm round my shoulders. 'Splendid, splendid.

You just let me know if Kathy starts to slack. She'll be across my knee within the hour.' He gave a wink, then turned for his office. But halfway across reception he stopped and turned back. He looked me up and down, like a photographer assessing a model. 'Y-e-e-e-s,' he said thoughtfully. 'Yes. I think you might very well be the chap for the job.'

'Job?'

He retraced his steps, put a hand on my shoulder. 'Very important job, Alex.'

'Really?'

'Really. Only thing is – no money in it.'

'Do you think that's the sort of job you should be getting for your clients?'

'There's no money in it, dear boy, because the job itself is its own reward.'

'What is it?'

'Coming to New York with me for three nights.'

'Miles – honestly – I didn't know you were that way inclined.'

He pursed his lips. 'Well, I've been trying to deny it to myself for years, but sometimes you just can't hide any more . . . No, seriously, Alex, New York. Me, you and my accountant.'

I began to see what he might be on about. For a few months now he's been talking to a big American agency about selling out to them. 'Ah, business trip?'

'Indeed. We're motoring along nicely, I think it's getting to the stage where we'll need to meet up again soon, have a detailed look at the books. So I'll have to ask Tony to come. But I've been mulling it over – all those bloody figures are enough to send anyone mad. Reckon what I need is someone from the cliff-face to mosey along with us, have dinner with the Yanks, a few drinks, tell 'em what it's like doing voice-overs, generally help with the charm offensive.'

'Are you sure?'

'Alex, my child, would I be asking you if I wasn't sure?'

No, but you might be asking me because you're pissed. Although, on second thoughts, this idea clearly pre-dated his lunch. 'Well, if you'd like me to come along, Miles, I'd be honoured.'

'Au contraire, au con*traire*. The honour is all mine.'

I laughed, shook his outstretched hand. A free trip to New York paid for by a man who won't even look at a hotel with fewer than five stars? At least some of the honour had to be mine. 'Thanks, Miles. I really appreciate that.'

'Glad to welcome you on board.' He leaned a little closer. 'We'll have a *blast*.'

Well, well. Something to look forward to.

She was at the cinema again today. This woman at the Saturday morning kids' cartoon thing I sometimes take Joe and Georgia to. I've seen her a few times before, she takes her little girl along. I don't know why but I've got it into my head she might be a single parent too; it's something about the way it's only ever her, I never see her with a husband or a boyfriend, so I thought maybe she's in the same position as me. Well, probably not exactly the same, because if she is divorced or separated then the girl will probably live with her, mothers normally get custody, don't they? But apart from that she's in the same position, I mean.

Anyway, we got to the cinema this morning and we started queuing up. Then the next person who turned up was *her*, and so she was in the queue behind us, and I thought, Come on, say something to her. I'd been worried it might be a naff thing to do, you know, trying to get talking to a woman just because you thought she was a single parent. But then I thought, No, there was that film where Hugh Grant did it, wasn't there, where he pretended to have a son so he could go along to a single parents' club and get off with all the women. I thought that was stupid, having Hugh Grant play a bloke who has difficulty with women, I mean, all he has to do to attract a woman is say, 'Look, I'm Hugh

14

Grant'. But I remembered the film was done from a novel, and everyone who read it said it was very good, you know, believable, so I thought maybe it wasn't such a naff thing to do. There are so many single parents around nowadays, they have to meet new people somewhere, don't they? (I haven't read the book myself, I've only seen the film.)

I got nervous, you know, wondering what I could say to get talking to this woman. When she said anything to her little girl (who's called Milly – obviously I don't know what the woman's called, her daughter just calls her Mummy) I felt relieved, in a way, because it stopped there being a possibility that I could talk to her, took the ball out of my court, if you like. I get that quite a lot when it comes to talking to women. Something'll happen that lets me pretend I could have chatted to them if only that thing hadn't happened. But you can't really pretend, can you? Not to yourself.

One of the first things you always say to people when you get talking – not just women, I mean anyone – is 'What do you do?', and I hate that bit of the conversation because I'm an accountant, and whenever you say that people go all quiet and say 'Oh'. Then they say 'Right', like they're trying to pretend it's an interesting job. Of course it isn't an interesting bloody job. I try to make it sound a bit better by telling them I work for an agency that represents actors and actresses and people who do voice-overs. Then they say 'Oh, that must be interesting', and it gives us the chance to talk about films and TV programmes. But I never seem to find the right things to say. It's not that I don't have thoughts about the films and programmes I watch. I do, all the time. It's just that I can never seem to remember them when it comes to talking to people.

Anyway, the queue was moving quite quickly, and soon it got to me being about two from the front. I thought, Come on, if you don't say something soon you'll have lost your chance, and I was trying like mad to think of something good to say. Why can't you just say 'Hello, I like you, please can I talk to you?', that's what I always want to say. But of course you're not allowed to do that. You have to say something clever to impress a woman, or at least something casual, you know, relaxed, something that lets you pretend you don't fancy her. Even though she must know you do otherwise why would you be trying to talk to her?

By now it was just the person in front of me buying their tickets. I thought, This is it, this is your last chance. I told myself I had to do it because if I didn't I'd spend the whole week thinking, Why didn't you say something to her . . . And then Georgia asked if she could have some popcorn. I told her yes she could, what kind did she want? She said the one that tastes like crisps (that's what she calls the salty kind), and then I asked Joe if he wanted any popcorn, and he said no, he wanted chocolate. So I asked him what sort of chocolate he wanted, and he said Maltesers. By that time the person in front of me had gone and it was my turn to get served. And of course I tried to pretend that I really had been going to say something to the woman, it was only Georgia asking about popcorn that stopped me. But like I say, you can't pretend to yourself.

I spent most of the time in the cinema telling myself it was all right, I could still talk to the woman at the end. (She sat about four rows in front of us.) But I wasn't sure that I would. I started to worry again about not being a very good dad. I think the problem is I haven't really grown up enough. I know it sounds silly, but I feel like I'm still a kid myself. Like this morning, when the cartoons were on, I was . . . well, I feel stupid saying it, but I really enjoyed them. They showed this Tom and Jerry one. Most of the cartoons are modern ones, but they show some old ones as well; all the kids love them. At one point Jerry was running along the edge of a carpet trying to get away from Tom, and Tom was pulling the carpet towards him really fast. Then when he got the end of the carpet in his paws Jerry was gone, and they showed you this little bump under the carpet and you knew Jerry must be hiding under it, and . . . well, the point is, I thought it was brilliant. I really loved it, it made me want to laugh. I bet you none of the other parents were thinking that. They were probably thinking responsible things, planning their careers and reviewing their finances and all that sort of stuff. They must have been really bored by Tom and Jerry.

I've been waiting for years to feel like I've grown up, but I'm thirty-three now and it still hasn't bloody happened. I wish I'd grown up before I got married. Definitely before we had Joe and Georgia. Blokes are supposed to sow their wild oats before they settle down, aren't they? which is just a polite way of saying shag lots of women, and I definitely didn't do that. You're not going to shag many women if you can't even talk to them. So this thing of still feeling like I'm a kid makes it really hard when it comes to thinking of myself as a dad. Last week, for instance, it was Joe's birthday (he was six), and I'd given him this toy. Georgia (she's four) could get it to work and he couldn't. He had a tantrum about it, and I told him it was OK, it didn't matter. But all the time I was thinking, That's how I get, frustrated and bothered because I'm no good with people. So really I'm no more grown-up than my six-year-old son. That can't be right, surely?

I do want to be a good dad. I miss Joe and Georgia. I get to see them every weekend and once during the week as well. My solicitor's told me we can soon apply for a new custody order which would let me see them more often than that, but I still miss them. I don't miss Anita. Not really. I don't think we ever really loved each other. I did try to make a go of our marriage, I really did. I think you should. Marriage isn't something you should treat lightly. But I don't think ours was ever going to work. I reckon Anita only married me because I'd got a secure job. She used to say she loved me, but that was usually only when I'd just bought her a birthday present or a Christmas present or I'd paid for her gym membership. I wasn't 'high-powered' enough for her. She got drunk one New Year's Eve and told me that. We never talked about it afterwards, but I've never forgotten it. She probably didn't like the fact I was an accountant. Even though it was steady it wasn't very exciting. Not like being the owner of a chain of gyms.

What I *really* want is the chance to be romantic. Anita never really liked my gestures. They seemed to irritate her. When I say 'romantic' I don't mean the corny things, like red roses or huge boxes of chocolates, I mean the little things you think of yourself. The other month, for instance, I bought a new camera, a digital one, and it turned out you could take films with it. Only short ones, fifteen seconds, and they don't have sound, but still, they look good. It gave me an idea, something I could do if I had a girlfriend. I'd hold the camera out at arm's length and take a film of myself holding up cards with my other hand. The first one would say 'Hello', the second one would say 'Just a short message to say . . .' and the last one would say '. . . I love you'. Then I'd download the film on to my computer, and when I was out I'd send my girlfriend a text, telling her to turn the computer on and play the film. I quite often have ideas for things like that. I'd love to be in a relationship with someone I could do those sorts of things for. I think I'd be good in a relationship like that, I'd be confident about it. It's just getting past that first stage I'm no good at.

I suppose that's why I've been thinking about this woman at the cinema so much. If I got talking to her I'd probably find there wasn't anything that special about her, not so I'd fall head over heels in love with her, I mean. I've probably got her on my mind just because she's an example of me not being able to talk to women.

Whatever the reason, when the lights went up at the end of the film, I got nervous again. I knew I should try and say something to her, and I was worried that I wouldn't do it. Then I'd end up hating myself for not taking my chance. While everyone was waiting for the aisle to clear I noticed her daughter had a Disney Princess toy. Georgia's got one of those too (she's mad about it), and I had an idea. I thought if I could get close to the woman and her daughter I could say to Georgia (so that the woman and daughter would hear as well), 'Look, Georgia, that little girl's got a Disney Princess like yours.' I thought this was a good idea, because it would be a natural way to start talking to her, not an awkward way that makes you sound like a prat.

So the aisle was slowly clearing and the woman was getting closer to our row, and we were getting closer to the end of it too. I was thinking, This is it, you've got to do this. She got a bit nearer, and we were almost at the end of the row. I thought, We mustn't get out into the aisle before she's up to our level, because if she's behind us I won't be able to do the line, so I said to Joe and Georgia, 'Hang on a minute'. I went back to our seats to 'check' we'd got everything. That slowed us up just enough so that when we came out of the row we were right next to the woman and her daughter.

By now I was really nervous, but I made myself go through with it. I looked down at the girl's toy, and I said, 'Oh look, Georgia, that little girl's got a Disney Princess just like yours', and Georgia said, 'Yes', and she looked at the girl. The girl looked back at her but Georgia wouldn't say anything, she was really shy. And I looked at the woman, and she smiled back at me, and I couldn't believe it, the plan had *worked*! I thought, Right, now you can start talking to her.

But I couldn't say anything. I was too nervous. I'd been so worked up about getting the comment about the toy right that I hadn't thought about what might happen next. And before I knew it the woman had moved to one side to get round some people, and so she looked away from me, and then it was too late, she was too far away for me to be able to have another go at talking to her. I suppose I could have chased after her and tried to say something else, but that would have looked a bit weird. It would have been obvious that I was trying to chat her up. That's what I meant earlier, to be good at chatting up, you have to make it look like you're not chatting up, otherwise you look like a prat.

Interesting evening. Met this Tony bloke. Miles fixed it up so we could get to know each other before New York. Then, being Miles, he couldn't make it (claimed it was a rearranged business meeting, but I bet it was a blonde). Told us to go ahead without him.

Miles had said six. I got to the office about five past. 'Hi, I'm here to see Tony Faulkner. He's expecting me – Alex Richards.'

The receptionist dialled Tony's number. 'There's no reply,' he said. 'It's just ringing out . . .'

At which point the door on the other side of reception opened. The man who appeared through it looked at me for a moment, but seemed unsure as to whether he should speak.

'Tony?' I said after a pause.

He broke into a smile. 'Are you Alex?'

I crossed over to him. 'Pleased to meet you.'

'Yes,' he said, shaking my hand, 'pleased to meet you too. I'm Tony.'

I'd seen him around the office once or twice before, without realising who he was – I'd never seen him talking to anyone, just carrying files around. Short and stocky, but good stocky, keeping-in-shape stocky rather than over-eating

21

stocky. His light grey suit was that of a man who doesn't take much interest in suits. His dark hair was cropped short. Although it looked good on him, I couldn't imagine, somehow, that he'd ever had it cut any other way.

'I wasn't sure whether you were here or not,' he said, 'so I thought I'd come down to reception and see.'

'Right, yeah. Sorry, I'm a couple of minutes late . . .'

'Oh no, no, no, sorry, I didn't mean that, I wasn't saying you were late, it was only five minutes after all, I wasn't saying that. I wouldn't even have come down to reception, I did try calling down,' he turned to the receptionist, 'but it was engaged, so I thought I might as well come down, save you waiting, you know . . .'

The receptionist smiled, not really knowing what to say.

'Anyway,' I said, 'not to worry, we're both here now. Shall we go for a drink?'

'Yeah, good idea.'

'Where do you want to go?'

'Anywhere, I'm not fussed.'

'How about the Pillars?'

He nodded enthusiastically. 'Great, yeah. Let's go there.'

'So – New York,' I said as we got the lift down. 'Not the worst place to go on a business trip, is it?'

'No, it's great. Well, I wouldn't know, to be honest. I've never been. But I imagine it's great. Have you been?'

'Yeah, a few times. I love it.'

'Great.'

'I've never had someone pay for me to go before, though. Pretty generous of Miles.'

'Mmm.'

'I know he's a bit larger-than-life at times, but you can't deny he's a good boss.'

Tony didn't say anything. Didn't he like Miles for some reason? I decided to skirt round office politics, talk about the merger as a whole. 'What does everyone think about it? Worried about their jobs?'

'No,' he said as we headed out on to the pavement, 'the Americans just want to get a foothold in the UK, that's all. They'll leave the firm pretty much as it is. If anything, they'll be giving us money to expand.'

'One last big payday for Miles, then.'

'Big? You mean enormous. Someone said to him in the office the other day, they said, "Miles, if this goes through will you buy yourself another Ferrari?", and he laughed and he said, "If this goes through I'll buy Ferrari".'

'I see what you mean.'

'Obviously that's not *literally* true. I mean, if you wanted to buy Ferrari you'd need hundreds of millions, well, probably billions . . . Miles won't have anything like that amount . . . but what he said about it being more than enough to buy just one Ferrari, that's true.'

'Right, yeah. I see.' I got the feeling I'd have to wait a few minutes for Tony to calm down, lose the meeting-someone-new nerves he seemed to have. Underneath his awkward exterior, I sensed, there was a fundamentally decent bloke trying to get out. I liked him already.

We got to the pub.

'Right,' I said, 'what do you want?'

'No, no, no, I'll get them,' replied Tony, reaching for his wallet.

'No, it's OK. What do you want?'

'Are you sure? I mean, I could . . .'

Behind him a couple were leaving. 'Look,' I said, 'you grab that table, I'll get the drinks. What do you want?'

'Oh, OK. Er, pint of bitter, please.'

As I waited to get served I looked over and saw him take a magazine and a ballpoint pen from his briefcase. He turned to a page near the back and studied it, making the occasional mark in the margin with his pen.

I took our drinks over and sat down. I chinked my Guinness against his bitter.

'Cheers.'

'Cheers.'

'Here's to New York.'

'Yes,' he said. 'Here's to New York.'

I saw that his magazine was *What Hi-Fi?* The page he'd been marking was the classified ads. 'Buying something?'

He licked a bit of beer froth from his top lip. 'I was thinking of getting a new amp.'

'Oh yeah? What sort?'

'There's a Harman Kardon they reckon's quite good. Three hundred and fifty.' He sounded less nervous now. I guessed he knew an awful lot about hi-fis, and would feel comfortable talking about them. As he talked me through some of the other amps on the market, I found that both guesses were correct.

'Right,' I said, when the mini-lecture was over. 'Between the Harman Kardon and the Sherwood, then, you think?'

'Think so.' He sniffed, kept nodding for a moment. 'But then, I think, you know, can I really afford it? Well, like, I *can* afford it. But what I mean is, I reckon . . . probably what I'd rather do is spend the money on my children.'

'I see. How many have you got?'

'Two. Joe, he's six, and Georgia. She's four.'

'Right.' I nodded. I never know what to say when people talk about their kids.

'You know, I'd like a new amp, but I can get by with my old one. I think I'll probably end up saving the money for August. I've got Joe and Georgia for a week then. Anita's going away. She's my ex-wife. We're divorced. Well, obviously we're divorced, otherwise . . . Anyway, I think, you know, probably I'll use the money when I've got Joe and Georgia. Treat them a bit.' He nodded again, as if he wanted to repeat 'treat them a bit' but couldn't think of another phrase.

We both sipped our pints. I felt as though I should say something more about the children, but I couldn't think of anything. So I picked up Tony's magazine and we went back to talking about hi-fis.

About ten minutes later some other people from Langley's turned up. The Bright Young Things, half a dozen or so budding agents in their mid-twenties (Miles has still got his eye for future talent). They spotted us, came to sit at the next table. I started chatting to Ross about the latest developments in what he insists on calling 'this wonderful industry of ours'. He's easy enough to get along with, but I always feel he only wants to talk to you to show he knows more than you do. Ross is a little too proud of the fact that he's quite so Bright while still so Young.

At first Tony tried chipping in with a few comments about the accountancy side of this wonderful industry of ours, but each time Ross would reply with a cursory 'yeah' (he might as well have added 'whatever'), and turn back to me to make a completely different point. He'd cover the rebuff with a smile, but a rebuff it certainly was. After a while Tony gave up and went back to flicking through his magazine.

The same thing happened three or four times: I'd get into a conversation with people on the other table, Tony would try to get involved but no one would take that much notice of him. I began to feel sorry for him, decided to get him talking about hi-fis again. He explained how CD players work. I'd never really understood it. Still don't, to be honest, but he seemed to enjoy telling me.

My mobile bleeped. Text message from a familiar number. *where r u?*

pillars. why?

Short wait. *exciting news*

The prompt couldn't have been more obvious. 'Tony,' I said, 'would you mind if a friend of mine joined us?'

"Course not.'

whenever u like

It took Rosie eight minutes.

'Hiya.'

'Hi there.' As we hugged, her hair tickled my face. It's naturally curly, tending towards wild, and she hasn't had it cut for a while. Not that that matters. It seems to complement her dress sense (which is the same whether she's at work or not): slightly . . . I can't avoid the word 'alternative', but not in a crap studenty way. Her clothes are always stylish, and often expensive. Tonight they were a vintage beaded top and DKNY jeans.

She broke away from the hug.

'Rosie, this is Tony. He's the guy I'm going to New York with, remember?'

She smiled at him. 'Oh yeah, hi. Alex told me about that. Free trip to the Big Apple, eh?'

'Yes,' said Tony, shaking her hand. 'That's right.'

'Not that I'm jealous, of course.'

Tony laughed. Rosie waited for him to say something. He didn't.

'What do you want to drink?' I asked.

'G&T'd be lovely.'

'Right. Another one, Tony?'

'Yeah, but I'll get 'em.'

'You sure?'

'Yeah, honest.'

Ah. Didn't want to be left alone with Rosie. 'OK.'

'Same again?'

'Please.'

When he was gone I turned to Rosie. 'Well?'

'My news, you mean?'

'No, I meant "well, what's the current temperature in Mexico City?"'

'You remember I was telling you about the Boathouse?'

'The what?'

'The Boathouse. That restaurant.'

'Oh, that – yeah.' Big Day Out do cookery courses at posh restaurants. Rosie had told me the other day that she was trying to line this place up.

'Well, I went to see them this afternoon, have a look round, chat with the owner, blah-dee-blah . . . and it went very well. *Very* well.'

'So you think you can do something with them?'

'A course? Yeah, probably. But that wasn't what I meant.'

'Oh, I see. The owner?'

'No. The owner's bank manager. Kieron.'

'On the handsome side, is he, Kieron?'

'Indeed he is. Very clean-cut. Gorgeous blue eyes. Maybe just a hint of cruelty around the lips.'

'You know you're getting old when bank managers start to look handsome.'

'Alex, I'd have gone for this sort of "handsome" when I was twenty-one.'

'So what happened?'

'He was there to see Max – that's the owner – after me. Max got held up on a call, so I started chatting to Kieron, then Max's assistant offered us both coffee, and we carried on chatting, then Max took another call, and . . . well, I'm seeing him next Tuesday night. With some of his friends.'

'Eh?'

'He said he was meeting up with a group of friends for a drink, did I want to go along? I liked him for that. We definitely hit it off – all the signs were there, Alex, eye contact, open body language, the lot – but even so, I think he might have thought it'd be a bit forward to ask me out on a date, I mean a "date" date, after just ten minutes. I liked the way he made it something with other people there, to ease the pressure a bit.'

'Yeah, I can see that.'

'But then on the other hand, you could say it's *more* forward to meet up while his friends are there, don't you think? Almost like we're doing the introduce-her-to-the-friends bit before we've done the . . . well, you know. And that's quite exciting too.'

'Rosie, I don't want to rain on anyone's parade here, but don't you think you might be reading a bit too much into this?'

She paused to consider it. Then, 'No. There was definitely something there. Those *eyes*, Alex. He never looked away from me. And besides – Susanna would approve.'

'Susanna?'

'That book.'

'Oh, *that*.'

'Yes. There's a section of the book about . . . well, it'd take a while to explain, but what I'm saying is Susanna would think me going on a date with Kieron is a good thing. Not that that would mean much to you, Mr Cynical.'

'Really? Mr Cynical, am I?'

'You know you are. You wouldn't buy that book in a million years.'

'Wouldn't I?'

'You haven't . . . you didn't . . . You haven't *bought* it?'

'As it happens, yes, I have.'

'Good God! I'm impressed, Alex. Really I am.'

'What, you thought I was too narrow-minded to read a self-help book?'

'What's the word I'm looking for here? Erm . . . oh yeah, that's it – "yes". Plus I thought you'd be embarrassed about it.'

'*Embarrassed?* Some of us are a little bigger than that, Rosie.'

I turned round to see Tony putting our drinks on the table. I reached for the Guinness. 'This mine? Cheers.'

'How are you finding it then?' said Rosie.

'Mmm? What?'

'This book – have you read any of it yet?'

I didn't say anything.

Rosie turned to Tony. 'Alex was just telling me about this new book he's bought.'

'Oh, really?' he said. 'What is it?'

'It's, er . . . it's that new novel everybody's raving about . . . you know, by that bloke . . . Smith. Kieron Smith.'

'Right. What's it about?'

'Well, it's, er . . . it's about lots of things . . . but, er, mainly it's about . . . this bank manager. With incredible eyes.'

Tony was struggling to open a packet of peanuts. I shot Rosie an 'all right, point taken' look, and decided to head off

29

the next attack before it came. 'You read any good novels lately, Tony?'

The plastic wrapping finally yielded to his efforts, and peanuts shot halfway across the table. 'Damn. Sorry.'

I brushed some peanuts back towards him.

'Er, sorry,' he said, 'what was that?'

'Novels. Have you read any good novels lately?'

'Not for a while,' he said, sweeping up the peanuts with the side of his hand. 'John Grisham, that's who I like. I've read all his.'

'What was the Grisham one I read?' said Rosie. '*The Pelican Brief*, that was it. I thought it was very good.'

Tony nodded. 'Yeah, it's great.'

'I must read some more,' she said.

'Yeah.' The peanuts were all tidied now, but he carried on rearranging the pile.

'Any you'd recommend in particular?'

He tidied one edge of the pile. 'Not really.' Then the opposite edge. 'They're all great.'

Rosie waited for him to say something else. But it was peanuts all the way now for Tony. She turned back to me. We both realised that with Tony there she couldn't tell me any more about Kieron, and I couldn't tell her any more about buying the book. Which suited me. I wouldn't have to admit to shaking as I'd carried it to the till. Or imagining that as soon as the assistant swiped the bar code a huge red light would start flashing behind the counter and there'd be a recorded message blasting out: 'SAD BASTARD AT TILL THREE! SAD BASTARD AT TILL THREE!' As I'd handed over my tenner I'd had to stop myself saying to the assistant, 'I have asked women out before, honest – some of them even said yes.'

So idle chit-chat it was. Mainly me and Rosie, although Tony did make the odd comment.

When she'd finished her drink she stood up. 'I'd better be going. Thanks for the drink, Tony.'

'That's all right.'

'Can I get anyone another before I leave?'

'No, I'm fine thanks.'

'Me neither. Thanks anyway.'

She smiled. 'Well, hope you enjoy your novel, Alex.'

'I'll try to. Hope your . . . meeting goes well.'

'So do I.'

I stood up to hug her goodbye. When I sat back down, Tony was watching something across the pub. Following his gaze, I saw Ross, who'd set to work on an attractive young woman standing next to him at the bar. From the way she was laughing it looked like she was a willing enough subject.

'Ross is up to his usual tricks,' I said.

'Yes,' said Tony. 'Women are never safe when Ross is around.' He opened his mouth as though he was going to say something else, then changed his mind and took a sip of beer. After a few moments he changed his mind again. 'What's . . . How . . . What would you say Ross's big attraction is for women?'

I thought about it for a moment. 'He's JGE, isn't he?'

'He's what?'

'JGE. Just Gay Enough.' Tony's blank stare told me he hadn't heard this theory. Neither had I until a couple of months ago. A producer I was working with had read about it in one of those women's magazines. 'Just Gay Enough means you can attract women because you're a little bit gay.'

Tony nearly choked on his beer. '*What?* I didn't know Ross was bisexual!'

'No, not literally gay. It just means being in touch with your feminine side. Women don't like overtly heterosexual men. You know, shirt open to the waist, medallion, leather trousers, any of that rubbish. It puts them off. They want a bloke who's not too threatening. They want you to have some of the characteristics of a gay man, without actually being gay. So they can talk to you about clothes, interior decorating, that sort of thing. But they still want you to be a complete animal in bed.'

Tony nodded slowly. 'Do you think there's anything in it?'

'Sure I do.' I looked at Ross again. I could just imagine the patter. That shade of make-up went perfectly with her eyes, he loved that top, who was it by . . .

'So you've got to do gay things even though you're not gay?'

'Sort of, yeah.' I tried to think of another example. 'Like . . . John Travolta. He's Just Gay Enough.'

'What, you mean in *Grease*? All that black leather? That's quite gay, isn't it?'

'No, not gay like that. I mean the modern era John Travolta. From *Pulp Fiction* onwards.'

'He shot a bloke's head off in that. That's not very gay.'

OK, I thought, forget *Pulp Fiction*. 'Think about *Get Shorty*, any of those films where he's tough without being macho. The way he talks, the actual sound he makes – it's almost camp, isn't it? Not very, just a fraction. But it's there, don't you think? The way he sounds his 's's.'

Tony nodded. 'Yeah. I see.'

I wondered if he did see.

Soon Ross was back with us, chatting and charming (I think a phone number had been taken). I threw in the occasional comment. Tony didn't say anything. He laughed in all the right places, but was obviously deep in thought. It struck me that he could be . . . let's say 'not unattractive' to women. His looks are what you might call 'dark and brooding'. But I get the sense that maybe the brooding's a little too real sometimes.

I gave Joe his new Scalextric set tonight. He was supposed to get it for his birthday but they didn't have any in stock and I had to order one. I spent all last night setting it up in his room (him and Georgia have still got their room here with all their stuff in it, they stay over sometimes). He loved it. We played on it for ages. He said he was going to be Jenson Button, and I could be Michael Schumacher, and we'd race each other. He thinks Jenson Button's ace. Whenever he gets a chance to press a button — if we're in a lift, or the channel needs changing on the telly, or I'm cooking something in the microwave for him and Georgia — he always presses the button and he says, 'I'll do it because I'm Jenson Button'. So we were racing the Scalextric cars tonight, and it was really good fun. They don't fly off the track as much as they used to with the one I had when I was kid.

While we were doing that Georgia watched her *Lion King* video. She said to Joe that he was silly for liking cars, and he said it was better than liking a stupid lion. I had to tell them to stop arguing otherwise I wouldn't let Georgia watch her video or Joe play with his Scalextric. That did the job.

When we got back to Anita's Shaun was outside, varnishing the fence. We said hello. I asked him how things were at the gym, and he said they were good, they'd signed up seventy new members last month. I thought about asking how many of them he'd shagged, but I didn't. Obviously I didn't because Joe and Georgia were there, but also because it'd make Shaun think I was bothered about Anita going off with him. Like I said before, I don't really miss her. No, what bothers me about Shaun is that I wish I was like him. Properly grown-up, I mean, not still feeling like I'm a kid. Tonight, for example, as soon as Joe got out of the car he was wheeling his Scalextric car everywhere (I'd said he could bring it home). Along the path, across the garden, doing the engine noise all the time. He wheeled it around Shaun's feet and said, 'Look, I'm Jenson Button.' Shaun just grunted, and I think he might have said 'very good', but you could tell he was only doing it because he was expected to, because he had to keep Joe happy. But when I was playing on the Scalextric with Joe I *loved* it. I think I enjoyed it as much as he did. That's what I mean. I wish I felt more like Shaun and less like Joe. Then I think I'd be more confident with people.

Mind you, I have made a bit of progress on that front. Or at least got a plan for making some progress. I'm going to New York, you see, on a business trip. I'm really excited about that. I've never been anywhere in America. As soon as my boss told me about it I went and changed ten pounds into dollars, because I wanted to see what they looked like. They were a lot smaller than I thought they'd be.

Anyway, the point is, I think the bloke who's coming with us, Alex, is a really good bloke. I found it easy to talk to him, easier than I usually find it with new people. I don't know what it was, I just seemed to feel like I could get on with him. I'd wondered what he'd be like, because I heard

Kathy (that's his agent) talking with her assistant in the office one day, they were talking about all their clients and saying which of them were good-looking, and they said Alex was good-looking but in a 'cute' way, not in a 'drop-dead' way. Another one of their clients was 'drop-dead' good-looking, they reckoned. Said he looked like Brad Pitt, but Alex looked more like Ben Stiller. I'd say that was a good description of him. He's taller than Ben Stiller, not really tall, but definitely taller than Ben Stiller. But I can see what they meant about Alex looking a bit like him.

Even though Alex is obviously more confident than me, I didn't mind. What happens quite a lot is that I'll meet someone and they'll be so confident and funny that it's almost like they're showing off. I get really intimidated by that; find I can't talk to them at all. But it wasn't like that with Alex. We had a really nice chat. He told me about this theory called 'Just Gay Enough'. I've decided I'm going to try it out.

The trick is going to be finding the right level of gayness. I've got a sheet of paper, and I've written a list of things, in decreasing order of how gay they are. So at the top of the page I've put the most gay thing I could think of – 'Actually having sex with another man' – and at the bottom I've put the least gay thing I could think of – 'Never having sex with another man' – and then in-between I've put a load of other things in order of gayness. I'm going to draw a line across the page, quite near the bottom but not right at the bottom, and then the thing that's one above the line, that's what I'm going to use as my 'Just Gay Enough' thing.

I've taken a lot of time to get this right, and put a lot of thought into it. This isn't something I've dashed off in ten minutes. I really want it to work. The first things I put down were the ones that came to mind straightaway, like 'having a big moustache', 'having lots of piercings on your face' (and other places too, if what I've heard is right, but I didn't need to go into all that), 'wearing your key ring on your belt' (I think there's some sort of code about which side of the belt they wear it on, relating to what they like to do when they . . . you know . . . but this was more detail I didn't need), and 'using poppers' (that's the slang for them, I think – it's some sort of drug – I think the proper name's 'animal nitrate' or something). I decided that all these things came into the 'very gay' category, so I put them near the top of the list.

Then on Friday night I had a bit of luck. There was an American comedy programme on television, I can't remember the title but it was one of those where there's a gay man who all the women like, so I made some notes on him. He was very well dressed, which I'm not; I'm not badly dressed but I could never be really trendy like he was. And he had very good taste in all the stuff in his home, which I haven't, and even if I had it wouldn't be much use because you can only show women how good your taste is when they've come round to your house and that's the bit I can't manage in the first place. But what was more promising was that he was very good at cooking, and although I'm not, I thought maybe I could widen it out to food generally. Because, for instance, it's quite gay to like quiche, isn't it, so I thought maybe I could pretend to do that. But the trouble there is that not many places serve quiche, and it'd sound strange standing next to a woman at the bar and asking the barman if they served quiche even though it didn't say so on the blackboard. But I put all these things down anyway, because I thought they were the right level of gayness, and might inspire me to think of others.

It worked, too. There was 'drinking cocktails', 'being good at dancing' – I knew I was on the right lines with that, because when Alex explained the theory to me he said John Travolta was a good example, and he was in *Saturday Night Fever*, wasn't he – and 'liking shopping' and 'liking Judy Garland' and 'buying lots of flowers' . . . I've come up with quite a few.

Now all I've got to do is draw my line across the page and choose my thing that's Just Gay Enough. Then I'll wait for a chance to do it.

Before you can plan your route to commitment, you first have to identify your 'Relationship USP'.

I'd been meaning to look at the book all week. If nothing else, I wanted to find out what Rosie had meant when she'd said the author would approve of her date with the bank manager. But you know how it goes, things crop up, you keep forgetting. What finally made me do it was Amy coming round.

It was Sunday. There were a few odds and sods of mine (CDs, that sort of thing) which had got mixed up with hers when we moved out of the flat, so she'd brought them over. She's only about half an hour's drive away, on the other side of Kent (a couple of streets from our old place). It was Amy's idea to get out of London when we shacked up together. We'd get more for our money, she said, but still be close enough to town for our jobs (she's a solicitor). When we split up I found I'd got used to taking London in small but regular doses.

Amy got to mine just after two. I heard the car outside, and by the time I opened my front door she was on her way up the path, carrying a big cardboard box. She smiled. 'Delivery for Mr Richards.'

I took the box and put it on the floor in the hall. 'Thanks for doing this,' I said.

'Invoice is in the post.'

'I'll file it under "B".'

A running joke whenever one of us does a favour for the other; the 'B' stands for 'bin'.

Amy's hair was different. Shorter, with light streaks in the chestnut brown. It looked good. Whoever she's favouring at Toni and Guy these days had done her proud. She was also tanned; from a holiday in Mexico, she informed me. New glasses, too. She'd mentioned those on the phone. The reactalite lenses had tinted slightly, making her eyes seem a darker brown than I knew they really were. Round the edges, I noticed, she'd developed a few more crow's feet. She started getting them a couple of years ago. Although of course she insists on calling them wrinkles. At first I tried telling her how sexy they look, but she refused to believe me, kept threatening Botox. Jokingly, I hope. Why any woman wants to look like she's been plugged into the mains is beyond me. Anyway, those days were gone now. It wasn't my place to tell Amy if she looked good or not, even though she did.

I gestured inside. 'Got time for a cup of tea?'

'I wondered when you were going to ask.'

While the kettle boiled Amy took a look round the flat.

'Nice place,' she said on her return.

'Not too bad, is it?'

'I like that old pine cabinet in the bathroom.'

'I bought that last week.'

It should have felt strange, having my new home judged by the person I'd shared my last one with. But it didn't. I valued Amy's opinions, even if she was now just a friend.

Only when I remembered that did I feel a bit sad. How could two people who'd once had sex behind a newspaper stand at Madrid airport end up like this?

I asked Amy about work.

'Miranda's still scheming away. There's a partnership up for grabs soon.'

'Do you think she'll get it?'

'Probably. Knowing her.'

I nearly asked whether Amy wasn't tempted to go for the partnership herself, but stopped myself just in time. She's keener on the title 'homemaker', even 'mother', than 'partner'. I don't see the rush, personally, seeing as she's only six months older than me. But I didn't fancy yet another discussion on the subject. We had enough 'discussions' on that before we split up. Tempted as I was to tell her about the book ('How can I be "scared of commitment" if I'm reading *The Road To Commitment*, eh?'), I kept quiet.

Then Amy noticed the object sitting on my coffee table.

'What is *that*?'

'Isn't it obvious?'

'Why the hell have you got a Wallace and Gromit mousemat?'

I rolled my eyes. 'Have a guess.'

'Your mum?'

'Who else?'

Amy laughed.

'It arrived in the post yesterday.'

'Bless her.'

'I must ring her later, say thanks.' As soon as I'd said it I could see the thought form in Amy's head. And I decided it wasn't such a bad idea. 'Actually, shall I do it now? You could have a chat with her.'

'If you want.' My mum and Amy liked each other a lot. I think Mum was more upset by us splitting up than I was. I wouldn't be surprised if Amy misses Mum more than she misses me.

Mum answered after the first ring, as if she'd been waiting for the call, which she probably had. 'Hello, seven-two-four?' She always answers with the old version of the phone number from when I was a kid, despite the fact that British Telecom, even in that sleepy little nearly-by-the-seaside village in Suffolk, have added several digits to the beginning.

'Hi, Mum.'

'Hello, son, how are you?'

'All right. You?'

'Fine, fine.' I could hear her trying to contain her excitement. *Has he got it yet, has it arrived?*

'I was ringing to say thanks for my present. It's great.'

'That's all right. It was only a little thing.' Trying to sound blasé about it, but obviously thrilled that she'd made her only child happy.

'No, it's just what I need.'

Then the explanation. There's always the explanation; ninety per cent of the fun of giving a present for my mum. 'Well, I knew you'd got that new computer of yours, and I was round at Jill's, and I was telling Malcolm all about it, and he said was it a toppy one, and I said I didn't know, he said there were two sorts, there were toppy ones and there were . . . no, hang on, was it . . .'

'Do you mean desktops and laptops?'

'That was it! Yes, he said was it a desktop, and of course I didn't know, but I knew you said you'd had it delivered, and Malcolm said then it probably was, because with . . . the other sort . . .'

'Laptops.'

'That's it, he said with them they're quite small – is that right?'

'Yeah.'

'Yes, he said they're quite small, so if you'd had it delivered it had to be a desk one, and he was telling me all about them, you know. Well, of course, I hadn't got a clue what he was on about, but I did remember him saying that one of the things was that with a desk one you had a mouthmat, and he pointed to his desk one – they've got it set up in that corner, you know, by the lamp, near the window. Not the big window, the window by the alcove, you remember?'

'Yeah, I know.'

'So he pointed to his desk one, and there it was, this mouthmat – and you'll never guess what – it had a picture of the Yorkshire Dales on it!'

'Never.'

'It did! You know how they like their holidays there. And I said I didn't know computer things had pictures of the Yorkshire Dales on them, and he said yes, you can get mouthmats with pictures of anything on them, and I said can you really, and he said yes. Well, anyhow, I didn't think anything more of it, not until the other day, I was in Woolies – and I noticed they had a section for computer things. Can you believe it, computer things in Woolies!'

'I know, they're taking over the world, Mum.'

'So I had a look, and of course I didn't know what half the stuff was, but eventually I saw them, they had a pile of these mouthmat thingies, and I had a look through them – all sorts they had, I couldn't believe it – they had ones with pop bands on, ones with David Beckham on, I thought I'm not getting one of *those* – him and that stupid wife of his – and then they had these ones with Wallace and Gromit on! And I thought, I know someone who likes Wallace and Gromit.' We watched *The Wrong Trousers* once when I was home for Christmas. 'Someone,' she continued, 'who likes Wallace and Gromit *and* has got a new computer.'

'That was really sweet of you, Mum. Thanks.'

'That's all right, son. You enjoy it.'

I traded smiles with Amy. No point in telling Mum that when you spend twelve hundred pounds on a desktop they tend to throw in a mousemat for free, or indeed that with the table the computer's on it's easier not to use a mousemat at all, and certainly no point in telling her that even if I was going to use a mousemat it wouldn't be a Wallace and Gromit one, enjoyable as the film was. No, better to just keep her happy by saying thanks, then put the mousemat with all the other well-intentioned but off-target presents she's bought me over the years.

Amy made a 'say hello from me' gesture. I thought I might as well go one better. 'Er, there's someone here you might want to speak to, Mum.'

Amy's happy look as I passed her the phone told me I'd done the right thing.

'Hello, June. It's Amy.'

I could hear the shriek from five feet away.

'I'm fine, June, fine . . . yes, I was just popping round to drop a few things off . . .'

I could sense the faintest tension on the other end of the line. Amy popping round to drop a few things off was a reminder that we weren't together any more, and I still don't think Mum understands why that's happened. Amy was, is and always will be a 'Lovely Girl' (June Richards ™), and therefore the perfect candidate for her son to marry. Why you would meet a Lovely Girl and then do anything other than marry her confuses, and I think, although she'd never say as much to my face, upsets Mum.

'Yes, still at the same firm . . . struggling along, you know how it is . . . Anyway, how are you, June? How are you getting along?' The tiniest pause before the last two words, because what she could easily have said instead was 'now that it's nearly a year since Brian died'. He was sixty-six. Liver trouble. Had an infection when he was younger. Things had never been entirely right since then. Maybe the knowledge that it was coming made it easier for me to bear when it happened. The funeral was horrible, though largely because I hated seeing Mum in such a state. Dad had been happy enough with his life. Started off as an engineer. Then, because he was very good at it, they stopped him doing it and promoted him to a job where he oversaw other people doing it. Mum loved him. He loved her. They both loved me, and I loved them back. But life doesn't stay like *The Waltons* for ever. My love for Dad never disappeared, it just stopped being 'won't be able to carry on if he's not in the world' love. He suffered a bit towards the end. I was glad he didn't have to go through that any more.

Besides which, I think his death concentrated my thoughts on this 'commitment' issue. It probably wasn't coincidence that Amy and I split up not long afterwards. She talks about commitment in terms of settling down, kids, etc.; I think of it more as being with someone you can share adventures with. Travel, live a bit. See some places you've never seen before, try some things you've never tried before. Great Wall of China. Scuba diving. Anything. Thinking about Dad's life made me scared of turning into my parents too soon. I'm only in my thirties, there's time for settling down . . . well, difficult to put an exact date on it . . . let's just say 'later'.

I do worry about how Mum's reacted to Dad not being around, though. About how she's getting on, even though with her friends in the village she never lacks company. Amy's sympathetic 'mmm's and 'I know's told me Mum was revealing more of her loneliness to her than she does to me. Wants to be strong for me, I suppose, doesn't want me worrying too much. Later, when the call was over, Amy agreed with me, but said that Mum was bearing up pretty well.

She left soon afterwards. A friendly hug when we said goodbye. The same tinge of regret that our relationship had dwindled to this.

Which was what made me get the book from the spare room, where it had been since I bought it, still in its bag. I read the back cover as I came downstairs again: *Dr Susanna Grove is one of America's leading relationship coaches. For over twenty years her private clients have benefitted from her incredible skills at analysing their relationship histories and helping them build successful long-term partnerships that LAST! Now you too can reap the rewards of her invaluable insights and wisdom, applying them to your own life and finding YOUR 'road to commitment'!*

Oh Christ, I thought. Here we go. The term 'relationship coach', for a start. Hardly like being a tennis coach, is it? Do you get people ringing you up at one in the morning when they're having an argument? 'Susanna, my girlfriend's got a problem with the way I behave towards her friends, and she says it's allied to wider doubts about my commitment to the relationship in general. I wonder whether you could talk me through some possible responses here?'

But, remembering Rosie's comments about my cynicism,

I vowed not to give up on the book before I'd even opened it. I poured myself a glass of wine, sat down, turned to the introduction. It was all about the book's central idea: your 'relationship USP'. As I soon as I saw that, I assumed Dr Grove was going to be one of those 'you are your own product' merchants, telling me to sell myself to potential partners. But 'USP', it turned out, stands for 'Unique *Staleness* Point'. Everybody, according to Dr Grove, has got something about them, a recurring factor – which nine times out of ten they themselves can't spot – that stops their relationships succeeding, means they keep going stale. The secret to getting your next relationship right is identifying that USP, then eliminating it.

Hmm. 'Staleness'.

On the floor were the Sunday papers. I'd bought two broadsheets and a tabloid, so it was a stack you could almost use as a footrest. They'd get me through what remained of the day. Sunday's the worst day of the week when you're on your own. All your friends retreat into the security of their coupledom, their roast dinners, their cosy afternoons cuddled up under a blanket with a good old film on the telly. While you're stuck on your own, making yourself read that article on shoes in the Style section because if you don't you'll be forced to stare at the wall and admit you don't have anyone to love you. You could ring your friends up, of course. They'd probably do the decent thing and invite you round for a drink. But you'd both know it was only under sufferance. Come the evening and you'd be expected to leave. Where you are and who you're with at eight o'clock on a Sunday night is a definition of 'home'. Outsiders, even friends you'd welcome with open arms on any other day of the week, are not allowed in.

But then I remembered the Sundays from the end of my relationship with Amy, when I'd been glad of the newspapers' many sections for another reason: they hid the fact that things felt wrong. Three years before, in the early months of our relationship, back when there was a thrill simply in being together, we used to fill our Sundays with sex. Now being together wasn't a thrill, it was a mundane familiarity. We'd chat about what we'd read in the Review section, or cut out a recipe from the magazine, meaning to cook it later but never actually getting round to it. The relationship was losing its passion, its freshness. As an anaesthetic against that we used the eight hundred and seventy-four sections of the Sunday newspapers.

So, yes, I could sort of see what the book was getting at. 'Staleness' is a very good word. But 'unique' – that was the word I had a problem with. Because try as I might, I couldn't get away from the feeling that relationships go stale anyway. Forget USPs, mine or Amy's or anyone else's, the fact is, if you get two people who like each other a lot, and fancy each other a lot, and you put them together, make them live together, allow them a couple of years to exhaust their back catalogue of revelations . . . hey presto, you'll have a relationship that's going stale. There's nothing wrong with the two people themselves; it's just that relationships tend to lose their passion after a while. That's what happened to Amy and me, to me and previous girlfriends, to lots of people I've known . . . that's just what happens.

I picked up the book again, flicked through the pages I'd read, realised I was thinking all this not in triumph but in sadness. I wanted to agree with it, but I couldn't. I wasn't boasting that I knew more than Dr Grove, I was scared that I didn't know anything at all.

It hit me, for the first time, that I'm thirty-four years old and I don't know a thing.

Saw Tony again last night. I was meeting Rosie in the Pillars; she was going to tell me about her date the night before, with the bank manager. She'd got delayed on the way back from a business meeting in Yorkshire (some airfield that does microlighting – she's thinking of signing them up), so I thought I'd call him, see if he was around for another drink before we jet off to New York tomorrow. He was.

'I'm really excited about it now,' he said. 'I've been looking it up on the Internet. All these sites have got all these things they say you've got to do while you're there. I'm just worried I won't get time for them all.'

'I'll show you round a bit if you want.'

'Would you? Really?'

''Course.'

'Oh, thanks, Alex, that's brilliant. It'll be really good to go with someone who knows what they're doing.' His enthusiasm was quite touching. 'What do you think's the best thing to go and see? What should we do first?'

'God, it's hard to pick just one thing. Empire State, Central Park, Staten Island Ferry – they're all worth a trip in themselves. If I had to choose one . . . I don't know . . . probably Grand Central, I'd say.'

'Is that the big train station?'

'Yeah.'

'I've seen that on all the websites.'

'It's beautiful.' I told him about the station, about those famous black and white pictures from the forties with the light streaming in through the huge windows, about the scene from *The Fisher King* where the commuters start to

49

waltz across the concourse . . . We agreed that was the first thing we'd go and see.

Soon after, Rosie arrived.

'Sorry I'm late,' she said. 'Motorway was a nightmare.'

'You should have got them to fly you back. Sit yourself down, I'll get you a drink.'

When we were all settled, I deliberately avoided mentioning Rosie's date. Didn't think she'd want to talk about it in front of Tony. But about the first thing she said was: 'Don't you want to hear about last night, then?'

'Of course I do. How did it go?'

'It was . . . interesting.' A strange smile crossed her face as she said it.

'That doesn't sound like a good sort of "interesting".'

'Doesn't it?'

'I don't think so, anyway.'

'Well, see what you think.' She took a sip of her Chardonnay. 'Kieron called me during the morning and said was I still on for meeting up with his friends, and I said sure I was, where were they all going to be, and he told me this wine bar just off Chancery Lane. I got there a bit early, and it was a great place, nice and relaxed, not too big. Being a Tuesday night it wasn't that busy, and there was a group of people in the corner, four of them when I got there, but a couple more turned up while I was waiting, and I thought, I bet that's them. I don't know why but they looked the sort of people who'd be Kieron's friends.'

'That'll be your feminine intuition again, Rosie.'

'Maybe you should hear the rest of what happened before you pass judgement on my feminine intuition.'

'So they weren't his friends, then?'

'Oh no, they were. Kieron turned up – looking, if

anything, even more handsome than when I'd met him before – he had this beautiful duck-egg-blue shirt on, I wouldn't be surprised if it was handmade, and the colour of it really set his eyes off. They are the most beautiful blue you've ever seen, I mean, really, he's up there with Paul Newman.'

'Praise indeed.'

'So he said hi, how was I, and there was a peck on each cheek, and he left his hand resting on my arm while we did some small talk, and all the time he was looking straight at me with those eyes. I mean, honestly, it was a good job I was sitting down because otherwise I think my knees might have weakened. Then he got himself a beer, and another drink for me, and we went across to his friends. There was Robert, who works for the same bank – different branch, same bank – and Alice, who sells pensions, and Dean, who's a surveyor, and Nancy who . . . blah-dee-blah. And they were all just like Kieron – in their thirties, smart, good-looking, you wouldn't complain if they were on your table at a wedding.'

'This is going very well: he's Paul Newman and you like all his friends.'

'I have to confess, Alex, at this point I was thinking along those lines myself. I got a bit worried for a while when I was talking to Alice – she was on my right, Kieron was on my left – because we seemed to talk for ages without Kieron paying me any attention. She thought one of her friends might have been a customer of mine last year, but we worked out it must have been another firm . . . Anyway, no sooner had the thought formed in my head that Kieron hadn't spoken to me for a while than I felt his hand on my arm again and he said, sorry to interrupt, Alice, but Robert's just been saying . . . so that got me talking to him and Kieron again, and then just Kieron on his own, and then he was facing me, his back was to the others, his eyes were working their magic again, and I thought, no, this guy definitely wants me here.'

'Always nice to feel wanted.'

'This is true. So, about half an hour went by, then Marcus turned up. Marcus is . . . oh, I can't remember what Marcus is . . . whatever it is I'm sure he's very good at it . . . and he said hi to everyone, and everyone said hi to him, and it was handshakes and kisses all round, and we moved up to make room for him. And then it all went quiet.'

'Quiet?'

'Yeah, like, no one saying anything. All the conversations were finished, then everyone looked at Kieron. He checked round the table, to see they were all paying attention, then he said, "OK, everyone, thanks for coming along tonight, good to see you all again," and turned to me, and said, "Rosie, a special thank you to you for coming along tonight," and I thought, ur-ur, something's not right here, but all I could do was smile back at him and wonder what the hell was coming next, and he said, "Let me explain about tonight," and he was doing the eyes again, and the smile, only now they weren't making me melt they were making me nervous, and then he said, "As you can see, tonight's just about meeting up and having a good time with a group of friends – a group of friends who have all accepted Jesus Christ into their life as their one true saviour."'

I'd got my glass to my lips at that point – and it froze there. I couldn't move, couldn't tilt it up to have a drink, couldn't put it back on the table.

'Funny you should do that,' continued Rosie. 'That's just

what I did. I looked round the table, and they were all smiling at me, you know, that really sickly, encouraging, "don't be scared" smile, and I was thinking, Scared? I'm fucking terrified. Then I looked back at Kieron, and he was obviously waiting for some sort of reaction, and I thought, No way, I'm not saying a word, you can make the running here, mate. He gave it a moment, then he said, "Now, the way it works is, we have these little get-togethers every Tuesday, and each week we take it in turns to bring one new person along, have a drink with them, get to know them a bit, have a good time, throw in the notion that maybe they could accept Jesus into their lives one day too." I said, "And it was your turn this week?" and he nodded.'

'Bloody hell,' said Tony. 'What did you do?'

'Nothing, I was still in shock at that point.'

'Don't blame you,' I said. 'So the intensity in his eyes wasn't sexual magnetism, it was religious fervour.'

'Yeah. I thought I was getting Paul Newman, turned out it was Billy Graham.'

'What happened?'

'I think he could tell I wasn't immediately going to jump up and shout "hallelujah", so he went for the next stage of his patter. Which was: "The reason we don't tell people why we're inviting them along is that they might get preconceptions, think, oh, it's a bunch of Bible-bashers, I don't want to know. We prefer to let them come along and see that just because you're a Christian it doesn't mean you can't be normal and have a normal job and enjoy a good time with your friends like normal people do." Then Nancy leaned across and said, "Whatever 'normal' means", and everyone laughed, a really smug, annoying laugh. That did it. The shock wore off. Now I was angry.'

'You wouldn't like Rosie when she's angry,' I said to Tony. Then, turning back to her, 'So what did you do?'

'I picked my bag up, finished my drink, then I looked at Kieron, looked right into those wonderful blue eyes of his, and I said, "I suppose a shag's out of the question, then?" And I stood up and left.'

I gave myself a moment to savour the image. Then, 'So you didn't feel the spirit of the Lord settling on you?'

Rosie fixed me with a 'don't even go there' look. I elected not to go there.

There was a very strange little incident a bit later. Tony was at the bar. Rosie had stepped outside to take a call on her mobile, and I decided to visit the gents. The pub was fairly packed by then, and I got momentarily stuck behind some people near the bar, only a few feet from where Tony was waiting to get served. He was studying a piece of paper – about A4 size, it was – I couldn't read what was on it, but it seemed to be some sort of list, with a line across it near the bottom. And he was muttering something to himself.

Next to him was a woman who'd just paid for her drinks. Tony folded the paper up, put it in his pocket, then tapped her on the shoulder. Perhaps he knew her? But no, when she turned round there was no look of recognition. She simply waited for him to speak. Which, after clearing his throat, he did. All he said, in a voice that sounded a bit . . . well, the only word I can use is 'camp', all he said was: 'Ooh, get you.'

I couldn't really believe what I'd heard. Neither, by the look on her face, could the woman. She stared at him for a moment, seemed to be on the verge of asking him to repeat himself, then thought better of it, collected her change, and went back to her friend in the corner.

Tony sighed heavily, then turned to the barman and said,

this time in his normal voice, 'Pint of Boddingtons, pint of Stella and a gin and tonic, please.'

When I got back to our table, I waited to see if he'd mention the incident. He didn't, so neither did I.

Very strange.

Oh, what's the bloody point? I really worked on this one as well. I had it all planned out. So much for Alex's bloody theories. OK, that's not fair. What I should really say is 'So much for bloody Tony trying to act on Alex's bloody theories'. I honestly thought I could make some progress with this. I'd gone through it all so carefully.

But I must try and not mope. Like I told Joe not to mope the other day, when we were in the park and there was an older boy on his bike who could do wheelies and Joe tried to copy him but he couldn't. Well, he could get his front wheel off the ground for about a tenth of a second, but only by really yanking the handlebars up, and when the front wheel came down the back one would bounce up and he'd wobble all over the place. After a bit I could tell he was in a mood about it, so I put my arm round him and told him it was OK, one day he'd be able to do a wheelie, and he shouldn't mope about it. I'll just have to try and take my own advice, won't I?

Tomorrow is when Alex and me and Miles go to New York. I'm really looking forward to it. I wouldn't have been looking forward to it nearly so much if it was just me and Miles. Because the thing about Miles is . . . well, it's about the deal with the American agency . . . actually, on second thoughts, you don't need to know about that. What I mean is, Alex is a really nice bloke. I find I can talk to him more easily than I can to most people. And I reckon his friend Rosie likes him as well. In fact I wouldn't be surprised if she's got a bit of thing for him. Mind you, what do I know?

Alex has said he'll show me around New York, which I think is really good of him. The first thing we're going to go and see is this big train station, Grand Central. Alex told me that it's not actually Grand Central *Station*, even though that's what people always call it, it's really Grand Central *Terminal*. I said it sounded brilliant, and then Alex told me about the scene in *The Fisher King* where all the commuters start waltzing through the station and I realised I knew which station he meant, because I've seen *The Fisher King*. I thought it was brilliant. The bit with the commuters was really beautiful. A tramp's chasing after a woman he's fallen in love with, and he's getting blocked by all the commuters, but then they all pair up and start to dance. And I'm going to see where they filmed it! In New York! Tomorrow!

Right, I must get some sleep now. Our flight's really early.

And so, as they say, to Manhattan. Tony and I flew over this morning. (Miles was to join us later – his secretary couldn't get us all on the same flight.) Tony spent most of the time going through his figures for the meetings. Six or seven huge ring binders, and about the same number of A4 folders, all crammed with closely typed pages of accounts, ready to answer any question the Americans could throw at him.

'Blimey,' I said. 'That might as well be in Urdu for all the sense I can make of it.'

He hadn't noticed me looking, and hurriedly shut the folder, made a clumsy attempt at changing the subject. Curious. Every so often he'd sigh theatrically, as though he wanted to draw my attention back to the figures and how much work they'd taken, but as soon as I asked him about them, to be polite, he'd clam up. I got the feeling he wanted to say something, but kept pulling back from it. I thought about asking him straight out, but decided if he really wanted to tell me he would.

Anyway, he soon forgot about the figures when we touched down at JFK.

'On behalf of American Airlines, I'd like to welcome you to New York,' said the pilot.

'This is it!' he whispered to me. 'We're here!'

His excitement level got steadily higher from then on. In the cab, when we got close enough to Manhattan to make out the Empire State Building, I pointed it out to him.

'Where, where?' he asked, craning forward so that he could see it.

'There,' I said, pointing. 'And that one just to the right is the Chrysler Building.'

'Really? Ace!'

'When they built it they were competing against someone down on Wall Street. They both wanted theirs to be the tallest building in the world. The other guy thought he'd won, but the Chrysler people had built the top bit of theirs in secret, inside the rest of the building, and they pushed it up at the last minute and won.'

'Honest?'

I nodded.

'Ace!'

There were delays in the Midtown tunnel, so the driver went across the 59th Street Bridge. I told Tony it was the bridge the cab used to drive across in the opening credits of *Taxi*.

'Was it really?' he said, pressing his head against the window so that he could see the top of the bridge's structure. 'Ace!'

By the time we got to the Paramount Hotel he was almost hyperventilating.

'We've got about an hour before Miles gets here,' I said to him in the lift. 'Why don't we dump our bags and go for a wander?'

'Great, yeah!'

'I'll see you in reception in ten minutes,' I said, getting out of the lift. Tony's room was a couple of floors above mine.

When I got down there he was sitting on one of the ultra-chic sofas.

'Alex!' he said, trying to keep his voice down, which given his state can't have been easy. 'By the lifts on my floor, right, there's this huge mirror – and it's got the *weather forecast* on it! There are five or six words written on the mirror, you know, all the things the weather could be, like "sunny" and "cloudy" and "rain", and whichever one the forecast is, there's a little light behind it that lights it up!'

'I know. They have them on all the floors.'

'Really? Wow!' Next to him was a copy of the *New York Times*. 'And I've just been reading this,' he said, picking it up, 'and over here, when they say something happened "on Wednesday" they don't write "on Wednesday", they put a comma and then they just write "Wednesday".'

'I know.'

'Don't you think that's weird?'

I laughed. 'I suppose it is.'

'Is that what they mean when they say we're two countries divided by a common language?'

'Yep. Talking of which – shall we hit the sidewalk?'

'Too right – come on!'

We turned left out of the hotel, and headed for Times Square. The Paramount's only a block away. As we rounded the corner, Tony's eyes widened and his mouth dropped open. He stopped dead in the middle of the pavement, turned a full circle, looking up at the billboards, the hotels, the enormous TV screens, struggling to take in the sheer scale of the place. I enjoyed the sight of him gawping for a moment, then gently steered him away from the busiest part of the pavement.

'Watch out, Tony, you're getting in everyone's way.'

'Have you *ever* seen anything like this, Alex?'

I looked around us. It was rush hour on a beautiful sunny day. Times Square, even by its own standards, was teeming, as much energy being given off by the human traffic as by the millions of light bulbs and pixels.

'No, I don't think I have.'

Suddenly he said, 'Hey, I've just remembered – can we go to Grand Central?'

'If you like.'

His excitement was really sweet. It was almost like he was a kid. Every few yards he spotted something new.

'Alex, Alex, look! There's a New York policeman! They look just like they do on the telly!'

'Look, Alex, look at the yellow taxis – there's . . .' He counted under his breath as a stream of them drove past us. 'That was *seven* cars in a line that were all yellow taxis!'

'Alex!' He actually tugged my sleeve for this one. 'Over there! There's steam coming out of the pavement! I thought that was something they made up for the films!'

The Paramount to Grand Central is a walk that would normally take me about fifteen minutes. With Tony it was going to take twice that. We passed a diner.

'I'm feeling a bit peckish,' I said. 'Fancy something to eat?'

'Yeah, sure. Great.'

We went in and positioned ourselves on high-backed padded seats either side of a window table. A waitress appeared within seconds.

'Hi. How are you today?' She offered us two menus.

'Actually I think I know what I want,' I said. 'Could I have a cheese omelette, please? With fries. And a coffee.'

'Sure.'

I thought Tony would want a look at the menu, but no. 'Could I have ham and eggs? Eggs over-easy, please. And a coffee as well.'

'Sure.'

When the waitress had gone, Tony leaned over to me and whispered, 'What does "over-easy" actually mean?'

I told him. While we waited for our food he stared out of the window, studying the commuters intently. And the cars emerging from the parking lot next door. And the newspaper vendor next to the subway entrance. And the huge chrome and glass office building opposite. It got me excited by proxy. Explaining everything to him – simple things like how Fifth Avenue was where the streets changed from East to West – reminded me of my own first time in New York, and helped me relive that sense of wonder.

A few people were waiting at the counter for takeaways. The guy at the front of the queue ordered his sandwich: 'Could I get a pastrami and Emmenthal on rye, with lettuce and tomato? No salt, lots of pepper, easy on the mayo.'

The woman who was serving had started collecting the ingredients before he'd finished listing them.

'You'd never get that in Britain, would you?' I said. 'It would have been, "Er, did you say brown bread?" and while he was saying, "No, rye bread", she'd have turned round because her mate didn't know how to work the till, and then she'd have come back to him two minutes later and they'd have to start all over again. And when he finally did get his sandwich it'd be coated in mayonnaise. Or she'd have forgotten it altogether.'

As it happened, a few minutes later a middle-aged British couple joined the queue.

'Erm, could I have, er . . .' said the man, who had a pale

face and a Midlands accent, 'erm, loike a baguette . . .' With his hands he was miming the shape of a baguette.

'She knows what a baguette looks like,' I hissed. 'She works here, remember?'

At that point our food arrived. But Tony kept watching the Brits at the counter, almost as though he was making mental notes on them. It was only when I commented on how good my omelette was that he dragged his attention back to the food and started eating.

'Mmmmmmm,' Tony said. 'This is fantastic. I'm having my eggs over-easy all the time from now on.'

When we'd finished we paid the bill (Tony was like lightning when it came to working out the fifteen per cent tip) and left. His rubbernecking at the skyscrapers continued. Combined with the fact that he kept forgetting that Americans drive on the other side of the road, it nearly got him killed at least twice.

'Watch it,' I said as another blaring horn disappeared down Forty-Second Street. 'If you're not careful I'm going to make you hold my hand.'

We reached the Vanderbilt Avenue entrance to Grand Central. It was very busy, and it took us a moment or two to get to the door.

'Are you ready for this, then?' I asked as we shuffled along in the crush.

Tony nodded. Already he was craning to get a look inside. Suddenly the blockage eased, and we were through the doors, standing at the top of the marble steps that lead down to the main concourse. For a good ten seconds Tony was totally speechless. He gazed around at the station's cavernous interior, at the ceiling, which seemed a mile up in the sky, painted with a map of the constellations, at the huge windows letting in shafts of daylight, at the ornate ticket booths and the ramps down to the platforms.

'They claim,' I said, leading him to one side so we wouldn't block everyone's way, 'that this is the world's biggest room.'

Still he couldn't speak. Instead he gave a slow, careful nod of the head.

'I always think to myself "that can't be true". But I can never think of one that's bigger.'

Suddenly he rediscovered his voice. 'That clock! In the middle! That's the one in *The Fisher King*, isn't it?'

I nodded.

'Ace! Let's go and have a look!'

And he was off down the steps, endangering the odd commuter who wasn't quick enough to get out of his way. I followed at a more sedate pace.

'It's beautiful!' he said as we stood in front of the circular information booth that the gold clock stands on.

'Certainly is.'

We wandered slowly round the booth to look at all four illuminated faces. Then, 'I bet the drinks are really expensive there, aren't they?'

Tony was indicating the bars on the upper level, either side of the door we'd come in.

'They're not what you'd call cheap. That one on the right's owned by Michael Jordan.'

'He's the baseball player, isn't he?'

'Basketball.'

'Oh yeah. I always get those two mixed up.' He watched the smart New Yorkers drinking at the bar. 'I suppose you have to book months in advance to get in there?'

I laughed. 'It's only a bar, Tony, not a five-star restaurant.'

'You mean anyone can turn up and have a drink?'

'Of course. Well, unless you were actually a tramp or something.'

'Like the one in *The Fisher King*?'

'Like the one in *The Fisher King*.'

'Can we go and have a drink there?'

'What, now?'

He nodded. I looked at the clock behind us. 'Actually, we'd better not. We should get back to the hotel, don't you think? Miles'll probably be there by now.'

'Oh,' said Tony gloomily.

'Don't worry, we're here for three days, aren't we? There's plenty of time.'

His face brightened.

'Come on,' I said, 'let's get the subway.'

Back at the hotel there was no sign of Miles in the lobby. Tony and I retired to our rooms. My voicemail light was flashing.

'Ah, Mr Richards, good day to you,' came the familiar voice. 'I expect you two are out whoring and drinking. Can't say I blame you. Just make sure you tidy yourselves up for tonight. Here's the drill – rendezvous with Uncle Sam downstairs at nineteen-thirty hours, ready for drinks and dinner. Then more drinks. Tonight is purely social. Give 'em the blarney and enough booze to float a small battleship, so that come tomorrow they won't know their balance sheets from their elbows.' Miles broke off for a chesty laugh. It turned into a major coughing fit. Somewhere in the middle of the hacking I thought I detected a 'bye', then the message ended.

When it came to it I was first down to the lobby, closely followed by Miles. As he strode over from the lifts I marvelled at just how well that man can raise his sartorial game when the occasion requires. His hair had been discreetly but expensively cut, so even though it still caressed his collar it had a stylish look, rather than its usual through-a-hedge-then-back-again one. The suit was a testament to Savile Row's ability to disguise even the largest of bellies. A silk handkerchief peeked tastefully from the top pocket. His cologne smelled wonderful. The man knew what would impress the Americans, and he was providing it by the silver champagne bucketful. Pure David Niven, only in a rather expanded format.

'Alex!' He purred the greeting, instead of booming it from twenty paces like he normally does. 'So good of you to come!'

'Really, Miles, it's my pleasure.'

'Pleasant flight?'

'Faultless. Yours?'

'Very relaxing. Rather a diverting pair of legs on the starboard stewardess.'

We sat down. Miles sighed contentedly. 'Is this city, or is this city not,' he said, 'the finest place on God's great earth?'

'I have heard rumours of it never sleeping.'

'There was a whisper that if you can make it here, you can make it anywhere.' He tapped me on the arm. 'Now remember, young Alex: tonight – anecdotes. Anecdotes and charm. Give the Yanks your "Confessions Of A Voice-over Artist" routine, soften them up for the kill.'

I gave a salute. 'Yessir.'

At twenty to eight the first two Americans arrived. Walter and Mary.

I'm *so* sorry we're late,' said Mary. 'I've never *seen* the Midtown traffic this bad.'

'Nonsense,' replied Miles, kissing her on both cheeks, 'we're on London time – you're five hours early. Walter, old chap, how are you? Good to see you again. Now I want both of you to meet one of my top artists, Alex Richards.'

We all shook hands. Both the Americans were in their fifties, and both were the word 'pleasant' made flesh. Medium height, neither slim nor fat, neither attractive nor unattractive. Greying, respectable, very good at their jobs. Which, as far as I could make out, were in the upper branches of the American firm's hierarchy. Both wore wedding rings, but they obviously weren't married to each other. I just knew there was absolutely no chance of them having an affair. Either of them, with anyone.

Walter and Miles fell into conversation. Mary told me how she adored London, how every time she visits she loves to go to the National Gallery, and I replied with something-or-other about Trafalgar Square, and from then on it was Fortnum's, Regent Street, the Globe . . . We were comparing notes on the British Museum when she suddenly patted her pocket.

'Oh, would you excuse me?' she said. 'That's my cell-phone.'

She took the phone from her pocket, but had some difficulty lifting the flip-up mouthpiece.

'Here, let me take your bag,' I offered. With both hands free she'd be able to do it.

'Thank you, you're so kind.'

Which meant that as Elisabeth arrived I was holding a lady's handbag. If we hadn't moved away from the sofas I guess I'd have put it down. But we had, so I didn't.

Elisabeth seemed the same as her colleagues. Twenty years younger, but essentially the same: pleasant. She had dark blonde hair cut to a respectably corporate length, and a fresh, slightly freckled face. Her mouth was set in a faint smile. It seemed to be her natural expression. It had been there since she'd arrived in the lobby (I'd seen her before she'd seen us), and even as Walter introduced her to Miles, who gave her the full-on Langley treatment, the smile didn't change that much. Her eyes were wide and blue and very bright, and she blinked quickly and regularly. It gave her the air of someone who was very good at listening politely but didn't have much of interest to say herself.

Then Walter introduced her to me.

'Hi there,' I said, shaking her hand. 'Very nice to meet you.'

She blinked. The smile remained set. Although her blue eyes never left mine, I knew she must have seen the handbag, and I felt awkward. There are people you can joke with about that sort of thing, and people you can't, and Elisabeth definitely belonged to the second group. Still she blinked. Still she smiled. It felt like an age since my 'very nice to meet you', and her only response had been to blink and smile. Blink and smile. Pleasant blinks. A pleasant smile. I began to feel even more awkward.

'You know,' came a female American voice, 'I really don't think that handbag goes with your shoes.'

I looked at Mary. She was still on her phone, trying to wrap up the call. There was no one else standing anywhere near us. I looked back at Elisabeth. She was still blinking in exactly the same way, still smiling in exactly the same way, and her eyes still hadn't left mine. Nothing had changed. Except, as I realised the comment had come from her, everything changed. I'd thought that Elisabeth's eyes were lights hiding the fact that there was nothing behind them. But now

I knew they were windows, and through them I could see a woman who was funny, confident, intelligent. And as I saw that, something clicked inside me, and Elisabeth was no longer just pleasant-looking, she was very, very sexy.

I smiled at Elisabeth's joke. Her smile increased in return, very faintly.

And the weirdest thing happened. I got two feelings, simultaneously, both of them in spades. One: the exact same feeling I've always had when a woman attracts me, I mean *really* attracts me. Two: the feeling that the first chapter of that book (I hadn't read any more of it since) had something to say after all. I couldn't tell you why, but the thought of those pages wouldn't leave my mind.

Somehow, I wasn't sure exactly how or why, I knew I was in deep trouble.

I was fifteen minutes late meeting the Americans last night, because I'd called Joe and Georgia to say hello. They were really excited about me being in America. I told them I was too. Joe asked me if I'd seen Will Smith yet, and I said no, but I was keeping an eye out for him.

By the time I got downstairs all the Americans had arrived and they were chatting to Miles and Alex. Then Miles introduced me to them. Then we all stood about talking for a few minutes. I didn't do much of the talking. Lots of the things they were saying were about New York, so I just listened. Then Miles said why didn't we have a drink, and we went upstairs to the bar. It's on the balcony overlooking the lobby, it's brilliant. We got a table and ordered some drinks. I didn't know what you should drink in a smart place like that, I knew they wouldn't have pints of bitter, so I had what Alex had, which was a whisky. Before I took my first sip I said, 'Mmm, I could use this', which is what they say in America, I've seen it in the films. But everyone else went quiet so I think I shouldn't have said it, I made a note not to say it again.

After we'd had a drink we went for dinner. It was at this really smart place on the Upper East Side (East means it's to the right of Fifth Avenue). We had to get two taxis – well, cabs, that's what they call them over here – because New York cabs are really small. (They've got this recorded message from the mayor which plays whenever you get in. I thought that was ace.) On the way there Miles said the restaurant was French, and I thought oh no, I'm not going to know what any of the things are, I'm going to end up ordering snails by mistake. But it was all right, there were English translations under everything so that was OK.

I carried on letting Miles and Alex do most of the talking. I thought it was better to let that happen, I'd only have said something wrong and messed it all up, and then Miles wouldn't have been happy. That was the reason I kept quiet. The main reason, I mean. The other reason was . . . well, the thing is . . . I mean, what I'm saying . . . Look, it was Elisabeth. I liked her. I mean really liked her. I thought she was very pretty. No, not pretty. Well, yes, she was pretty, but I mean more than that. 'Pretty' is a word for when you're just being polite about someone. No, what I mean is I really . . . well, fancied her. In fact I'd even go so far as to say I thought she was beautiful.

I knew I liked her when Walter and Mary said she'd be going through the figures with me. On our own. They were going to talk about all the big general stuff with Miles, and leave me and Elisabeth to look at the books, because she was the accountant. I could take her through everything and she could ask me questions. And when they said that I got excited, but nervous as well, about being left alone with her. That was when I realised how much I liked her. I don't normally like people this quickly, but she seems warm and kind and interested in me and my life. And I felt I could talk to her for hours, if only I knew what to say.

71

It was funny, I would have thought Alex would like her as well, you know, at least chat her up a bit, but he didn't pay her any attention at all. It was almost as though he was trying to ignore her. He wasn't rude or anything, but whenever she said something to him he'd answer her as quickly as he could, then move on to say something else to one of the others, or even to me. (He was still making sure he talked to me. I like him for that.)

I have to say, though, I was quite glad about Alex not fancying her. For my own sake. I started to feel like that this morning, when I was round at her office going through the accounts. Last night it didn't even occur to me to do anything about the fact that I liked her. But this morning, when I was with her in her office, and she'd realised that I knew what I was talking about with the accounts and we were getting on quite well, I started to get a bit more confident. Only a bit, mind you. It was still making me really nervous even being in the same room as her. She's so beautiful. I think I noticed it even more this morning because we weren't out in a posh restaurant, we were just in her office, but she still looked really beautiful. She doesn't wear very much make-up, which I think is good. I think sometimes women wear too much make-up, it's like they're trying too hard. Elisabeth doesn't. There's something very . . . well, I'm not really sure what word to use . . . I think I'd say 'natural', there's something very natural about the way she looks and I think that's why I find her beautiful.

So when we were going through the accounts I decided I was going to ask her out. I made myself a promise that I wasn't going to chicken out of it. I got very nervous thinking about it, and there were several times when neither of us

72

was saying anything, when I was waiting while she looked through figures, that I nearly managed to ask her if she'd like to go out for a drink but I couldn't. After a bit, though, I began to tell myself it'd be all right, because Miles and me and Alex are supposed to be seeing the Americans for meals and drinks as well as just talking about the deal. So if I asked Elisabeth out for a drink she could just see it like that, she wouldn't have to know that I was asking her out. In a way that was bad because I wanted her to know I was asking her out, otherwise she wouldn't know I thought she was beautiful. But in another way it was good because I was scared of her knowing I thought she was beautiful. If she didn't like me in the same way I'd have embarrassed myself. It's like half of you is thinking, 'I won't know if I don't ask', but the other half's thinking, 'I don't want to make a fool of myself'.

In the end I plucked up the courage and asked her. I'd mentioned earlier on how Alex had taken me to Grand Central Terminal (I made sure I used the proper name), and that I'd liked the bar there but we hadn't had time to go. Then when it came to it I said I didn't suppose she'd want to go to Grand Central after we'd finished the work so we could have a drink at Michael Jackson's bar, and she laughed at me and said it was Michael Jordan not Michael Jackson. Honestly, I could have kicked myself. But it didn't seem to matter. She said yes!

As soon as she said it I felt really excited, and I was glad I'd had the courage to do it. But also I began to get nervous, because now I was going to have to go through with it. Impressing Elisabeth was going to be really difficult. I'd have to try really hard. I almost wished she'd said no because then I wouldn't have had to be so nervous about

73

doing it. But I told myself that was silly, I'd never get anywhere if I didn't try. I'd just have to cope with my nerves and give it as good a shot as I could.

When we'd finished working on the accounts for today (we've still got quite a bit to do tomorrow) Elisabeth said she had some calls to make, so why didn't we meet at the bar later. I was glad about this because it meant I could go back to the hotel and do some planning about the date, make sure I was prepared. When I got to my room I sat down with a pen and a sheet of the headed notepaper that hotels give you in that little plastic wallet thing, and I wrote some notes. There were two main things I wanted to remember. The first was something Alex said when we first got here and we went to a café (or I should say a 'diner'.) He said that Americans never use their hands when they're speaking. I remembered that, and all last night I was watching Walter and Mary, and Elisabeth herself. In fact Miles was the same as well: none of them wave their hands about when they're speaking. I decided Alex is right, it's much more impressive when you don't do that. It makes you look calm and in control.

So that was the first thing I wrote down: 'Keep your hands still.' The second thing was something else I noticed last night, which was what Miles or the others would do if the conversation dried up for a moment: they'd always ask a question. For instance, Miles would ask Walter how long the American firm had been in their office building, or Mary would ask Miles if he lived in London . . . simple things, not really that interesting but they're ways of getting everyone talking again. And the really good thing about a question is that the other person answers it; you're making them do the talking so you don't have to. As far as

I'm concerned that's always a good thing. I wrote down a list of questions I could ask Elisabeth, basic ones like 'How long have you been an accountant?', 'Have you got any brothers and sisters?', 'Have you always lived in New York?', things like that.

I decided to leave plenty of time to get to Grand Central from the hotel just in case I got a bit lost. The last thing I wanted to do was be late, but actually I didn't have any trouble finding it at all, and I was fifteen minutes early. I went and sat at a table on the right. They're the ones that overlook the station, you get a really good view.

I hate waiting for someone on my own, you feel like people are looking at you even though you know they're not. It always reminds me of what actors say about doing nothing being the hardest thing to do on stage. While I was reading the drinks menu I tried to make sure I was sitting in a relaxed way, not sprawled out like you would be at home watching TV, but also not uptight like someone who's nervous. This is the worst thing about waiting for someone. You have to look good all the time because they could turn up at any minute and see you before you've seen them. You can't take even a second to do something that isn't cool, like scratching the back of your thigh, because if you do you can guarantee that's the moment they'll arrive.

The waitress came up and asked if I'd like a drink while I was waiting, and I said yes. Then I realised I'd been reading the drinks menu for a good five minutes and I couldn't tell you a single thing on it, because I'd been so worried about how I looked. (I bet Alex never has things like this happening to him.) I decided I'd copy what we were doing last night, and I asked for a whisky. Then, just as the waitress

75

was about to leave, I asked if I could have quite a lot of water with it. I didn't want to get drunk in front of Elisabeth.

The waitress brought my drink, and I concentrated on only sipping a tiny bit each time. I sat there thinking, Hands and questions, hands and questions, hands and questions. Eventually Elisabeth arrived a few minutes late ('fashionably late', that'd be, I suppose). She was still in her work clothes, but she looked great even in those. I got really, really nervous when she was walking across to me, and I made an extra special effort not to knock anything over when I stood up. She said hello and sat down opposite me and smiled. Because the table was between us it meant we couldn't kiss each other hello. I didn't know whether we were going to anyway, but I was glad we didn't because often I get it wrong. I don't know whether you're supposed to do one or two, different people seem to do it different ways. I started by saying, 'Hello, how are you?' I worried it might have sounded a bit strange because we'd only seen each other a couple of hours ago, but Elisabeth didn't seem to think it was too strange, she said, 'Fine, how are you?' And I said, 'Fine, how are you?' Then I realised what I'd done and I felt a prat. I quickly asked Elisabeth if she'd like a drink and she said yes, she'd like a spritzer.

Then I asked if she'd made all her calls OK, but while she was answering that I had to keep one eye out for a waitress so I didn't really catch what she said. I had to hope she hadn't asked me a question. When she stopped speaking I just said 'great'. Then there was a bit of a pause, and Elisabeth asked me if everything was OK back at the hotel, and I said yes. But just as I said it a waitress appeared from behind me, which meant that Elisabeth got her attention before I could and asked for a spritzer. This wasn't good because I should have ordered the drink, but I tried to forget about it, and instead got on with the conversation.

I was determined to make as good a job of this as I could, especially because I was quite encouraged by the way Elisabeth had smiled when she'd turned up. It was a genuine smile, you know, when you can tell someone really means it, not like they're only there because they have to be. I knew I looked OK. I know I'm not really good-looking but also I'm not ugly or anything. I'm just sort of neutral. So it was up to me to try and interest Elisabeth, try and prove myself to her. That's what I mean about having to make a good job of the conversation.

I'd decided that a good way to start would be commenting on the surroundings, so I said, 'Great place, isn't it?' (I also remembered about my hands, and instead of pointing towards the station I nodded towards it with my head.) Elisabeth said yes it was. Then I said the thing I'd got ready, this was going to be my first really good comment, I said, 'They say it's the biggest room in the world.' But Elisabeth wasn't as impressed as I'd hoped she'd be, in fact she nodded and said, 'Yeah, I know.' Then she said, 'Although we had a talk from a motivational guru last year who told us that the biggest room in the world is the room for improvement.' I hadn't heard of this room, so I just nodded and said, 'Really?', but then I realised that it was a joke, you know, 'room for improvement', and I laughed a bit and said, 'Oh, I see'. Then Elisabeth said, 'We were not impressed by the motivational guru', and I tried to think of something to come back with, to agree with her about motivational gurus not being very good. But I couldn't really, we haven't had any at our firm, Miles doesn't go in for that sort of thing. So all I could say was 'no'.

This wasn't the start I'd been hoping for. But I tried to keep calm, and remember the things on my list. While I thought of something else to say I had a drink of my whisky. To avoid too much hand use I kept my left hand on my knee and picked the glass up with my right hand. This made me feel a bit more confident because I knew I was doing something right. But when I put my glass down again I realised I'd been too busy thinking about that and hadn't actually thought of anything to say. So I had to take another drink. This was when I remembered about my questions. I asked Elisabeth the first one I'd written down, which was, 'How long have you been an accountant?' She said, 'Six years.' She didn't say anything else. I thought, bugger, that's not how it's supposed to happen, the whole point of a question is it's meant to get her talking. So I had to think of a reply.

Six years didn't seem very long to me, because I thought she was about the same age as me and I qualified ten years ago. I thought maybe I could pursue this line, but then I realised it'd mean asking how old she was, which obviously you can't do to a woman. Then I had a few seconds sweating about how close I'd come to asking her that, and by then the silence had set in. This is what happens, you see. I get so worried about thinking of something good to say that my brain freezes, and then the panic begins, and it becomes a vicious circle. I try telling myself that if I relax it'll all be OK. But 'trying to relax' is a contradiction in terms, isn't it?

Just at that point the waitress showed up with Elisabeth's drink, and she also brought a bowl of nuts that she put on the table in front of us. Not peanuts like you get in pubs in London but those big brown ones, oval they are, I don't know what you call them. Elisabeth picked up her drink and I picked up mine (keeping my left hand on my knee) and we clinked our glasses together. Elisabeth said 'cheers' and I said 'cheers', and that was good, that got the conversation rolling again. I managed to think of something to ask Elisabeth: how long does it take to qualify as an accountant in America? She explained a bit about it, and then said she hadn't become an accountant until she was twenty-seven because she'd gone travelling after college (I think that's what they call university in America). Also, she'd lived in Rome for a couple of years.

This was good, it gave me something to go on. I asked her why she'd lived in Rome. She just said 'a guy' and gave that look people do when they shrug their shoulders except she didn't shrug her shoulders, it was like she was saying 'it didn't work out'. Now this *wasn't* good, because I got the feeling she didn't want to talk about it, like it had been a big, passionate affair. It would have been too prying to ask about it, so that killed off that bit of the conversation. Annoying, because that's the thing I can never do: move on from the polite, boring stuff to the interesting stuff, you know, talking about boyfriends and girlfriends and all that type of thing. That's when you can really make progress with someone, isn't it? When you can really 'flirt' with them. I wish I could do flirting.

I decided I'd better switch back to the questions I'd got ready, and tried to remember what the next one was on my list. While I did that I took another drink of whisky (this time I picked the glass up with my left hand and kept my right hand on my knee, just to be different). There was only a bit left, so when I put the glass back down it was empty. The waitress was passing and she said, 'Can I get you another?' I said, 'Yes please', and asked Elisabeth if she wanted another but she'd hardly had any of her first one yet, so she said no.

What with all of this happening I still hadn't remembered what the next question was. The whisky must have affected me a bit because no matter how hard I tried I just couldn't remember it. I decided to go to the toilet to have a look at the list. I told Elisabeth this (except obviously I didn't mention the list) and she told me where the toilet was, it was through some double doors and then you have to turn left. When I got in there I felt in the pocket I thought I'd put the list in, but it wasn't there. So I tried my other pocket but it wasn't there either. I tried my trouser pockets as well . . . I'd only forgotten the bloody list, hadn't I? This was where I really started to panic. I took some deep breaths and tried to remember the questions I'd written down, but even though I tried really hard I couldn't, not one of them. Then I tried to make up some new ones from scratch, but that was no good either, I was panicking so much I couldn't think straight. It was all going wrong. I was in a brilliant bar with a brilliant woman who I thought was really beautiful and I couldn't think of anything to say.

I stayed in the toilet as long as I could, but after a bit I had to go back out, Elisabeth would have thought something had happened to me. She smiled at me when I sat down, and by that time the waitress had brought my second drink so I had a sip of that. Well, I think in my panic it was more of a gulp actually. Elisabeth asked how the whisky was and I said 'very nice'. So then it was my turn to ask something, but like I say I couldn't think of anything good. I said the only question I could think of which was, 'What's your middle name?' Elisabeth looked a bit confused, and said she didn't have one, and I said, 'Oh'. Then I said, 'My middle name's Michael', and she said that was funny, that was her dad's middle name as well. I said, 'Oh, is he an accountant too?' and she said, 'No, he's a dentist.' But then I couldn't think of anything to say about dentists so that was the end of that.

All the time, though, Elisabeth was still smiling nicely at me. It was like she wanted the conversation to go well, I think she really did want to get along with me. It wasn't like she was bored with me or anything. She probably realised I was nervous. She started talking again, she told me a bit more about qualifying as an accountant. This was good, because it meant there wasn't that bloody silence any more. I had one of the nuts, and then another, and I noticed that I really liked them. I'd better be careful, I thought, I can't sit here eating all of these, I'll look like a complete pig. So I pushed them towards Elisabeth. Well, I had one more before I did that, but it was only one.

She was still telling me about how she'd qualified, and that gave me an idea. I decided to get my next question ready *before* she finished speaking. What always happens is I leave it until I have to say something before I start thinking what that something might be. So I got a question ready, it was: 'How long have you been at Annenberg's?' (That's the American firm.) I practised it in my head as Elisabeth was speaking. I said to myself, 'How long have you been at Annenberg's?' over and over again. Elisabeth was telling me about the college she went

81

to and some of the people there. All the time I was nod-ding and smiling and looking interested, and saying to myself 'How long have you been at Annenberg's? How long have you been at Annenberg's?' Then I could tell Elisabeth was about to wind up, she'd picked up her glass and she had it nearly to her mouth, and I was thinking, How long have you been at Annenberg's?, and then the last thing she said was, 'And then I joined Annenberg's, that was three years ago.'

This was just going from bad to bloody worse now. All I wanted to do was tell Elisabeth how beautiful I thought she was. But you're not allowed to do that, are you? You have to impress women and say clever things and make them laugh, then you're allowed to tell them you think they're beautiful, but not before. I wish I was like Alex. I mean, I'd seen last night he didn't think Elisabeth was beautiful, otherwise he'd have talked to her more, but I bet you if he did think she was beautiful he'd have been able to impress her by saying clever things.

To be honest with you I can't really remember what we said after that. The conversation never dried up completely, but it never really got going either. One thing that kept hap-pening was I'd find myself having a drink at the same time as Elisabeth so neither of us could say anything. I tried to make sure that when she finished saying something I hadn't got my glass to my lips, but the more I tried the more it seemed to happen. It was like if someone tells you not to think of a white horse, the first thing you think of is a white horse (an advertising bloke told me that at the firm's Christmas party last year). I didn't make a complete prat of myself with Elisabeth, but I didn't really get anywhere, either. It was very frustrating.

After a bit Elisabeth asked what Miles and Alex were doing, and we decided we should see if we could meet up with them. As we were leaving I promised myself that somehow, at some point, I'm going to have another go at making some progress with Elisabeth. And I'll make a real effort to get it right.

I really do like her.

When someone takes your mind off Manhattan, you know they're special. All day I wandered the town that thrills me every time I visit it and hardly noticed a thing. Tony and Elisabeth were holed up in her office talking figures, Miles was schmoozing the bosses, I had the day to myself. But no matter where I went or what I did, every thought led back to Elisabeth. I window-shopped on Fifth Avenue – how would that Tiffany necklace look on her? I went to the Metropolitan Museum and gazed at a painting worth more than my street – what would Elisabeth think of it? I did something I've always meant to do but never got round to: I took the subway under the East River and walked back across the Brooklyn Bridge. But it's a hell of a walk. All the more time to imagine doing it with Elisabeth's hand in mine.

Maybe I should have made more effort to talk to her at dinner. Or should I say made less of an effort not to talk to her. Perhaps she'd have bored me, been less irresistible than my imagination was telling me. But who was I kidding? I'd overheard her conversations with Miles and Walter and Mary, and with every word she hooked me in a little bit more.

And all the time I kept thinking about the book, what it had said about my past relationships, repeating the mistakes in my future ones. Not that I was expecting a relationship with Elisabeth, of course; I didn't know what she thought of me, whether she'd noticed me as much as I'd noticed her. That wasn't the point. The point was I was *imagining* being in a relationship with her, dreaming of how thrilling it would be, that thrill you get in the first few days and weeks of being with someone new. It was the first time I'd been this bowled over by anyone since I split up with Amy. The way I felt about Elisabeth was what I thought I'd had with Amy, before we started arguing too much. The worry that caused me made me think about the book, made me wonder if I hadn't dismissed it too easily.

No one had made plans for the night. I was back at the Paramount waiting to hear from Tony. As I watched the same CNN report for what felt like the thousandth time, my phone finally rang.

'Alex? It's me.'

'Hi there. Where are you?'

'I'm at Grand Central Terminal. I'm with Elisabeth, you see, and we were wondering, do you fancy meeting up?' I wasn't sure, but he sounded a bit drunk.

'Sure. Jump in a cab, I'll see you in the bar in ten minutes.'

'Right you are.'

I changed my shirt. I checked that my hair looked OK. I put on some aftershave. I tried to tell myself I'd have done these things whoever I was meeting.

So Tony had taken Elisabeth for a drink without asking me along? I thought back to the night before, his expression as he watched her talking to Miles, the fact he'd kept looking at her even when it was Miles who was speaking, like someone watching only one of the players in a tennis match. I'd suspected as much. I wasn't alone in my feelings for her.

I reached the bar just as they were entering the lobby, so I stood and waited for them to climb the stairs. Tony was walking in front of Elisabeth, looking back at her as he spoke, turning round every few seconds to check he wasn't going to bump into anything. (He nearly did, but saw the table just in time.) She was calmness itself, though, walking at her own pace, smiling politely at whatever Tony was saying, all the time exuding that unflappability.

They reached me. I smiled.

'All right, Alex?'

'Fine.'

As I said it Tony moved to one side, and there she was, still blinking, still unflappable, still sexy.

'Hello, Elisabeth.'

'Hi.'

I stepped towards her. The previous night we'd shaken hands. Was that too formal now? Should we kiss? We were getting closer, my hand found hers. But only because I'd stepped forward – she was still motionless, waiting for me to come to her. Now my head was bowing forward, my lips heading for her cheek. They brushed it, and I could feel her lips on my cheek too. How long did we stay like that? Enough time for me to catch her scent as I breathed in. Did we prolong the kiss beyond normal polite levels? Or was it just my nervousness making me feel like we did?

'How was Grand Central?'

Tony bobbed beside us. 'It was OK.'

'Did you go and see the Whispering Gallery?'

Elisabeth looked at Tony. 'I didn't know you wanted to see that. You should have told me.'

'I didn't know about it,' said Tony.

'Yes you did,' I replied. 'I told you about it yesterday.'

'No you didn't.'

'Didn't I? Sorry, I thought I had. It's an archway down on the lower level. Outside the Oyster Bar. You can hear someone whispering from the other side of it.'

'Like the wall in St Paul's Cathedral?'

'Yeah.'

'I tried that when I went to London,' said Elisabeth. 'Couldn't get it to work.'

'Really?' *Who did you go to London with?*

'We couldn't hear a thing. Maybe it was the atmospheric conditions.'

I nodded wisely.

'Then again, it could have been the two dozen screaming schoolchildren.'

I continued to nod wisely before realising what she'd said. Her expression was so deadpan that even after she'd said something funny you couldn't believe she'd said something funny. Which, once you realised she had, made it all the funnier. And that made her all the more sexy.

We moved into the bar and found a table. Elisabeth sat on a sofa, Tony and I were on chairs facing her. Once we'd ordered drinks I asked how the day's book-checking had gone.

'Fine,' said Elisabeth. 'Your man here certainly is thorough in his work.'

'So you didn't spot the million-pound hole in the accounts?'

Tony seemed to flinch; must have been the booze. 'I'm sure Elisabeth doesn't want to talk about work,' he said, looking at her as he did so.

'You're right, it'd be boring for Alex.' She turned to me. 'How did you keep yourself busy today, then?'

I thought of you. 'Wandered around.' I told them about

the museum and the shops. The bridge. How I'd continued down Canal Street when I'd crossed it. Elisabeth mentioned a Chinese restaurant she always goes to there. We started trading New York comments. Tony, of course, couldn't really join in. I felt bad. The only thing more obvious in his eyes than his drunkenness was how he felt about Elisabeth. He was still doing his half-a-tennis-match routine. A couple of times I tried to include him in the conversation, but it was never going to work. Elisabeth mentioned the Woolworth Building, and he asked me if that was the one where they pushed the top up at the end to win the competition. I reminded him that was the Chrysler.

I went to the gents, hoping it would allow him to strike up a conversation of his own with her. But when I got back they were sitting there in silence. And someone had taken my chair, which meant I had to sit next to her on the sofa. Whenever she reached forward for her drink I could smell her perfume again.

We ordered another round. Then another. Miles showed up, looking like he'd had plenty of rounds of his own.

'Thought I'd find you in here,' he boomed. 'Well, well, if it isn't the best accountant in the world. And you're here as well, Tony.'

Tony joined in the laughter. I think I was the only one who noticed the effort he had to make.

'How did it go today?' asked Miles. 'All the figures making sense, are they?'

'Sure,' said Elizabeth. 'Everything looks shipshape.'

'Splendid, splendid.' I could almost see the dollar signs appearing in his eyes. He gestured towards me and Tony. 'And I trust these two reprobates are behaving themselves with you?'

'Sadly they are,' replied Elisabeth.

Miles grinned at her, then added a wink for good measure.

'What can I get you, Miles?' I asked.

'No, no, I'm only popping in to say hello. You youngsters don't want a granddad like me hanging around, cramping your style.' Obviously he had other plans. 'Besides, there's an old friend I said I'd have a drink with.' I bet she wasn't all that old. 'I'll catch up with you tomorrow, OK?'

With an elaborate bow he was off. But as he got to the staircase he looked back at us. Seeing that Elisabeth was bending to move her handbag out of someone's way, he signalled her with a nod of his head, and gave me a leery 'Bit of all right, isn't she, why don't you give it a go?' look. From where he was sitting Tony couldn't see. Even though Miles's look had nothing to do with me, I still felt guilty about it.

'My bet,' said Elisabeth quietly, 'is that they work together, his wife thinks he's out with the guys, and her dependable but boring boyfriend is waiting for her at their home in New Jersey.'

'Sorry?'

'Two o'clock.' She flicked her eyes, but not her head, to the right. I turned discreetly and looked past Tony at a couple sitting a few tables away. She was twenty-five or so, he must have been twice that. They were both wearing expensive business suits, although the way they were flirting you wouldn't have bet on that staying true for very long. Everything Elisabeth had said seemed totally believable.

'I think he's her boss,' I said, 'but even if he wasn't she'd still want to sleep with him.'

Tony turned round to see who we were talking about. He did it in a totally obvious way, but I didn't mind, in fact I wanted him to attract the couple's attention. Then Elisabeth and I would have to stop our game.

'They haven't slept together yet,' she said. 'But tonight could be the night.'

'That's incredible, Agent Starling, how the hell do you deduce that?' What was I doing? Why was I playing along? How could I do this to Tony? Why didn't I get him back into the conversation?

Elisabeth gave me a mock-disapproving look, but didn't say anything. This was my chance. 'What do you reckon, Tony?' I asked.

'They certainly seem quite fond of each other, I have to say.'

That did a good enough job of killing off the discussion. The three of us chatted about . . . well, I can't remember, everything we said was so mundane. Remarks became dead-ends, the conversation had no flow to it. Tony – I hated myself for thinking it, but I had no choice – was a weight around our necks, he was stopping Elisabeth and me from . . . something. I didn't want to think what that something could be.

She stood up. 'You must excuse me.' I noticed her glass (like mine) was empty. Would she be having another drink when she got back, or was this the end of the night? *Please don't go. Please stay with me. With us.*

'You all right, Tony?' His glass was still half-full. He hadn't touched it for ages.

'Mmm. Feel tired.'

'Jet lag?'

'I think it's the whisky. Think I'm a bit drunk.'

'We should go and get something to eat.'

'Don't want to eat. It'll make me ill.'

'It won't make you ill, it'll make you better.'

But you could tell he'd made his mind up. 'No, I'm going back to my room.'

Don't do this to me, Tony. 'Come on, this is New York City, you can't go to bed at half past eight.'

'Need some sleep.'

Elisabeth came back. 'What's happening?'

What's happening is that I'm desperate to stay with you. And wishing I wasn't. Not just because of Tony, either. There's something about this – about us flirting, about me being attracted to you – something that's bad news . . . 'We were just talking about going for dinner.'

'Great. Where do you want to eat?'

'How about Joe Allen's?' She'd mentioned it earlier.

'Sure.' She turned, ready to leave.

I stood up. 'Come on, Tony.'

'Nah.' He wasn't going to be railroaded. 'I'm really tired. I'm going to call it a night.' He looked up at Elisabeth. 'I think it must be the jet lag.'

'Are you sure?'

'Yeah.'

'Well, I'll see you in the morning,' she said. 'Thanks for all your help today.'

He nodded. "S all right. See you tomorrow.' He looked undecided about saying something else, but then just mumbled goodnight.

He walked off to the lifts. I wanted to follow him, make a show of solidarity with him. I was going out to dinner with the woman he fancied. I hated myself for being so excited about it.

As we left the bar the all-over-each-other couple were ordering another bottle of champagne. 'Poor Duane's going to be waiting up late tonight,' said Elisabeth.

'Duane?' I replied. 'I had him down as more of an Eric.'

'Mmm. Perhaps you're right. Then again, what about Howard? He could be a Howard.'

I wrinkled my nose. 'I'm sticking with Eric.'

The restaurant was close by, so we walked there. We chatted, not about anything important, just the sort of stuff we'd been talking about with Tony, but a million times more relaxed. No awkward pauses while we sat down, looked at the menu, ordered. Then, when we'd got our wine, Elisabeth raised her glass.

'Here's to . . . Here's to a dinner where you've got no choice but to talk to me.'

I tried to play dumb. 'I'm sorry?'

'Seeing as this is only our second dinner together, it's not a hard one to work out, Alex.'

'Oh, last night?'

'Yes. Last night.'

'Did you think I wasn't talking to you? I'm sorry, I didn't . . .' But her expression told me not to bother insulting her intelligence. 'It was . . .' *We both know what it was, Alex.* 'You see . . .' *Yeah, she does see. She sees how attracted I am to her. But if she was bothered by last night, she wouldn't be here, would she?* I gave up.

We reverted to chit-chat for a while. When we were on our main courses, Elisabeth said, 'So, Alex. Alex Richards.'

'I don't remember telling you my surname.'

'There's a complete list of Langley and Langley's clients as an appendix to the accounts.'

'Ah, I see.'

'So, Alex – what's Mrs Richards doing while you're in New York?'

'Oh, you know, knitting, watching television, keeping

92

the house tidy. The sort of things pensioners do.'

She smiled. 'OK – girlfriend.'

I could lie. But you can check with Tony tomorrow. 'Girlfriend? Moi?'

Silence.

You want me to ask if you've got a boyfriend, don't you? Not going to. Don't want you to know I'm interested. Well, I think you know I'm interested. Just want to hide it. From myself if not from you. 'How's your food?'

'Great. Yours?'

'Lovely.' *I'm glad we didn't do the 'trying each other's food' thing. There's some formality left here at least.*

'Mind if I try a bit?'

'Sure.' I cut her some steak, she swapped it for some duck. We both agreed they were both delicious.

Neither of us bothered with dessert.

Elisabeth sipped her coffee. 'I bet they're still there.'

I pretended not to know who she meant.

'Probably on their next bottle of champagne.'

I can't pretend any more, can I? 'They're finding it difficult to make the final move.'

'Enjoying the anticipation too much. But I bet they're sitting on one of the sofas now, instead of at that table.'

'No, I think they liked the table.' *Of course none of this means anything unless you come back to the hotel with me to check, does it? Well, I'm not inviting you. I'm not giving in. I'm just going to sit here and drink my coffee.*

Elisabeth played with the lump of sugar on her saucer. 'I bet you they're on a sofa.'

I can't play a stupid game like this then suddenly get serious. 'Table.' I paused. 'I'll give you a call tomorrow to let you know who won.'

She smiled, a calm, self-confident smile, then asked our waitress for the bill. She didn't have to tell me that the smile meant she was coming back to the Paramount. Or that she knew that's what I wanted.

Sure enough, when we got to the hotel the couple were still there. On a sofa.

Elisabeth laughed. 'I win.'

'I guess it's my round then.'

'It was your round anyway.'

So what's the stake?

We found somewhere we could spy on the couple, and sat down. It was a sofa. The night had obviously reached its 'sitting together on a sofa' stage. Elisabeth wasn't too close to me, but our bodies were certainly angled towards each other. It felt comfortable.

'She knows deep down he'd never leave his wife for her,' said Elisabeth.

'But she still resents Eric for being boring. She knows that . . . We haven't got a name for him yet.'

Elisabeth studied the man. 'I think he's . . . James.'

'Yeah, I can see that. Definitely James, though, not Jim.'

'Definitely.'

'She knows James is exciting, intelligent, an achiever. She thinks she deserves someone like him. Someone who can satisfy her intellectually. Which Eric can't.'

'Or maybe her resentment about Howard . . . it's no use arguing, he's called Howard, that's all there is to it . . . is because secretly she knows she's not as intelligent as she'd like to be. Really she's a Howard kind of girl, even though she wants to be like James.'

'Maybe. Reflected glory. Yeah, you could be on to something.'

We watched them for a while. A waiter brought our drinks. We both leaned forward to take sips, and when we sat back found ourselves slightly closer to each other. Not in each other's personal space yet, but it was noticeable.

'Tell me about London,' said Elisabeth.

'Quite big. Pretty noisy. Romans invented it.'

'I meant you in London.'

'There isn't a me in London. I work there, but I don't live there.'

'No?'

'Used to. Live out in Kent now. Small town. Not even the centre of a small town.'

'Really? I imagined some hip bachelor pad on Piccadilly.'

'Piccadilly? How much money do you think there is in voice-overs? No, boring, small-town boy.' *Why did you say that? Sounds like you're fishing for compliments. Switch it to her, ask about her. No, don't, that'll only make it worse. Pretend you're not interested in her. Even though you want to know every last detail about her.*

We lapsed back into silence. After a while I could hear her breathing. It was steady, regular, unhurried. Like everything else about her.

The middle-aged guy stood up, took his mobile from his pocket. He examined the screen, then stepped out of the bar before answering the call.

'She's checking up on him,' I said.

'Do you think she suspects anything?'

'Could well do. He should have left his phone switched off.'

'Then she'd definitely be suspicious.'

'Good point.' I looked back at the girl. 'Do you think she's the only one he's fooling around with?'

'At the moment, yeah. He's definitely been unfaithful

before, but only ever with one woman at a time.'

'Never struggles to attract women.'

'No, I'm sure he doesn't. There'll always be girls who fall for men like him.'

'But you wouldn't?'

'Not my type.'

Don't say it. Take a drink. I took a drink. Put the glass down. Sat back. 'What is your type?' *I tried, didn't I?*

Elisabeth thought. 'I don't really have one.'

'Well how can you say he's not your type?'

'You can have a type you don't go for without having one you do go for.'

'Can you?'

'Of course. The ones you like are always the ones who surprise you.'

I nodded, the sort of nod that shows you're thinking about it but aren't going to respond. *Stay away from this. Don't put any more fuel on the fire.* Eventually I breathed in, a deep, changing-the-subject breath, and said, 'So how long have you been at Annenberg's?'

There was no reply. For a moment I wondered if Elisabeth hadn't heard me. Then I felt her looking at me, a look that was burning the side of my face. I turned towards her. 'You can claim to be a boring, small-town boy if you like,' she said. 'But please don't try and pretend you're *that* boring.'

Suddenly I was on the inside of Elisabeth's bubble. The one she keeps around her, the bubble of calmness that protects her from everyone else. No one gets inside, no one gets close to her. Unless she wants them to, of course. And I was inside it. It was just me and her, side by side, knowing we were attracted to each other, both knowing that we both knew it. It was secure and terrifying at the same time.

The man had returned from his phone call.

'It was definitely his wife,' said Elisabeth. 'Look at the way they're sitting.'

The couple weren't even touching any more, let alone mauling each other. 'That's ruined their evening.' *Unlike us. How have we got this close? Our legs will be touching soon. I haven't made a deliberate effort to move. Have you? Or are we doing it without realising?*

'Kind of makes you feel sorry for them. Must be a serious thing, for them to be that guilty. More than just a casual office-fuck.'

It was a shock hearing Elisabeth swear for the first time. But then again not really, not with what she was swearing about. It felt easy talking to her about sex. Was she the sort to indulge in casual office-fucks? Casual fucks of any kind? Somehow I knew she wasn't.

We watched them for a bit longer. Then I said, 'Tell me about New York.'

'New York? Hmm.' Elisabeth crossed her legs. Now her foot was dangling close to my shin, occasionally brushing against it. 'What can I tell you about New York?'

I turned more towards her, put my elbow on the back of the sofa, rested my head against my hand.

'Lots of men in New York. Many of them like our friend over there.'

'You mean attached?'

She nodded her head.

'And you don't . . .' I put on a cod American accent, '". . . do the attached thing"?'

'I don't,' she turned up her own accent, '"do the attached thing".' As she said it she rested her arm on the sofa, mirrored my pose. Her hair fell back on one side, revealing her neck. I wanted to kiss it.

'Surely there must be some unattached men in New York?'

'Yeah, there are. Nine times out of ten you can see why.'

'And the tenth?'

'Gay.'

'Oh well. At least that gives you someone to go shopping with.'

She gave a little laugh. It died away, leaving a smile. I smiled back at her, our eyes not leaving each other's for a second. Then the smiles died away. Neither of us moved. She'd brought me down to her level of stillness. Her gaze flickered to my lips for a second. Mine did to hers. Then we locked stares again. I knew my heart should be racing, but it wasn't. This felt completely natural. Still neither of us moved, or said a word. We stayed like this for . . . oh, I don't know, it's impossible to measure time when you're feeling like that. It was sublime. But scary too. My doubts were growing, breeding by the second. Why? I didn't really understand it. It was just a feeling I'd got. You know when you begin to feel nauseous, that bit before you actually feel sick, before you even get the dryness in the mouth, before there's any physical sign at all? Those few moments when you know something's wrong but you can't put your finger on it, almost as if there's a ghost in the room with you? It was like that.

I made myself look away. The couple we'd been watching were standing up.

'All bets are off for tonight,' I said.

Elisabeth took a second to realise what I meant. 'Oh, them. Yeah. I wonder how they've left it?'

'They'll be back for more. Sooner or later.'

'They do work together, after all.'

Now the couple were walking out of the bar. 'Look how close they're staying to each other,' I said. 'I bet their good-night kiss will be more than just a peck on the cheek.'

'Mmm.'

'Shall we follow them and see?'

Elisabeth laughed. 'There's a line where "curious" becomes "Peeping Tom", you know.'

'Yes, your Honour.'

'Besides, this sofa is really comfortable. Don't you think?'

Too comfortable. 'It's a comfortable hotel.'

'Except the rooms are small. From what everyone says.'

Don't respond, Alex. Don't fall into her trap. 'You've never stayed here?' *Didn't you hear me? I said don't fall . . .*

'Seems kind of dumb to pay for a hotel room in your hometown.'

'Yeah, but you could have . . .' *What? What can you possibly mean by that, Alex, apart from 'gone back to the room of someone who was staying here'?*

'You're right. I could have. But I haven't.'

Are you going to supply the 'until now' or are you waiting for me to do it? I tried to think of something to say that would change the subject. I could pick any comment I wanted. I didn't have to talk about the rooms at all. 'My rooms have never seemed that small here, I've got to say.'

'Really? The phrase people always use is "postage stamp".'

'I know, I've been lucky, I guess.'

'You mean you think they,' she magnified her accent once more, '"just *adore* your cute little English accent"?'

I laughed. 'Did I say that?'

'You didn't have to. Just how huge is your room, Mr Big Shot? To the nearest hectare?' She waited for me to respond to the teasing. I refused to play ball. 'I bet it's not a big room at all. I bet you're just boasting.'

She was smiling. So was I. The smiles drifted away. We fell silent again. Stared into each other's eyes again. Still I fought against it. I thought about playing the 'been a long day' card. But even though it had, I still couldn't produce a yawn. I broke away from Elisabeth's gaze and looked round the bar, trying to find someone else yawning, hoping it would be contagious. But it seemed yawns are up there with policemen in the 'can't find 'em when you need 'em' stakes.

I looked at her lips, then back into her eyes. I could feel myself giving in. That sense of unease was still there. But the thought of kissing those lips . . .

'There's only one way I can think of . . .' I began.

'Ye-e-s?'

'. . . of proving to you that I'm not lying about the room.'

Elisabeth nodded thoughtfully. 'I certainly can't think of another.'

I left the slightest pause. Then: 'You call the lift. I'll sign for the drinks.'

When the lift came another couple of people got in with us. That dulled our flirting, but as we got out and walked along the corridor to my room Elisabeth said quietly, 'It's actually quite embarrassing for me, having to call your bluff like this. I can only hope it'll stop you lying to impress people in the future.'

I laughed, but didn't say anything. We reached my door. I unlocked it, stood back to let Elisabeth through. She walked into the room. I followed, letting the door close behind me. Three possible places to sit. The white leather armchair. The smaller chair in front of the desk. The bed. I decided to stay standing.

'Well, well, well,' said Elisabeth. 'It looks like I owe Mr Richards an apology. This is no far-as-the-eye-can-see suite, but it's certainly no postage stamp either.'

'I think it's what you might reasonably call a hotel-room-sized hotel room.'

She sat in the armchair. Its back was incredibly high, way higher than it needed to be to support even a giant's head. It was the sort of thing you'd see in a pop video. The other chair was right next to her. If I sat there we'd be within touching distance. There was still fight left in me, that feeling of unease telling me this was a bad idea. I sat on the end of the bed, remembering just in time how stupid you look if you lean back with nothing to support you. I leaned forward, elbows on knees.

'I feel terrible now,' said Elisabeth.

'I'm sorry?'

'For doubting your word.'

'So you should. Disgraceful slur on my name.'

'I really don't know how I can make it up to you.'

'No ideas at all?'

She grinned. 'Well, maybe the one . . .'

She stood up. I kept my gaze fixed on the chair. She walked towards the bed. I felt her sit down next to me. There was a moment, as I stared ahead, when the fight stayed in me, when I listened to my doubts. But they still wouldn't give me a straight answer, wouldn't tell me exactly what the unease was all about. How could they expect me to resist Elisabeth if they weren't going to give me the whole picture?

She leaned towards me. 'About that idea . . .' The words were whispered, so that I could feel her breath on my neck. I gave in. I turned, and our mouths met.

*

My doubts stayed away for a long time. All of yesterday, for certain. The day started at about seven a.m., when Elisabeth woke me to kiss me goodbye. She was going home to get changed, ready for another (as she put it) 'exciting session with the accounts'. Although she did admit Tony was sweet, if a little shy. Again I wandered the streets all day, but this time my thoughts weren't about what it would be like to sleep with Elisabeth, they were about what it had been like to sleep with Elisabeth. And how much I wanted to sleep with her again. Last night we all had our farewell dinner. Once in a while my eyes would meet Elisabeth's across the table, and for an instant there'd be the thrill of our shared secret. Then it was back to routine conversation, and the anticipation of what lay in store later.

As the British and American parties exchanged goodbyes outside the restaurant, Elisabeth slipped a folded piece of paper into my pocket. The first chance I got to read it was when I paid for our cab back at the Paramount (the journey felt like hours). It said: 'I'll come to your room at eleven-thirty.' This gave me time for a nightcap with Tony (Miles was off, presumably seeing his 'old friend' again). I tried not to feel too guilty as we talked. I thought about telling him what had happened the night before, but decided not to. If nothing comes of it, I thought, which it might well not, what's the point in him knowing? What he doesn't know can't hurt him.

We finished our drinks and called it a night.

Elisabeth was three minutes late.

Six-thirty this morning was when my doubts came back. Good time of day, that, for doubts. The little bastards know your defences are down.

Elisabeth and I had woken earlier, and made love in that wonderful still-half-asleep-but-somehow-more-alert-because-of-it way. Then she drifted back to sleep, but my jet lag kicked in and kept me awake. And I began to feel depressed. 'All animals are sad after sex.' It's a Latin phrase (*omne* something or other). If people have been saying it for two thousand years there's got to be something to it. There's the chemical explanation, of course. All the endorphins, or whatever it is your brain produces during sex, disappear, and you get the emotional equivalent of a rainstorm after sunshine. But there was more to it than that this morning, I know there was. I had the same feeling of unease I had in the bar the other night, the same thoughts about that book.

I got out of bed, pulled on a dressing gown and went over to the window. I stared down on Manhattan. Then at my reflection in the glass. Why did I feel so down? The more I tried to grab it, the more it eluded me.

I went to Grand Central again this morning. It was our last day in New York, and I'd woken up early and couldn't get back to sleep, so I put the television on, but I couldn't find anything interesting. Then I remembered about that Whispering Gallery thing Alex mentioned the other night, and I thought I might as well get up and go for a look at it.

I thought about Elisabeth a lot. I've been thinking about her all the time, actually. I felt a bit down yesterday when we were working in her office, after the way I'd messed up my chance with her the night before. She was still nice to me and she asked me lots of questions about Joe and Georgia. But I want her to be more than nice to me. I want her to like me as much as I like her. Maybe it's just that she's really hard to impress. I mean, even last night, when we all went out to dinner again, even Alex didn't seem to impress her that much. She hardly paid him any attention at all.

I walked over to Grand Central. With it being so early there weren't too many people about, which was good because it meant I could stand and look up at it all without getting in anyone's way. I looked for signs to the Whispering Gallery, but there weren't any. Then I remembered Alex had said it was outside the 'Oyster Bar', and I found a police-man who told me where that was, down some stairs off the main bit of the station. It took me a while to work out where the whispering bit was, but I think I got it right, there are two tunnels that cross each other, I think it must be there. The thing was, though — and I hadn't really thought about this on the way across, which I suppose was pretty stupid — I couldn't try the whispering thing because I didn't have anyone to whisper to, or anyone who could whisper to me. I thought about asking a passer-by if they'd stop and help me, but that would just have looked weird.

So all I could do was stand there and look at it. It was still early (half past six), so it wasn't that busy. I stood under the arch and imagined what it would be like if Elisabeth was there, whispering to me, me whispering to her. That made me feel depressed, though, because that would never happen, so I tried to stop imagining it. But I couldn't.

Never mind travelling the road to commitment; even finding it is a hard enough task for today's thirty-somethings. You're the generation I like to call the 'change generation'.

I lasted five hours after I'd got back to England. Tried telling myself I could ignore what had happened with Elisabeth – or rather what I'd felt while it was happening – because it had all taken place in New York, a fairytale place where strange things happen all the time. Almost persuaded myself it hadn't happened at all, it had been a dream.

Almost, but not quite. My worries hung around, niggled me, kept telling me I had to take another look at that book.

Chapter Two of *The Road To Commitment* was headed: 'USP and the Change Generation'. Ignoring the thought that this sounded like a little-known Motown act, I read on. What the Good Doctor Susanna meant by the 'change generation' was that our parents, certainly our grandparents, had it easy when it came to choices: they didn't have any. The local cinema showed one movie a week, there was one style of clothes everybody bought, everyone drove the same sort of car. In other words, there was only one sort of person you could be. So it didn't really matter who you got married to (something you did at twenty-one): everyone was the same anyway. But now, there are a million choices to be made – our lives are full of change. Employment, fashion, entertainment – we define who we are by making our choices in each of them. Which makes it all the harder to pick someone who's right for you.

Susanna obviously wasn't saying your ideal partner is someone who likes the same cut of jeans as you. But she did say that almost all her clients have failed in their past relationships because they keep being attracted to the same kind of person; there was something those partners had in common (something the person themselves hadn't spotted) that ruined the relationship every time, became their Unique Staleness Point.

'The change generation', I ask you. But I gave my irritation a moment to depart. I didn't want the jargon blinding me to the underlying message. This book had got me intrigued. Going for the same sort of person all the time; maybe that's what Rosie had meant when she said Susanna would approve of her trying a bank manager? I can't remember her ever having a boyfriend with such a conventional job.

I remembered that Manhattan dawn, my ghost-in-the-room feeling. I wanted to take this seriously, work it out, decide what I felt. Had Dr Grove got something to tell me after all?

Sunday evening. I'd gone to see Mum for a couple of days. The two of us were sitting in the kitchen, finishing our Individual Chocolate Mousses.

'That was lovely,' I said. 'Thanks.'

'Nice, aren't they?' said Mum, standing up and taking my empty pot. 'Normally they're forty-five pence, and I wouldn't pay that for them, but Morrisons had them on special, three for ninety-nine, so I thought why not?'

On the table in front of me was a cheque for a five-figure sum. The latest instalment from Dad's life insurance payout. I allowed myself a quiet smile, but made sure it was gone before Mum turned round again.

'Do you want anything else?'

'No thanks, Mum. Couldn't eat another thing.'

From the portable TV in the corner came the opening music of *Who Wants To Be A Millionaire?* At the same time there was the sound of a car pulling up outside.

'Ooh, that'll be Jill,' she said, heading for the front door.

While she was gone I took over making the tea.

'Hurry up, Jill,' came Mum's voice from the hallway. 'You're just in time for *Millionaires*.'

After a few seconds they both appeared in the kitchen.

'Hello, young Alex,' said Jill. She always calls me that. 'How are you?'

'Oh, mustn't grumble, you know.' I always say that to her.

'Now you sit down,' said Mum, taking the teapot from my hand. 'I'll do that.'

I raised my eyebrows and gave Jill a 'what can you do?' smile.

'Your Mum told me she spoke to Amy the other week,' beamed Jill. She made it sound as though Mum had been granted an audience with the Pope.

'Yeah, she was round dropping some stuff off.'

'Ahhh. She's a . . .'

I braced myself.

'. . . lovely girl.'

I didn't dare look up. I knew Mum and Jill would be smiling and nodding at each other.

There was a tinny round of applause as the first contestant took the chair. He was carrying on from the last programme with two thousand pounds.

'Did you see that one who lost the quarter of a million the other night?' asked Jill.

'I *know*,' said Mum. 'Why didn't he take the money? Did you know it, Alex?'

'No. I knew it wasn't Henry the second, but apart from that I'd have been guessing. Except I wouldn't. Not with two hundred and fifty grand. Well, two hundred and eighteen.'

Jill shook her head. 'I bet he's regretting it now.'

And so on. Occasionally I watched the two of them watching the programme, and marvelled. Forty years of friendship, and they still saw each other nearly every day. What did they find to talk about?

Monday afternoon. Sitting in the main room, Mum on the sofa, me in one of the armchairs. Dad's empty chair – that's what it still seems like, what I suppose it's always going to seem like – between us. We were watching a documentary about lions. After a while I started doing what I'd done the night before, watched Mum as she watched the TV. She was fascinated by it. And I saw how this world – her world, the world that existed within this house, within this village – had never changed. I used to be part of it. I used to sit here with her and Dad, doing silly voices to nature programmes, watching quiz shows, saying 'mustn't grumble'. But then I grew up, and I moved away, changed.

Yeah, OK, 'the change generation' was a crappy bit of jargon. But the idea behind it . . .

I looked over to the table, where the lunch things had all been tidied away, the pepper pot with its three tiny holes in the top, its fine brown powder. That's what pepper used to mean to me. Now it means hard black peppercorns, mills instead of pots. Through the doorway I could see Mum's coat hanging up in the hall. Bound to be Marks & Spencer. That's where she always gets her coats.

I feel horrible saying all this, because it might sound snobbish. It isn't meant to. I'm not saying I'm better than I used to be, or better than Mum. Of course I'm not. She's happy as she is, which is just the same as she always was, and I love her just as much as I always have. I'm just pointing out that when I was back there, in that world, the world that hasn't changed, I got my coats from M&S too, because . . . well, because where else do you get your coats from in that world? I mean, even if it wasn't about me being a kid and my mum buying my coats for me, I'd still have been an M&S coat-buyer. But now I'm not. I've got four coats, one of which was from Boss and one of which was from a second-hand shop years ago but which I still like, and none of which are from M&S. That's all I'm saying: I've changed, broadened my horizons, tried new things.

I remembered something from my childhood. I was nine or ten, watching the news with Mum and Dad. There was an item about a near-miss over Heathrow Airport, and because TV graphics were so basic in those days they'd done the little picture in the top-right hand corner by getting a photo of some blue sky with clouds on it, and sticking on photos of the two types of plane involved.

'Good God!' Mum had said. 'They really were close, weren't they?'

I'd laughed at her and explained how they'd done it and

110

said, 'You didn't really think that was a photo of it actually happening, did you?', and Dad had laughed and said, 'Sometimes I despair of you, June', and Mum had laughed too. And I can remember feeling different from Mum (and Dad), even then. I think I already knew that one day I'd leave that village of theirs, I'd go off into the big wide world and change.

'The big wide world.' The phrase stuck in my mind (time for a bit of jargon of my own, perhaps). It is a big world. I've seen quite a bit of it, there's still lots I want to see. But Mum – she's never been west of the Costa del Sol or east of Great Yarmouth.

The change generation. Yeah, I thought. There's something in that.

'No.'

'*Please.*'

'*No.*'

'Just a quick look.'

It was the following weekend. Rosie was over at my flat. We were going to Kathy's barbecue. Kathy had said I could bring a friend.

I'd told Rosie about Elisabeth. Then I made the mistake of adding that Elisabeth had sent me an e-mail.

'No,' I said. 'Absolutely not.'

'Oh, go on.'

'Rosie, I've told you, I can remember the bloody e-mail word for word. I've read it enough times. She said—'

'*Don't* tell me. It won't be the same. I need to see it on the screen.'

'Why?'

'To really get a feel for what she's like.'

'It's nothing to do with you being the nosiest woman in the world, then?'

'Alex, you're the one who's just spent three-quarters of an hour talking about her.'

'Yeah, but what I don't understand is how you're going to get any more of a "feel for what she's like" by seeing whether she uses Arial or Times New Roman.'

We carried on like this for a few minutes before I decided to end the argument by doing what I always do to end arguments with Rosie. I let her win.

'Before you're allowed to look at the e-mail,' I said as we sat in the spare room, waiting for the computer to boot up, 'you've got to let me edit it first.'

'Embarrassing bit, is there?'

I didn't reply.

'Glad to hear it,' said Rosie. 'I'd be disappointed in you if there wasn't.'

I made her turn away while I used the return key to edit two particular sentences off the bottom of the screen. 'Right,' I said, 'all done. You can turn round now.'

What confronted Rosie was:

well, i never expected my investigations into langley and langley to be quite that detailed! not that i'm complaining, and i'm certainly not complaining about that coffee from room service. waiter was kinda handsome, i thought. hope he was happy with the tip i gave him.

how's england? too long since i've been there. (hmm . . .)

went back to the bar at the paramount the night you left — some of the girls at work wanted to go out

drinking, i said i knew just the place — no sign of the
lovers, but when i'm there again i'll keep a lookout.

xx

ps . . .

'"PS" what?' asked Rosie. 'Oh. That was the bit you edited.'
'Yep.'
She grinned. 'Let's have a look.'
'Don't even waste your breath.'
'Pretty please?'
'Pretty no-way-in-a-million-years.'
She shrugged. 'Fair enough.' Then, looking back at the
screen, 'What's this about room service and coffee?'
'The hotel's got a Dean and Deluca, and Elisabeth had
said the night before how much she loved their coffee. So
while she was still asleep I got dressed and went downstairs
and fetched her one.'
'And the tip?'
'Rosie, you have a very fertile imagination. Why don't
you use it?'
'I have. I want to find out if I imagined right.'
'See previous answer about PS.'
'Killjoy. I have to say though, Alex, top marks for
romance. Getting up early to bring the girl her favourite
coffee.'
'I couldn't sleep.'
'Stop it. False modesty doesn't become you.'
'It's not false modesty. Really, I couldn't get back to sleep, so
I thought I might as well go and buy us both a coffee. I wasn't
romantic, just jet-lagged. Well, jet-lagged and worried.'

'Worried?'

'About Elisabeth. About falling into bed with her so easily.'

'I don't follow you.'

'The book, Rosie, the book.' I pointed to my copy, which was on the desk next to the computer. 'Come on, you were the one who got me into it in the first place.'

'Oh, the book.' She picked it up.

I nodded. 'All that stuff about change. There's something in it. Definitely. The only thing is, I don't know what. Not exactly. That chapter about not going for the same sort of person you've gone for before – I keep thinking about that. Was that why you thought it'd be a good idea to go for a bank manager?'

'Yeah. For all the good it did me.'

'You can't give up because of one God-botherer. Trial and error, Rosie.'

'Bloody big error.' She gave a chuckle. 'No, you're right. Onwards and upwards. That's my new motto. Stop dwelling on past mistakes.'

I reread the e-mail, remembering how wonderful the previous week had been. 'Everything about Elisabeth,' I said, 'about what happened in New York, reminds me of the beginning of just about every other relationship I've ever had. Like when I first got together with Amy. The thrill of . . . well, not even of being together, it's just the thrill of thinking about them and knowing they're thinking about you. You know what I mean?'

Rosie nodded.

'And then gradually that thrill fades, and fades a bit more, and eventually there's no thrill at all.'

'Uh-huh.'

I left it a few moments, but it was obvious Rosie wasn't

going to say any more. She never does say much about Amy. They met, of course, and Rosie was civil, but I don't think she ever really liked her. Probably spotted before I did that Amy wasn't right for me.

So I changed tack. 'I can imagine exactly the same thing happening with Elisabeth.'

'Yeah, but she lives in New York, doesn't she? It's not as though she's going to be moving in with you next week.'

'No, but this merger looks pretty well sorted now. They're going to want someone moving over to London to watch the books, aren't they?'

'Did you and Elisabeth discuss that?'

'Nah. We only slept together twice. Would have sounded a bit forward, wouldn't it, talking about long-term plans?'

'I suppose so. But it was obviously more than just a two-night stand for her.' Rosie tapped the screen. '"Too long" since she's been to England. "Hmm." Angling for an invite. What did you reply?'

'What could I reply? I sent her an e-mail saying if she came over I knew this lovely little hotel she could stay at in Kent. Not very luxurious but the rates were good.'

'And you weren't just saying it to be polite?'

'No. That's the worrying thing. I really want her to come over. And if she did move over permanently I'd want to carry on seeing her. But if that book's got anything to it, which, like I say, I think it has, then carrying on seeing her isn't a good idea. I've got a suspicion my "Unique Staleness Point" would kick in. Whatever it is.' I stared at the key-board, tapping the Caps-Lock key very quickly again and again. It was only when a polite cough from Rosie brought me to my senses that I realised I was in danger of breaking it.

'Sorry, Rosie. Going on a bit, I know.'

'No you're not. Why should any of this be easy? As you said, don't give up. Trial and error.' Her face took on a 'plan-hatching' expression. 'Starting this afternoon.'

'Eh?'

'You'll see. I'll explain when we get there. In the mean-time – any chance of another coffee?'

'Sure.' I took her cup and headed for the kitchen. I was nearer the door than she was. Only halfway through it did I realise what she was doing. I quickly turned round, and just caught her hand before it reached the 'down' arrow on the keyboard.

'I've told you,' I said. 'You are *not* looking at that PS.'

At the far end of the garden the band were performing 'All Right Now' by Free. The lead guitarist, Kathy's brother, had his eyes closed, obviously imagining that he was playing at Wembley Arena. When the song ended everyone applauded. The rhythm guitarist announced that the next song would be 'Sultans of Swing' by Dire Straits.

Rosie cut herself a piece of burger, taking care that her plastic knife didn't bend the paper plate too much as it rested on her lap. 'You ready for this trial and error, then?'

'Depends what it is.'

'It's going on a date, that's all.' She looked round the garden. 'This lot seem a fairly decent cross-section of the population. There should be at least one person here for each of us.'

'Eh?'

'You and I have got to get into the habit of looking for people who aren't like our previous partners. So why don't we start now?'

'What about Elisabeth?'

'What about her, Alex? She's someone you slept with twice. You don't know for sure that you're ever going to see her again. And even if you do, you said it yourself, she's the sort of person you should be getting away from.'

I picked at my potato salad.

'Look,' Rosie continued, 'I'm not seriously suggesting that either of us is going to find our ideal partner this afternoon. I'm just saying we have to start going on dates, meeting new people. Try and work out where we were going wrong with the old ones. It's called "forcing the change".'

'Is it?'

'Yeah. Haven't you got to that bit of the book yet?'

'No.' I cast my eye over the fellow guests. Tried not to think about Elisabeth. Just going on a date? Couldn't do any harm, could it? 'OK. Go on then.'

'Right.' She put down her plate. 'We meet back here in an hour and a half, each having got the phone number of someone who we wouldn't normally think of going on a date with.'

Which is exactly what we did.

'OK,' said Rosie. 'You go first.'

'Maya. She's a teacher.'

'Where is she?'

I pointed her out.

'Ah,' said Rosie. 'A teacher with nice legs.'

'You said someone I wouldn't normally go out with, not someone I wouldn't go out with if you paid me a million pounds. Maya didn't immediately strike me as a woman I'd normally pursue, but she was perfectly pleasant and humorous. Said she thought the band were quite good, and she happened to know they were playing at a pub near her next week. I said there were worse things to do on a Wednesday night, and so there we are, we're going to see them.'

'Yes, all right, Mr Touchy. You're right, you've never been out with a teacher. Like I've never been out with a rugby player.'

'A rugby player?'

'Well, he's a barrister. But it was the rugby he talked about most. That's him.' She gave a subtle nod of her head. 'Gerry.'

'Christ, how many times a week does he play?'

'Only Saturday afternoons. But he also trains on Tuesdays and Thursdays.'

'You can tell.'

'Yes, well you're allowed legs, I'm allowed pecs.'

I tried. Honestly I did. But the date was 'lukewarm' at best. Maya was pleasant enough, but we didn't have that much to say to each other. In the end I was glad we were watching a band. We only had the gaps between songs to fill.

The 'date' had been designed to take my mind off Elisabeth, but it had the opposite effect. It had been like all the other first dates I've ever had. Or – and this is the point – all the first dates I could ever imagine having. When you start off with someone you're nervous, on your best behaviour, trying to say the right things, bothered about the impression you're creating. You make an effort. If they mention a philosopher you've never heard of you pretend that you have. The best girls, of course, are the ones where on the second or third date you can pluck up the courage to tell them you haven't heard of the philosopher and they don't mind. Or the really best girls (like Amy and Elisabeth), the girls you end up having relationships with and living with, the girls you really love, are the girls who don't mention philosophers you've never heard of in the first place, because they're your sort of people; they're like you and interested in the same things as you and they laugh at the same things as you. That's why you're naturally attracted to them. Except that Dr Susanna's telling me the people I'm naturally attracted to aren't the ones I should be with.

But then once you've been in a relationship with someone for ages the not making an effort with them becomes a bad thing not a good thing. You get 'cosy' and 'familiar' and 'comfortable' and all those other words that mean there's no excitement in your relationship any more. I want someone I don't have to make an effort with, but always in the good sense. Or is that what Dr Susanna's saying? That if I don't have to make an effort with someone the relationship's doomed from the start?

God knows. I think it's time I had another read of the book.

This is really good. I'm really pleased about this. It's definitely a step in the right direction. Because today – I talked to the woman at the cinema!

Not that anything came of it. But that doesn't matter. I saw her when I was queuing up to buy some sweets for Joe and Georgia. She was with her daughter again, and they were still in the queue to buy tickets. Luckily the timing worked out, because her daughter didn't want any sweets, so they skipped that bit and we all got to the door into the cinema itself at the same time. What was even better was that the daughter had her Disney Princess with her again, so that meant I could make another comment about it, try and do what I did before, get talking to the woman by saying something she could overhear. I said, 'Look, Georgia, that little girl's got a Disney Princess.' But then to stop it being exactly the same comment as before I also said, 'She's got a blue dress on hers, yours wears a green dress, doesn't she?'

Georgia looked at the toy, and then at the girl, and the girl looked back at her, not smiling but not looking unfriendly either, just sort of curious, the way kids do. Georgia looked up at me and gave a little nod, but she wouldn't say anything, she'd gone all shy. And that's what I said. I looked across at the woman, and she was looking at me, and I said, 'She's a bit shy.' That's all. I didn't say anything else. It was almost like I didn't realise I'd said it. It was a thought in my head, and then, whoosh, out it came. Thankfully the woman replied straightaway. That was good because it meant I didn't have time to realise what was happening and panic about it. At first she spoke to Georgia rather than me. She said, 'Your Disney Princess has a green dress, does she?' But Georgia got super-shy then, she hid behind my leg. I looked up at the woman, and she smiled at me, then she said, 'Milly keeps on at me to buy some more dresses for hers.'

I said, 'I know, that's the thing with toys, isn't it? It's not just the thing itself, they always design them so you have to keep buying other stuff afterwards.' The woman said, 'Tell me about it. We spent a fortune on madam here at Christmas, thought she'd have enough new things to keep her going for ages. It wasn't even the end of January before we had to start buying more stuff.' Then I told her how I'm thinking of buying a new bit of track for Joe's Scalextric (obviously I kept my voice down, I didn't want him to hear), and we carried on talking for ages after that. Sat in the same row and everything.

It was only when the cartoons had started and I'd got time to think that I realised what had happened. I'd spoken to her! OK, I'd found out she had a partner, but that isn't what I meant. What was important was I'd done it: managed to talk to someone! It made me think of Alex in New York, how he was relaxed about talking to Walter and Mary and Elisabeth. And I realised it's just starting off that's the difficult bit. If you say something simple at the beginning (like the thing I said about Georgia being shy), everything else can flow from that. I think maybe I've learned that from Alex. The reason he's good in social situations is that he's just relaxed. He's not a smoothie, a charmer, anything naff like that. He's just relaxed.

Although obviously there's more to it than that if you're actually trying to get somewhere with a woman, in the romantic sense, I mean. Perhaps I could learn about that from Alex as well. Especially because – this is my other big news at the moment – Elisabeth's coming to London! Miles told me yesterday. Her and Walter and Mary are visiting soon (they haven't fixed a date yet – he thinks it'll be in about a month or so). They're going to take one more look at the premises and everything, check the accounts again, work out the final details ready to go back home and draw up the contract. I hope that goes all right. Miles has said it will. It better had.

Anyway, I'm not going into all that. That's all very complicated. What I'm concentrating on now is Elisabeth. It's three weeks and two days since we got back from New York, and I've thought about her every single day. I've decided that when she's over I'm going to ask her out again. Once I've done that I think I'll ask Alex for some advice. What I should do, how I should behave, all that sort of stuff. I feel like I could talk to Alex about things like this and not be embarrassed. I'm sure he'd help me.

You have to reflect on yesterday and experiment today. You have to 'force the change'.

So this was the bit Rosie had mentioned. Dr Susanna telling us how to improve our chances of working out our USPs. The 'experimenting today' part was what she'd set up in the garden – the dates. The 'reflecting on yesterday' part, according to the book, was a case of looking back on your past relationships, analysing them, seeing if you could spot any patterns, anything your ex-partners had in common. For example, said Dr Susanna, several of her female clients had realised they were 'nurturers': they kept being attracted to men who needed a lot of attention. But the thing about men like that is that they always end up taking their partner for granted, not paying any attention to *their* problems and needs. As soon as they went for a man who didn't need so much nurturing, the relationship was a lot stronger.

To help analyse your relationships, said the book, you should use anything you can to jog your memory. Something a lot of people find useful, apparently, is looking at diaries they kept at the time. Only one problem with that: I don't keep a diary. Never have. Apart from a couple of months when I was fourteen, and unless I wanted to remind myself how unfair the world was then and how it really didn't understand me, that wouldn't be any use. But then I had an idea: photographs. Maybe they'd jog my memory. Pictures are supposed to be worth a thousand words. Diaries by Kodak.

I fetched down the big cardboard box I keep on top of the wardrobe. It contains all my old photos. None of them labelled, of course – that'd be far too organised – but I could guess which were the most recent by how dog-eared the packets were. I worked my way back through my thirties, then my twenties. Through Amy, Sonia, Louise, Rebecca, Natalie, Sheena. That's a pretty arbitrary list, by the way. Not all of them were relationships with a capital 'R', although I suppose they all meant something at the time.

I tell you what I did notice, though. There were only happy photos. Photos of when a relationship was going well. Photos of drunken nights in Barcelona, smiling embraces at friends' weddings, the two of you in paint-splattered overalls decorating your new flat. Which weren't the photos I needed. I needed photos of the end of a relationship, when it was petering out. But of course you've stopped taking photos by then. That's what I'm saying. It's a sign. If it's a long time since you took a photo of your partner, maybe you need to sit down and talk. (Perhaps I could write to Dr Susanna with that? She might put it in the next edition.)

Anyway, I thought and thought about it, but nothing came to mind. I couldn't spot a single recurring factor that might tell me where my relationships had foundered.

I did get an answer in the end, though. From a very unexpected source. Jill.

I was at Mum's for a couple of days. It was the weekend before her birthday (I'd taken her present over early because of a tentative arrangement to help Mick move house.) Mum was fussing over the stove, refusing to allow either me or Jill to help. Laying the table was as much as she'd let us do.

'And how's work?' asked Jill.

'Oh, you know, struggling along. I've been offered a new cartoon. It's called Mr Wiggle. Educational thing, apparently. At least twelve episodes, and there'll probably be more after that. Otherwise it's ads as usual. Did one for Electrolux last week.'

Jill's reaction was the same as it always is when I tell her about my work. She smiles a lot, nods a lot, and when she's certain I've finished she says, 'Lovely'. I don't think much of what I say means anything to her. When Jill was growing up, there were only three jobs a man could have. He could make something, he could drive something or he could wear a suit. Mine doesn't fit into any of those categories. I sense Jill can't entirely understand why 'saying the words in adverts' counts as a proper job. And I'm not really sure I don't agree with her.

'There we are,' said Mum, placing two huge plates of sausage and mash in front of us.

'This looks gorgeous,' I said. 'Onion gravy as well. Fantastic.'

'Are these the sausages from Morrisons you were telling me about?' asked Jill.

Mum nodded. 'Three for two.'

'They sell sausages in pairs?' I said.

'No, three *packets* for two. I've frozen the others so I can—'

'Mum, I was joking.'

'Oh, get away with you, you silly sod.' She and Jill exchanged 'isn't he a rascal' smiles.

We all began to eat. 'This is just what I wanted, Mum. Real comfort food.'

'Real what food?'

'Comfort food.' I looked at Jill. Her face was as blank as Mum's. 'You know – comfort food. No? Sausage and mash, shepherd's pie, apple crumble. It's like . . . well, it's comfort food. Food you really like.'

'Why would you eat food you didn't like?' asked Mum.

'No, it's not that . . . it's . . .' I gave up. There was no way I could think of to explain it. The conversation turned to a local hedge dispute that had recently come to court.

After the meal Jill and I persuaded Mum to let us do the washing-up. Negotiations were like an Arab–Israeli peace conference, but we got there in the end.

'Listen,' whispered Jill while Mum was out of the kitchen. 'About your Mum's birthday . . .'

'Yeah?'

'Well, you see, Sylvia and me were talking yesterday . . . we were waiting for the bus to go shopping . . . your mum wasn't there, it was only us . . . well, Sue was there as well, but she can't . . . she's going away with Vic . . . they're going to Cornwall with the caravan . . . already booked at the campsite, you see . . .'

'Jill, what can't Sue do?'

'Well, that's it, that's what I'm asking . . . What I meant was . . . that's why I said Sue can't do it, you see, on account of her being away . . . what Sylvia and me were thinking was . . . well, we rang your Uncle Norman, and he asked Margaret and they said they can both come . . . and Betty's fairly certain she can make it, that's if her son'll drive her, you know she doesn't like getting the train on her own, not at her age . . . and—'

'Jill, are you suggesting a surprise party for Mum's birthday?'

She looked confused. 'How did you . . . ?'

'Just a guess.'

'Well, yes, that's what I was going to ask, you see . . . do you think you could make it?'

No contest, was it? I hadn't given Mick a definite 'yes', and he could soon find someone else. 'Of course. I think it's a lovely idea.'

'Oh *wonderful*, it'll mean so much to her for you to be here.'

'I'll still leave the present now, like I was going to. That way she won't suspect anything.'

'Good thinking. What have you got her?'

'A nature book.' It was the book-of-the-series from that lion documentary we watched the other week.

'That sounds good. She'll like that.' Jill looked away, fiddled with the edge of her tea-towel. 'Sylvia was saying it's not going to be easy for your mum, you know, with it being her first birthday since . . . since your dad . . .' More fiddling.

'She is OK, isn't she, Jill? She always seems OK when I speak to her, but I do worry sometimes . . .'

'Yes, she's fine. Well, as fine as you can be when . . . I mean, I suppose there's . . . she's started to forget little things here and there . . . nothing important, you understand, just . . . oh, I don't know . . . whether she's put sugar in a cup of tea or not, that sort of thing . . .'

'Blimey, Jill, I do that and I'm thirty-four.'

She laughed. 'Yeah. She's all right, the old girl . . . I mean, it's bound to be a shock, isn't it, losing your husband after so long? I can tell you, it's really made me appreciate Malcolm a bit more.'

'Never thought I'd hear you say that.'

'I never thought I'd hear me say that.' From upstairs came the sound of the toilet flushing. 'Ooh, now, I was going to say as well, Alex . . . I was thinking . . . maybe you'd like to ask Amy along too? You know, if you'd . . . if she'd . . .'

I might have known. Who better to make a party go well than a Lovely Girl? Oh well, if it'd make them happy . . . and I'd quite like to see her again too. 'Yeah. Why not?'

'That'd be *wonderful*. You know how your Mum likes her.'

'Yeah.' I *liked* Amy. It was loving her that got tricky.

We heard Mum's footsteps on the stairs.

'Now listen,' said Jill quickly, 'Sylvia's doing the sandwiches, I'm in charge of sweets – do you think Amy would do one of her cherry cakes? Your mum would like that, I know she would.'

Amy has made one cherry cake in her entire life. Did it while we were up at Mum's a couple of years ago. Don't know why – something to do, she saw the recipe in one of Mum's books – but it turned out superbly, became a bit of a talking point.

'OK. I'll ask her.'

Mum appeared in the doorway. 'Have you two finished that washing-up already? You are good.'

'Least we could do after a dinner like that, Mum.'

'It was nothing special.' Buried deep beneath the denial I could just make out her pride.

It was only later that evening that I realised what a favour Jill had done me. You never know, I thought, spending some time with Amy, remembering what she's like, might help with my 'force the change' thinking.

The following Wednesday night. I was looking over Rosie's shoulder at Miles. 'Let's Twist Again' by Chubby Checker was playing, and he was trying to dance.

'These *fucking* shoes!' he yelled as, for the third time, he fell over. His natural padding was coming in useful. 'They keep sticking on the *fucking* floor!'

'That's the whole point of them, Miles,' said Kathy, laughing. 'They're designed to give you more friction.'

It was the latest Langley and Langley get-together. Ten-pin bowling. About thirty of us, a mixture of staff and clients plus a dozen or so guests (we're allowed to take whoever we want – I'd asked Rosie). All paid for by Miles. He does it once in a while. Team morale and all that. Plus he'd wanted to tell everyone how well the talks in America had gone, the merger was well on track, etc.

'Well friction's no good for the fucking *twist*, is it?' he shouted. He took off the red shoes and hurled them away. Just as well. They'd been clashing with his bright orange corduroy trousers. 'Ah, this is more like it!' Now that his green socks were in direct contact with the highly polished floor, he shimmied violently from side to side. 'This brings back some memories!' he boomed, arms jutting out at an alarming angle, his left hand hanging down in a very camp fashion. His right would probably have done the same but for the fact that it was holding a half-empty bottle of wine. 'Those were the days!' With each gyration his field of movement was growing. There were shouts and whistles of appreciation from his employees, which egged him on even more.

Rosie and I enjoyed the show for a moment, then returned to what we'd been talking about. Dates. I'd told her about my non-event with Maya, she was telling me about Gerry, her rugby-playing barrister. Their first drink had gone 'quite well', Rosie was thinking there might be something there after all. Then, on the morning of their second date, Gerry had cancelled because he had to work late in the office.

'The last thing I wanted,' she continued, 'was to sit around my flat feeling miserable, thinking, "I should have been out with Gerry tonight", so I made sure I went out with a friend.'

In the distance, Miles twisted into my field of vision. His face was now puce, but he still managed a cheery wink as he passed by. I gave him a smile of encouragement, and he disappeared off to the right.

'I called Trudi, she said she'd love to come out. So there we were, having a high old time, cocktails aplenty, and we ended up passing the bar Gerry had taken me to on our first date, which was a really good place, so I said to Trudi why didn't we go in there, and as we got through the door guess who I saw on the other side of the room?'

Miles came into view on his return trip from right to left. He was still grinning at the others as they cheered him on, but this time I ignored him. 'Someone who'd told you they were working late in the office, perhaps?'

'The very same.'

'Maybe he was taking a half-hour break?'

'Alex, you wouldn't have said that if you'd seen him.'

'Bit of a state?'

'More than tipsy, let's put it that way.'

'Well, perhaps he'd finished his work in the office and was carrying on his preparations in the bar.'

'Yes, the girl he was with might well have been helping him on the case. As part of a school project. And yes, maybe he was telling her what his tactics were going to be in court. But I really don't see why his hand needed to be where it was. Unless she'd stored the files in a very unusual place.'

'Ah.'

'Yes, Alex. Ah.'

'Had he seen you?'

'Nope.'

'Did you point him out to Trudi?'

'Yep.'

'And did you discuss with her how you were going to handle the situation?'

'Yep.'

'So what was it? Headbutt? Or pint of lager in the lap?'

'Neither. We turned round and left the bar.'

'What? You turned . . . Oh, I see. Playing the long game?'

'Oh yes. Oh yes indeed.'

I rubbed my hands together. 'I'm listening.'

'Two days later Gerry calls and says, "Hello, Rosie, how are you?" And I say, "I'm fine, Gerry, how's the case going?" and he says it's all finished now, it was hard work while it was on but now he's got time to play again. So I tell him great, why don't we get together and play? He says he'd love to, what do I fancy doing? I tell him there's a lovely pub my friend Trudi's told me about – which is true, she has – and it's out in the countryside, quite a long drive, about an hour from London, but well worth it apparently, why don't we go and check it out? He says that sounds great. We fix it for the next day, which is a Saturday, and I say I don't mind driving, why don't I pick him up at seven?'

'Why do I get the feeling that you've got someone, or something, waiting for him at this pub?'

'No, nothing like that. The pub's absolutely genuine. Trudi's right, it's lovely. Bit difficult to find, but really lovely. Obviously the best place for miles around because it's packed, but Gerry manages to find us a table in the corner – very intimate – while I get the first round in. Pint of the local ale for him – he's really entering into the country pub spirit – vodka and tonic for me. Except I ask the barmaid to give me the vodka neat, I want to pour my own tonic in. Which I do. After I've poured the vodka into Gerry's pint.'

'Rosie, you're a wicked woman.'

'Thank you. So I take our drinks across, and Gerry starts to tell me about the case – took a *lot* of preparation, he says, had to do a *lot* of groundwork . . . I can imagine, I say – and what with all the details, by the time he's finished it's time for another drink, what would I like? Vodka and tonic, I tell him. When he gets back from the bar he says enough about him and his court case, what have I been up to, and I say oh, you know, this and that, here and there, and we have a good old chat, and all the time the pub's getting more and more crowded so once or twice he has to move his chair a little bit closer to mine, and then after a while it's my round again.'

'Your vodka goes into his pint again?'

'You're a quick learner, Alex. And not only does it go into that pint, but when Gerry buys the next round he brings the drinks back then goes straight off to the gents, so hey presto, I tip that vodka into his pint as well. We talk some more, he shuffles his chair some more, I laugh at some more of his jokes – but you know, for some reason he's having a bit of difficulty remembering the punchlines by now – and then before you can say "lying little shit" I'm back to the bar again and I've got us another drink. When I sit down he says, hang on, you've had all these vodka and tonics, you're driving, aren't you? And I say, oh, didn't I mention, they do rooms here as well, sorry, I should have said, I've been having such a good time I just assumed we were going to stay over and go back to London in the morning. And his face lights up – even though his eyes are crossed you can see his face light up – and he says no, that's fine, that's absolutely fine. Then I say, "Actually I've just asked at the bar and as it happens they've only got one room left tonight, but the bar-maid told me it's got a sofa as well as a bed, so if you don't mind sharing then I don't."'

'Call me a cynical old goat if you will, Rosie, but I'm guessing you delivered that information in a way that led him to assume the sofa wouldn't be needed?'

'Alex, you're a cynical old goat. It's one of your best qualities. By now, Gerry's on his fifth pint of beer and his fourth vodka, while I've had the grand total of one vodka and a lot of tonic. And it's getting near closing time, which is my cue to deliver the *coup de grâce*.'

'Namely . . . ?'

Rosie gave a quiet chuckle. 'I say I'm going to the ladies, would he keep an eye on my handbag? Then I do indeed go to the ladies. But when I come out, instead of returning to the main bar I go into the back bar. And from there, I leave the pub. And get into my car. And open the glove compartment, where I've left my mobile phone, and dial the number on the card that I took from the board near the toilets in the pub.' By now she was almost singing the words. 'Which was a card for a local cab firm. And I order a taxi in Gerry's name, going to London. I ask them how much that's going to be. They ask which part of London, and I say the far side, which is where Gerry lives, and they say they're really busy at the moment, and I say we don't mind paying a bit more to jump the queue. They don't sound too surprised at that, because they know – like I do – that the nearest train station is eight miles away and the last train to London left five minutes ago. They say how does eighty quid sound if they're there in quarter of an hour, and I say that's fine. Then I drive off.'

'Eighty quid? Wouldn't it have been cheaper for him to stay at the pub and get a train back in the morning?'

'It would have been. Assuming I was telling the truth about the pub doing rooms.'

'You cunning fox, you.'

'I have my moments.'

'Hang on – what about your handbag?'

'My real handbag was in the glove compartment with my phone. The one I left with Gerry was an old one I was throwing out. At the beginning of the evening all it contained was enough money for the drinks I bought, and a note. The note read: "Who knows, the next time you work late on a case she might even be old enough to vote."'

'You haven't heard from him since, I suppose?'

'Not a squeak.'

I shook my head in wonder. 'Beautiful, Rosie. That was absolutely beautiful.'

She gave a sigh. 'No it wasn't, not really. I'm supposed to be on the road to commitment, not the road back from pubs in the middle of nowhere.'

At that point we were interrupted. By Miles. He appeared at what was almost literally breakneck speed, crashing right into the middle of our group. He ended up flat on his back on the floor, staring up at everyone.

'Are you OK, Miles?' asked Kathy.

He was by now the colour of an overripe beetroot, and had to take several gulps of air before he could reply. When he did, it was by lifting his bottle of wine and showing it round proudly. 'Look at that,' he gasped. 'Didn't spill a drop.'

There was a round of applause as he struggled to his feet.

'More drinks!' he shouted, making everyone cheer as well as clap. He saluted them with the bottle, then took a swig from it.

'I hope these nights out are going to carry on after the

merger,' said Hazel when the noise had died down. She's one of Miles's longest-serving agents, senior enough to say things like this in front of him.

'Too bloody right they are,' he replied, a trickle of red wine running down his chin. 'I'm going to make it part of the deal. Specific clause guaranteeing "team bonding". Or whatever it's called now.' He collapsed on to a seat. 'Getting pissed up, that's what it was called in my day.'

He took out his wallet, gave a couple of people a wad of notes each, and dispatched them to the bar.

'You know what,' he continued, as though the sight of the money had inspired him to make a spontaneous announcement, 'we should all have a *really* special celebration when the deal goes through. Something more than chucking a few balls at pieces of wood. What about . . . a day at the races? Loads of bubbly, slap-up meal, hundred quid gambling money for everyone.'

The cheering had only just started when Miles held up his hand for silence. 'No, forget that, a mere *day* will not accommodate our need for revelry. A weekend away, that's what's called for.'

This time he let the cheering continue.

'Where?' shouted someone.

'It's got to be the seaside, hasn't it?' came a reply.

'Fuck that,' said Miles. 'This is the culmination of my long and, if I say so myself, which I do, illustrious career. This event will commemorate my final involvement with the firm I have nurtured, crafted, poured my very *soul* into. It will NOT take place in some godforsaken dump on the English coast with us sheltering from the rain, eating cold chips out of plastic cones. No, this weekend demands a venue of class, of excitement, of sophistication. This weekend demands . . . Paris!'

'Bravo!' yelled Hazel, after which everyone else joined in, shouting, cheering, clinking their glasses against Miles's wine bottle. As people took on board what he'd just said – he was going to treat a hundred employees to a weekend in one of the most thrilling cities in the world, a city not known for its low prices – the noise grew and grew. A very out-of-tune rendition of the 'Marseillaise' was struck up, which prompted Sheila from personnel, who's old enough to know better, to jump on to a table, gather her skirt round her knees and start performing the cancan. Hazel, meanwhile, wandered around kissing everyone and saying, 'We'll always have Paris.'

I turned to say something to Rosie. But Ross had come across and was talking to her. ('Good luck, mate,' I thought.) Over at another table I saw Tony, sitting on his own. I went over to join him.

'Nice move by Miles, eh?' I said.

'Yeah.' Tony was smiling, but only just.

'I hope he doesn't regret it when he wakes up in the morning and remembers. It may have been the drink talking, but now everyone's reacted like this he'll have to keep his word.'

What there was of Tony's smile disappeared completely. 'Miles came into my office this afternoon. He said if he took everyone away to Paris for the weekend, how much of it could he claim against tax?'

'Oh. Not such a spontaneous outburst after all, then.'

'No.'

'Still, that doesn't take away from it being generous, does it?'

Tony didn't reply. What *is* it that he doesn't like about Miles?

*

Amy put her seatbelt on and I pulled away. 'Thanks for doing this. I know it must be a drag for you.'

'Don't be silly. It's not a drag at all. It'll be good to see your mum again.'

'Did you manage the cake?'

'Yeah, it's in there.' She pointed to the bag she'd put on the back seat. 'Took me ages to find that recipe book. I had to go to five shops.'

'If it was one of Mum's I'm surprised it was still in print at all. I'll give you the money for it.'

'Alex, it was only a fiver. Anyway, there are some good recipes in it. I might have a go at one or two.'

'You sure? Aren't they full of stuff like lard and starch?'

'It's not *that* old.'

It was funny having Amy with me on the familiar route again. It was good to see her, and she kept making me laugh. Until her mobile bleeped with a text. She read it quickly, gave an involuntary giggle, put the phone back in her bag.

I left it a few seconds. Then, 'Oh yes?'

'Oh yes, what?'

'Come on, Amy, when a woman reacts like that to a text it can only mean one thing.'

She smiled.

'What's his name?'

'David.'

'Right.'

'Met him through work.'

'I see.'

I sensed Amy didn't want to say any more. After all, what can you say about someone you've just started going out with? You can talk about how you met, what your first date was, what their hobbies are. But all people really want to know is, 'Is the sex any good?' and 'Do you think you'll stay together?'

'How about you?' asked Amy.

'Mmm? Oh, I see . . .' Should I tell her about Elisabeth? Seemed presumptuous, kind of tacky to mention a one-off. OK, it's not going to stay that way – the Americans have got the trip sorted – they get here a week on Wednesday. Elisabeth called to tell me the other day. Said she was looking forward to seeing me again, could she still stay at mine, I said of course, I was looking forward to it too (which I am, despite my misgivings). Then she asked why it was so noisy, I said I was in Rossi's (a café near the office) having my lunch. Elisabeth made me promise to take her there when she's over.

So she isn't a one-off. But even so . . . 'Nah, no one.'

We got to Mum's just before one. There were a couple of cars in the drive already, so I had to park out on the road. I looked over the hedge. In the kitchen I could see Uncle Norman talking to Sylvia. They were drinking tea – the best china had been called into service. Jill was taking the cling film off two enormous plates of sandwiches, helped by my aunt Margaret. At the back of it all, standing by the sink, was Mum. She wasn't talking to anyone, just watching them all. But not with her usual everyone's-happy-so-I-am-too expression. She looked sad. Or at least bored. Distant, perhaps. It shocked me. I remembered what Jill had said the other week, about Mum losing a bit of her spark. Was she? No, Mum's all right. Probably just fazed by the surprise of the party, that's all.

I knocked on the door. Jill opened it. As soon as she saw Amy she went into raptures. 'Hell-O dear! How are *you*?' The hug was like something you'd expect from the mother of a freshly released hijack victim.

Amy tried to reply, but she could barely breathe, let alone talk.

Jill lowered her voice. 'Ooh, now I mustn't let June hear me . . . don't want to give the game away. Just you *wait* till she sees you're here.' She took a step back. 'My, you *are* looking well, dearie. Are they new glasses?'

Amy nodded.

'They suit you, honestly they do.' There was barely room on her face to contain the grin.

I gave a small cough. 'Hello, Jill.'

'Oh, hello, Alex dear. How are you?'

'Mustn't grum—'

'Right then,' she continued, beckoning us in. She closed the door and lowered her voice to a whisper. 'Pop your bags down there. Now, Amy love, have you got the cake?'

'Yeah, it's in here.'

While Amy rummaged in her bag, Jill looked along the corridor to check the kitchen door was still closed. 'Stay quiet, won't you, we don't want to ruin the surprise! Come on, let's go and see the birthday girl.' She squeezed Amy's arm. 'Ooh, she's going to be *so* thrilled to see you!' She set off in front of us, a sort of pensioner mother hen on steroids.

Edging the kitchen door open, she put her head round it. Through the gap we could hear Sylvia talking about last week's lottery draw.

'Hang on a second, Sylvia, love . . .'

The kitchen went quiet.

'June – you'll never guess who's here to see you!'

Amy looked at me, smiled and shook her head.

Mum hadn't replied. 'Come on,' said Jill, 'who do you think it is?'

'Bloody get on with it,' came Uncle Norman's gruff voice. 'It's not *This Is Your Life*, you know.'

Jill couldn't contain herself any longer. With one hand she thrust the door wide open, with the other she virtually yanked Amy into the kitchen.

'Hello, June,' said Amy.

Mum gasped. '*Arrrggghhh*! Hello *you*!' She launched herself at Amy, who just had time to pass the cake tin to Jill before Mum enveloped her in a hug.

'It's Amy!' cried Jill.

Margaret and Sylvia looked on, waiting for an introduction to the new guest, smiling at the sudden explosion of joy. Norman did the same but without the smile.

'I didn't know *you* were coming!' said Mum.

Amy pulled away, keeping her hands on Mum's shoulders. 'That's the idea of a surprise party, isn't it?'

Mum, Jill, Margaret and Sylvia all howled with laughter. Norman was wide-eyed, partly with bemusement, partly because his glasses are so strong. He turned and saw me moving into the doorway. We nodded 'hello' to each other. The laughter was too loud for us to speak.

'No, you daft thing,' said Mum, 'I mean, I knew Alex would be coming, well, once Norman and Margaret got here, they were the first you see, that's when Jill told me what she'd done – she's such a devil . . .'

Jill let out a tiny shriek of delight.

'So I knew Alex would be coming,' continued Mum. She still hadn't looked at me. 'But I never guessed . . . Oh, it's *lovely* to see you again, it really is!'

'It's lovely to see you too, June.'

They hugged again. Looking over Amy's shoulder, Mum finally saw me.

'Hello,' I said. 'Don't know if you remember me. I'm your son.'

She laughed. 'Come here, you silly sod.'

We hugged. 'Happy birthday, Mum.'

'Thanks, son. Thanks for coming.' Then she turned back to Amy. 'Oh, this is such a lovely surprise! Fancy you coming all the way out here!'

Amy started to say something, but at exactly the same moment as Jill, who still hadn't calmed down.

'Sorry, Jill.'

'No, no, no, love, I'm sorry, after you!' She added another shriek.

'I was just going to say, June – it's not much, and I've got you a proper present in my bag – but I thought you might like a bit of cherry cake on your birthday.' She took the tin from Jill and handed it to Mum.

Mum prised the lid off and looked inside. 'Oh, Amy! Oh, you *shouldn't* have!'

'Really, June, it was nothing.'

Jill peered into the tin. 'She's done a cherry cake!'

Mum held out the tin so that everyone could take a look. 'She does a *lovely* cherry cake!' said Jill.

Amy and I exchanged the faintest of smiles.

Margaret examined the cake. 'Ooh, that looks delicious!'

Then it was Sylvia's turn. 'Lovely! That looks really lovely!'

Then Norman. 'Aye.'

Mum put the tin on the table. 'That's something to look forward to for later. Now, Amy, let's get you a cup of tea. And do you want some sandwiches? There's egg and cr—'

'You just sit yourself down, you,' said Jill. 'You're the one whose party it is. I'll look after the guests. Now, what do you want, Amy? There's egg and cress, coronation chicken, cheese, cheese and ham . . .'

'Those coronation chicken ones look tasty,' said Amy.

'Is that all you want, love? Go on, have a cheese and ham as well.'

'OK, thanks, I will.'

Jill put the sandwiches on a plate, then arranged some crisps on one side and two lettuce leaves on the other. 'Help yourself to salad cream and pickle, won't you? Now, let's get that kettle on.'

Amy sat next to Mum, who introduced her to the others. Soon all the women were chatting. Norman, who was standing, now looked more bored than bemused.

Right, I'll get my own sandwiches, shall I? I loaded a plate with sandwiches, then went and stood next to Norman.

'Hi, Norman.'

'All right, Alex lad. How you doing?'

'Not bad. You?'

'Aye.' He took a sip of tea. 'What you driving nowadays?'

This is always, without exception and no matter who he's talking to, Norman's opening conversational gambit. You could introduce him to someone with a guide dog and he'd ask them what they were driving nowadays.

'Same as last time I saw you, Norman.'

'That Renault?'

He *remembers*, that's the thing.

'Yeah. How about you?'

'Got a Corolla at the moment. Nothing special, you know, but it does the job.'

I pray that Norman never thinks back and realises I've only ever owned two cars. The shock might kill him. It'd be tantamount to him finding out I was gay.

'Toyota,' he continued. 'Always know where you are with a Toyota. Japanese, you see. Say what you like about 'em during the war, but they know their cars.' He paused. 'Weren't you doing one of those ads of yours for a Toyota, last time I saw you?'

Was I? 'Oh yeah, that's right . . . Yeah.'

'Which model was it?'

Oh come ON. 'It was . . . do you know, it's slipped my mind . . . I think it was . . .'

'The Yaris, wasn't it?'

'Of course, that was it.'

'The one with central locking?'

'I don't think the ad was quite that specific, Norman. They normally just do a general one, leave the details for when people show an interest.'

He nodded sadly. Norman probably dreams of a world where there are no TV programmes, only separate adverts for the Toyota Yaris with central locking and the Toyota Yaris without.

There was a pause. Maybe I could get us off cars? Ask him if he'd got a holiday planned—

'Hey, I tell you what, Alex, there's a bloke at work's just got one of those Audi A6s . . .'

Give up, you know you're along for the ride. I set myself to nod every five seconds and smile every ten, and switched off. Norman burbled on harmlessly. Across the kitchen Mum and Jill were still hanging on Amy's every word.

'. . . they had it in the green, but I didn't even bother trying that on, I knew it wouldn't be me.'

'No, love, I know what you mean,' said Jill. 'You have to be sure, don't you?'

Mum tapped Amy on the knee. 'And how's work, dear?'

'Oh, OK, you know. I'm doing a big commercial con-
veyance at the moment. This charity are buying a disused
store and turning it into one of their shops.'

*That's it, you've killed the conversation there. Mum's going to
tell you she doesn't understand all that complicated solicitor
stuff.* 'Ooh, I bought something at a charity shop the other
day.'

'Really, what was that?'

'That little egg timer there.'

Jill passed Amy the item in question. 'Have a guess how
much.'

'Let's see . . . two pounds?'

'Seventy-five pence.'

'Never!'

Mum nodded excitedly.

Jill took the egg timer and put it back by the stove. 'You
can't beat a charity shop for bargains, that's what I always
say.'

'Seventy-five pence,' said Amy. 'I don't know. When this
place I'm working on opens up I'll have to see what bargains
they've got.'

Mum and Jill laughed loudly. *Comedy goddess, isn't she? I*
tuned back to Norman. '. . . which is all right if you're in traffic, of course, but once you get out on the motorway . . .'
What have I done to deserve this?

Eventually I escaped and moved across for a chat with
Sylvia. More guests arrived – some of Mum's friends from the
village, aunt Betty, a few distant cousins (I managed to
remember *most* of their names) . . . After a while we all
moved through to the main room.

Jill, who was on glass-topping duty with Amy, said, 'Isn't
it about time you opened your presents, June?'

'Oh, I can do that later. Everyone's having a lovely time, they don't want to watch me unwrap—'

'Do as you're told,' said Amy. 'It's your party and you're going to enjoy it whether you like it or not.' With her foot she nudged the pile of presents towards Mum. 'Now get cracking.'

'Yes, come on,' said Sylvia.

'Oh, if I have to.'

Amy poured her some more wine. 'Yes, you have to.' They smiled at each other. *Just open the bloody presents, will you?*

Mum worked her way through the pile. There were cardigans and book tokens and chocolates, and people gasped and cooed and said 'Isn't that lovely?' Mum said all the chocolates were going to ruin her diet. Margaret said what was she dieting for, there was nothing on her. Which wasn't true, it's never true of any of us. Although Mum did look a bit thinner than last time I saw her.

She reached Amy's present, which was a Cliff Richard greatest hits CD. 'Cliff!' shrieked, Mum. 'Is this the one with . . .' She scanned the track listing. 'It is! "Mistletoe and Wine"! This is the one I was telling you about, Jill, you know, the other day . . . the one I saw the advert for . . . It's got "Mistletoe and Wine" on it. I love that song.'

There were hums of agreement from around the room.

'Such lovely words,' said someone.

'Yeah,' said someone else, 'really gentle and . . . and *nice*.'

'Who is it?' said Norman.

'Cliff Richards,' said Margaret.

Norman nodded. 'Oh.'

Mum unwrapped my present. 'Ah, that's lovely. Thanks, son.'

'It's the one with the lions, Mum. You know, the one we watched?'

She nodded, and flicked through a few of the photos.

Sylvia had picked up the Cliff Richard CD. '"Move It" – that's the one I like.'

'Ooh yes,' said Mum, letting the book close. 'And what's that other one I like?'

'"Living Doll"?'

'No, no, one of his other ones . . . you know, later . . .'

Sylvia examined the list of tracks. '"Miss You Nights"?'

'No, that's not it.' Mum put the book on the floor. 'Here, let me have a look.' Sylvia gave her the CD. 'Where are we? That's it – "Devil Woman". "She's just a devil woman . . ."' She didn't know any more of the words, so settled for '"nah-nah nah-nah nah-nah"'.

'Ooh, you old rocker you,' said Jill, and everyone laughed.

Amy reached me. 'More wine?'

I'd have loved another glass. 'No,' I said. 'I'm switching to beer.' I pushed past her on my way to the kitchen.

Things didn't get much better the next day. My mood wasn't improved by having had to sleep on the sofa (Amy had the spare room). Jill came round on the pretext of helping tidy up, but really because she couldn't bear to be apart from the weekend's star guest. The four of us had some of the leftover party food for lunch. There was still a stack that needed freezing, and Jill set to work labelling it all. Mum took Amy into the garden to show her some new flowers she'd planted. I sat in the main room, pretending to read a magazine, but really keeping an eye on them.

From the way Mum kept glancing my way I could tell they were talking about me. I felt my hackles rising again.

This wasn't like the start of a relationship, when your mum and your girlfriend say nice things about you to each other. Family life being what it is, that's the only way your mum ever tells you what she really feels. You'll be driving home from a weekend with the parents and your girlfriend'll say, 'She's proud of you, you know?', and you'll say, 'Yeah, I suppose so', and she'll say, 'No, really, she told me when you were having your bath'. Then you'll say, 'That's nice', as though it doesn't mean anything, but really you're desperate for a line-by-line report. Now, though, I felt like a young offender who'd been sent out of the room while his probation officers discussed him.

Jill came through from the kitchen. 'That's that lot done.' She looked at the clock. 'What time did your mum say Morecambe and Wise were on?'

'Quarter past three, wasn't it?'

'Oh blast, we've missed the start.' She opened the window. 'Come on, June, you're missing your programme.'

I switched the TV on and flicked through the channels. Two familiar figures appeared, with huge sideburns and 1970s suits.

'There they are,' said Jill, as Mum and Amy came in and sat on the sofa. 'Proper comedians for you. Not like that rowdy lot you get nowadays.'

The programme was a compilation. Most of the routines I'd seen before. Even the ones I hadn't contained the trusty old stand-bys: Ernie talking about his latest play, Eric waggling his glasses, the two of them humiliating a star guest. The last sketch was the Grieg piano concerto. Eric playing the right notes but 'not necessarily in the right order'.

'Oh, I love this one,' said Mum.

Suddenly the house felt very small. I thought back to

Grand Central, standing there with Tony, thinking how far it was from Suffolk, what a big world we live in. And even though I hated myself for feeling this – hate myself even more now I've calmed down – I felt totally different from Mum, almost as though she couldn't be my mum. There's this big world out there, millions of places and billions of people . . . and she's content to stay in this tiny village, where everything stays the same and nothing ever changes. And she watches the same TV programmes again and again and again, and still they keep her happy, still they're completely new to her every time. Like a goldfish with a seven-second memory happy to stay in its little bowl.

Do you think I'm a bastard to say something like that? I wouldn't blame you. I do. But that doesn't mean it isn't what I felt.

I was still angry at eight o'clock that night. Not that I realised, until Amy's intake of breath made me look down at the dashboard. I was doing nearly ninety. I looked up again. The car in front wasn't that far away.

'Don't you think you should slow down a bit?'

I'd been going to until she said that. 'I know what I'm doing.' But the gap was still narrowing, and the middle lane was too busy for the other car to pull over. I eased off to eighty-five. Then eighty. 'Happy now?'

'What's your problem, Alex?'

'I haven't got a problem. You were the one with the problem.'

'Ending up in the back seat of that Jaguar would have been a problem for both of us.'

I went quiet. Arguing with a girlfriend can feel exciting, sexy, life-affirming, but bickering with an ex-girlfriend made me feel stupid, like a drunk picking fights at a bus stop. I hated myself because I'd got angry with my sixty-five-year-old mum, I hated the fact that Amy had a new relationship sorted while I was pissing about with self-help books, and I was angry because I couldn't understand why I was so angry.

'I suppose David never goes above fifty.' *Shit.* Now she'd think I was jealous. If I tried to tell her I wasn't it'd only make her think I was. Why had I said something stupid like that?

'As it happens, David doesn't drive.'

Uncle Norman wouldn't like that. All the cars up ahead braked heavily. We slowed to sixty. I pulled into the middle lane. Maybe that would help me calm down, stop me saying anything else I'd regret.

'Oh. I see.' *Come on, say something else. Show you can be polite.* 'Where does he live, David?'

'Greenwich.'

'Must be doing well for himself.'

'He shares with two others.'

'Right.'

We both knew I was trying to make up for the original comment. I felt uncomfortable, resentful, like a schoolkid who's just been told off by his teacher then given the chance to prove he can be civil.

'What does he do?'

'He's an architect.'

'Great.' I worried it had sounded sarcastic. I still felt on edge, my anger was still there. I'd have to be careful. 'You said you met him through work?'

'Yeah, he's working on this charity shop. He wants to set up his own practice in the long term, specialise in sustainable energy projects.'

Sustainable energy? I felt the red mist coming down again.

'Lovely. Sounds perfect. Sounds like he's the one. I bet you're really happy, eh? Bet he even wants kids as well, you won't have to nag him into it.' Where the hell had *that* come from?

Amy sighed, the disappointed teacher. She wasn't even going to pay me the compliment of getting angry. 'Alex, I never "nagged" you, and you know it. I simply pointed out that having children isn't exactly the most unnatural thing in the world for couples to do.'

'No, it just fucks up your life for about twenty years, that's all.'

'That's nice. Optimistic.'

'Realistic. I mean, look at Jim and Linda. Dead-end jobs, both of them – that was the only reason they had Jemima.'

'Jennifer.'

'Whatever. They had that kid because their own lives were so boring they needed to create another one to get interested in. I'm sorry, but my life's got more to it than that.'

Such as?'

'Such as seeing a bit of the world. Having some new experiences. Like . . . like . . . going mountaineering.'

'*Mountaineering?*'

'All right, that's not a very good example.' I was frustrated at not being able to think of a better one. 'But the point is . . .'

Amy cut me off with another sigh, bigger than her first. 'Oh, what's the point in us going through all this again, Alex? What's the point in us having the argument when we're not even going out together?'

'There wasn't much point in us having it when we were.'

'Exactly.'

Well done, Alex. Pretty comprehensive job of ruining the

journey there. I said sorry a couple of miles later, and Amy said it didn't matter. But the fact that she was right – it didn't matter because we weren't going out any more – made the whole thing even more miserable, and our small talk for the next hour and a half was horribly artificial. She couldn't wait to get out of the car. Not surprising, really. I'd been a total shit. All in all not exactly a weekend to remember. Not for any of the right reasons, anyway.

I got home, tried to hide from the disgust I was feeling about myself. But Sunday night television doesn't give you much cover in that respect. The vile, petty way I'd treated Amy kept haunting me. What had she done to deserve me sniping about her boyfriend? Especially after she'd agreed to go to the party and bake a cake in the first place. What had Mum done to deserve me sulking? She'd liked someone, that's all. She'd liked Amy and been pleased to see her. She'd liked Cliff Richard. She'd liked Amy buying her a Cliff Richard CD. All that liking, and I'd been hateful.

It made me pick up the phone.

'Hello, seven-two-four?'

'Hi, Mum.'

'Hello, son. Get home safely?'

'Yeah, no problems. There wasn't much traffic.'

'Oh, that's good.'

'Door to door it wasn't even three and a half hours. And that included dropping Amy off .'

'That *is* good. There was once me and your Dad did it and we were still on the motorway after five hours, do you remember?'

'Yeah. Bank Holiday, wasn't it?'

'That was it, yeah.'

'Listen, Mum . . .'

'Mmm?'

'I just wanted to say . . . I mean . . . I wanted to . . .'

She waited.

'I wanted to say thanks for the weekend. You know, putting me up. Putting us up.'

'You don't have to say thanks, silly. I'm the one who should be saying thanks to you, for coming all that way. Lovely surprise like that.'

'No, but . . .'

'I mean, you can't even have been that comfortable, sleeping on the settee.'

'I was fine.'

'And I hope Amy didn't mind me not having clean sheets in the spare room.'

'Mum, they were clean. Just not fresh on, that's all.'

'No, but you like to put fresh on, don't you? For visitors . . .'

'It doesn't matter, Mum.'

'Mmm, well . . .'

I paused. 'Mum, I wanted to say . . .' *Go on, say it. Say the word. It's not difficult.* 'I wanted to say . . . thanks.'

'You just did, you daft thing.'

'No, but . . . well . . . anyway, that's it . . . thanks for a lovely weekend. I really enjoyed it.'

'I enjoyed seeing you, love. And Amy. It was a wonderful surprise.'

'Well, it was your birthday. If you can't have a surprise on your birthday when can you, eh?'

'Yeah.'

'All right, Mum, I'd better be off.'

'OK, son. Speak to you soon.'

'Yeah, lots of love. Night.'

'Night.' Then her usual thing of repeating it a dozen times until she was sure I'd gone.

I'd rung up to apologise because I thought it'd make me feel less guilty. The fact that I couldn't bring myself to do it had made me feel even more guilty. But then again, what was the point of apologising to Mum? She probably hadn't even noticed my sulk, there were so many people there. Saying sorry would only have alarmed her, ruined her weekend. It was Amy who deserved the apology. But even if she took the call – which was doubtful, she'd probably leave it to the answerphone – anything I said would only make things worse. I should just let it lie.

So I went to bed. Couldn't sleep. Funny that.

Eventually I did drop off. But I woke two hours later. Not drowsily, either – I was wide awake. But very calm. At peace. Somehow all the self-loathing and guilt had left me, like a pile of dirty clothes in the corner of the room. I turned the pillow over and rested my face against the coolness of the new side. At first all I could hear was my own breathing. Then, as the stillness became more perfect, the ticking of my watch on the bedside table. Then a gurgling sound from the radiator.

And I remembered my nastiness to Amy in the car. Children. That was it. That's where I've been going wrong, that's my USP. I've always gone out with women – well, I don't know about always, but instantly I could think of at least three girlfriends who'd talked about having children. Not that I'm saying I don't ever want to have children. Just not yet. And they did. We never had huge arguments about it, but now I can see it was always there, this assumption that kids are what a relationship's all about. Kids tie you down, stop you experiencing new things and generally enjoying life.

I suppose that's what my irritation with Mum was all about. Because I'm different from her. She's happy to stay in her little village, watching the same TV programmes endlessly. That's all she's ever wanted. Get married, become a mother. By the time she was my age she'd done it. But I want to get out there, into the big world. See as much of it as I can. Keep changing. Of course, in Mum's day it wasn't as easy to jet around the world, do different things, change all the time. That's what the book said. Now it is easy, and I want to do it. The mistake I've been making is going out with women who are just waiting to have kids. I need a woman who wants to come and see the big world with me.

The truth coming out in anger, I guess that's what it was. Same as the truth coming out when you're drunk. Except instead of being left with a hangover you're left with a feeling of calm. I lay there, perfectly still, the pillow cool against my cheek, thinking it through.

And wondering about Elisabeth.

I took Joe and Georgia to the fair the other night. There's one that's set up in the park near me. We had a brilliant time. Joe's favourite thing was the dodgems. We had three goes on them. Joe wanted even more, but Georgia said she was feeling sick. I wouldn't have minded another go, to be honest. Of course all the time we were on them Joe was pretending to be Jenson Button. I said it wouldn't be very good if Jenson Button drove like that, would it, bumping into people all the time. Joe said that didn't matter, whenever we bumped into another driver it was Michael Schumacher and we were knocking him out of the race so we could win it.

Anita called me and said she was out late-night shopping with Shaun, why didn't I drop the kids off at the shopping centre, it was nearer than her house. We found them in the sports shop. Shaun was buying a new golf club, the assistant was talking him through all the different ones, so he didn't really notice us get there. I talked to Anita for a bit, told her about what we'd done at the fair, and Georgia told her about going on the 'horse ride' (she meant the merry-go-round). Joe had wandered off and found this framed picture of Jenson Button, they've got pictures of loads of sports stars on this one wall. He came back and pulled at my leg and said, 'Daddy, come and look at this, come and look at this.' So we went over there, and I lifted him up so he could see it better, and we read all the sponsors' names on Jenson Button's overalls, and when I said each one Joe would point to it and he'd say the name himself.

While we were doing that I looked over at Shaun; he was being really serious with the assistant, asking him lots of questions about the golf clubs. He looked so grown-up, the complete opposite of what I'd been feeling like all night, having a good time with Joe and Georgia. But for the first time I didn't really mind that. Right at that moment, I realised I didn't want to be like Shaun. There was something about his grown-upness that made me think he wasn't really enjoying himself that much. Obviously he was buying something that would make him happy, he loves his golf, plays all the time. But I got the feeling it was a very routine sort of happiness, no . . . what's the word . . . no real *joy* in it. But the happiness I got from holding Joe and reading Jenson Button's overalls with him – that had lots of joy in it. I realised I'm glad that's how I feel when I'm with him and Georgia. In fact I feel a bit bad about what I've said before, about resenting the fact that I feel like a kid. I think maybe with them I'm supposed to. Maybe other parents do that too. I'd never seen it that way before.

But obviously that only applies when I'm with them. When I'm with adults I shouldn't be like that. Especially not with Elisabeth. She's here now – they got here today. The good thing is she's going to be based in my office, because that's where we keep most of the accounts she'll need to look at. So I'll have lots of time to talk to her.

She came to put her laptop and her folders in my office, ready to start work tomorrow, and while she was there I asked her if she'd like a coffee, and she said yes, she'd love one. So I buzzed this work experience lad we've got in at the moment, and he put his head round the door and I said could he get us two coffees please. I wasn't all high and mighty with him, I hate people who do that, but I thought it would help if Elisabeth saw me in a position of authority, might help her take me seriously. I asked if we could have one white with one sugar, the other one black with no sugar, and when I said the second one I looked at Elisabeth and said, 'That is right, isn't it?' and she looked surprised and said, 'Well remembered' and I said, 'Attention to detail, that's what accountancy's all about, isn't it?' (I'd got that one ready) and she laughed and said, 'Yes, I suppose it is'. I felt really good when she laughed. It made me all happy inside.

But I wish I could have kept us off the topic of children. I forgot to take the picture of Joe and Georgia off my desk. I meant to do that, put it in my drawer so Elisabeth wouldn't see it. Wouldn't give the right image, I thought, her seeing me as a boring old bloke with two kids. I wanted her to think of me as young and exciting. Well, not young exactly – she knows I'm the same age as her – but young at heart, that's what I mean. If she thought I was the sort of bloke who spends his weekends helping a four-year-old read nursery rhymes it wouldn't do much for my chances of impressing her, would it?

Of course she bloody well noticed the picture, didn't she? Asked me when it had been taken. I had to tell her. It was only a few months ago. The three of us had gone to the seaside, and we'd built this enormous sandcastle, it was almost as tall as Georgia. We got this bloke who was walking his dog to take a picture of us all standing next to it. Well, Joe and Georgia were standing, I was kneeling down, obviously. Bloody freezing it was.

I told Elisabeth all this. I was cringing inside, wishing I'd remembered to hide the picture. Although actually, now I come to think of it, she seemed fairly interested. She kept asking me about it, and it made her smile when I told her about Joe saying 'brawbridge' 'cos he couldn't say 'drawbridge'. I mean, I'm sure she was just making conversation, while she finished her coffee. But still, things could have gone worse.

I've decided what my next move is going to be: I'm going to ask her to dinner at my house. I think if I'm on home ground I might feel a bit more confident. There's one little spanner in the works, which is that Elisabeth isn't staying in London. Walter and Mary are in this hotel on Park Lane, but she isn't with them, she's staying with a friend who lives about three-quarters of an hour outside town. Old friend, apparently, someone she hasn't seen for a while, she said she wanted to catch up with them, so she's staying at their flat instead of at the hotel. Probably someone she used to go to college with or something. Anyway, I don't think that'll matter too much.

The mistake, looking back on it, was to have the discussion in front of Elisabeth. She was sitting at a spare desk, checking some figures in one of Kathy's ledgers. It was her first full day in the office. She'd come in to the room when I was already there, and we did our 'Hi there, good to see you again, how are you?' routine pretty convincingly, I thought. Modest peck on each cheek, then Elisabeth got on with her work. Kathy would never have guessed that Elisabeth and I had in fact spent the previous afternoon, evening and night in my flat. Almost all of it in the bedroom.

'Three o'clock, isn't it?'

Kathy consulted her computer. 'Yeah, that's right . . . but, oh, I forgot to tell you.'

'What?'

'I've swapped this afternoon with Friday. It's the cartoon you're doing today, not Rover.'

My private alarm bell went off. 'Eh?'

'The agency called and said the ad's still being edited, could they put it off a couple of days.'

'And you agreed?'

'Yeah. Why not? Both sessions are in Mick's studio. It doesn't make any difference to him, why should it to you? You were going to do Rover today and the cartoon on Friday, now it's the other way round, that's all.'

'And you didn't think to tell me?'

'I meant to, Alex, but I forgot, I'm sorry. It didn't really seem that important. What does it matter which way round you do the ads?'

'Kathy, it's this afternoon that Walter and Mary are coming to watch me.' More PR from Miles.

'So?'

'So – these very important Americans, on whom I've somehow managed to make a half-decent impression – God knows how, Kathy, but I have – who were going to come and see me record a nice, sober advert for Rover's new executive car, are now going to come and see me record the voice of a cartoon character called Mr Wiggle.'

'Oh, calm down. It's only a cartoon.'

'No, Kathy, it's a cartoon called Mr Wiggle. Have you seen it, by any chance?'

'How could I? It hasn't started going out yet. And even when it does it's going to be on at ten o'clock in the morning, isn't it? I know that's the middle of the night as far as you're concerned, but some of us have to be in the office by that time. Getting you work, in case you've forgotten.'

'For which you get handsomely rewar—'

'Don't even think about saying that, Alex. I've told you before, I don't take ten per cent of your earnings, you take ninety per cent of mine.'

I was getting sidetracked here. 'Kathy, all I'm saying is I'd rather do the Rover session this afternoon, not the cartoon. If at all possible.'

'And I've told you, it *isn't* at all possible. If it was I'd swap them back for you. Gladly.' She gave a sigh. 'Look, if you're that bothered about it why don't you tell Walter and Mary to come on Friday instead of today?'

'Yeah, that's an idea.' I turned to Elisabeth. 'They could do that, couldn't they?'

But I knew from the grin she was almost – *almost* – suppressing that Elisabeth had formed a plan. A plan with yours truly at the centre of it. She pretended not to have been listening. 'I'm sorry?'

I swallowed nervously. 'Walter and Mary – they were supposed to be coming to see me do a session this afternoon, remember?' *Come on, Elisabeth, don't do this to me.*

'Were they? Oh yes, of course, I remember now. Is there some sort of problem?'

You bloody know there is. You heard every word. 'Well, what it is . . . you see . . . I think it'd be better if they came to the one I'm doing on Friday instead. You're still around then, aren't you?'

'Yes. We don't fly home till Sunday.'

'So there wouldn't be any problem in them coming along on Friday? Instead of today?'

'Er, I'm not sure . . .' *How did I know you were going to say that?* 'We're meeting up for lunch, I'll ask them then.' *Yeah. Right. Of course you will.* 'Now you must excuse me, I've got to go back up to Tony's office. You don't mind if I take this print-out, Kathy?'

'Of course not. Give me a call if you need anything else.'

I followed her down the corridor. 'Elisabeth, please . . .'

She stopped. 'Yes, Alex?' Then, checking no one was around, she kissed me quickly on the neck. 'I mean "Mr Wiggle".'

'Look, please . . . you haven't seen this cartoon . . . trust me . . . *please* . . .' But I knew it was no good. Pleading would only make her more determined. Instead I let her kiss me again, this time on the lips. Then she headed for the stairs.

All I could do was go for lunch and expect the worst.

Which was just as well, because it was exactly what I got. At two-forty I went back to the office. Walter, Mary and Elisabeth were in reception.

'Hi!' said Mary, kissing me on both cheeks. 'Good to see you again!'

'Likewise. How's London treating you?'

'Wonderfully, just wonderfully. I *love* these offices.'

'Good, aren't they? Over a hundred years old. Lots of character. Or is that Miles?'

Walter gave me a manly handshake. 'And I understand we're going to have the pleasure of seeing you at work?'

'Erm, yes, so I believe . . . although I'm not so sure about the "pleasure" part.'

'Nonsense,' he replied. 'Without you none of us would have jobs. You're the one who pays the bills, remember!'

Yeah, it's just that I'd rather you watched me paying the bills via Rover instead of Mr Bloody Wiggle. 'Well, I do my best . . .' I decided to give it one last crack. 'Listen, I was wondering . . .' I cast a nervous glance at Elisabeth. She was biting her lip. 'I'm doing another session on Friday, and I've been thinking . . . that one would be much more interesting for you than today's . . . the director who's doing it is a really creative guy, I think you'd enjoy watching him work . . .' I stopped. Any more and I might have dropped to my knees and begged.

'You're the expert,' said Walter. He turned to Mary. 'What do you say? I think we could rearrange that conference call with Bruce, couldn't we?'

'Yeah, I don't see why not . . . I'm sure we can do it some-time tomorrow . . .'

'Er, actually . . .' said Elisabeth. Walter and Mary looked at her. I looked at the floor. 'Actually, I was speaking to Bruce

162

just now. He happened to mention he was going upstate tomorrow. So, I'm afraid . . .'

There was no point perservering. Whatever I said, Elisabeth was going to find a way round it. 'Oh well, it doesn't matter. This afternoon it is, then.'

'This afternoon it is,' said Mary. 'I'm sure we're going to enjoy it just fine.'

Not as much as your accountant is. 'Yeah.' I looked at my watch. 'Well, session starts in fifteen minutes. Shall we get round there?'

At the studio I introduced everyone to Mick. He gave them a layman's guide to some of the equipment. Walter asked him a couple of questions about woofers and tweeters. Mary and Elisabeth chatted about something or other. I sat in the corner, sweating.

By ten past three there was still no sign of Dorothy, the cartoon's producer.

'I meant to say, she called from her car,' said Mick. 'Said the traffic was looking bad.'

'Not to worry,' said Mary with a smile.

'You'll like her,' continued Mick. 'She's lovely. Looks like your dotty grandmother, but underneath she's sharp as a knife. Got her own production company. Specialises in educational cartoons. This one's doing really well. Selling it all round the world, she is.'

'All round the world, eh, Alex?' said Walter. 'I bet that keeps the royalty cheques rolling in.'

I did my best to smile. 'Makes a few quid.' *And I'd give you every penny if you'd leave now and not watch me do this recording.*

Soon Dorothy showed up. Five foot nothing of hyperactivity bursting into the control room, spluttering apologies

163

for being late. She was wearing a bright purple raincoat (it was one of the sunniest days of the year), and carrying a huge tartan bag over her shoulder. Even though it was almost the same size as her, Dorothy had packed it to over-flowing. In the half-dozen paces from the door to the chair, she lost a hairbrush (although to look at her you wouldn't think she used one), a set of keys, two half-eaten tangerines and a dog-eared sketchbook. We each fielded the item that fell nearest to us.

'Thank you, thank you . . . I'm so sorry . . . thank you, so sorry, so sorry,' said Dorothy as she collected everything.

Once order had been restored, I introduced her to Walter, Mary and Elisabeth. 'They're over here from New York,' I said. 'And they wanted to see what actually hap-pens in a voice-over session. You don't mind if they sit in, do you?'

'Of course not! More the merrier!'

Really? You can tell them to get lost as far as I'm concerned.
'That's very kind of you, Dorothy.'

'Yes, thanks, Dorothy,' said Elisabeth. 'We really appreciate it.'

I bet you do.

'Rightio . . .' said Dorothy, rummaging in her bag, '. . . one copy of the script . . .' I took it from her. On the front page, in bold 48-point, it said:

MR WIGGLE, SERIES ONE, EPISODE THREE
MR WIGGLE GOES TO THE POST OFFICE.

I couldn't bear to look at any more.

'And here's the disk . . .' continued Dorothy, '. . . although . . . is it the right one?'

My hopes rose. *Please* let her have brought the wrong episode.

'Episode three – is that the script you've got, Alex?'

Bollocks. 'Yeah, that's the one.'

'OK,' said Mick, 'do you want to go through and get your cans on? I'll load the programme.'

I did as I was told, feeling more like a condemned man entering the execution chamber than a voice-over artist entering a studio. My headphones on, I stood at the mike patiently. Nervously. Through the glass I watched Mick and Dorothy sit at the mixing desk. Walter and Mary occupied the sofa on the raised level behind them. Right at the back stood Elisabeth. I fixed her with a stare. She smiled and gave me the thumbs-up. I wanted to respond with a different gesture. It wasn't one Mr Wiggle would use.

'OK,' came Mick's voice in my headphones, 'give me a bit for level?'

I counted to ten and back down again.

'That's great.'

'All right then,' said Dorothy. 'Let's make a start, shall we?'

Fixed to the wall above the glass was a big plasma screen. It crackled with wavy lines for a moment. Then the words 'Mr Wiggle, Series One, Episode Three' appeared, together with a load of technical info about what format it was in and the like. On the left of the screen was a clock, counting down from fifteen seconds. When it got to zero the opening credits appeared, with a time code across the bottom. Although the voice-over wasn't yet on the tape, the music was. Mr Wiggle's theme tune is played by a small brass band. It's a pleasant little tune, the main melody taken by a trumpet. It fits Mr Wiggle's character perfectly. He's an essentially cheery but sometimes quite pompous character.

He's on the rotund side, with a head that's bald in the middle but with patches of curly white hair on either side. He wears round tortoiseshell glasses and a blue pin-striped suit. Each episode starts with him having breakfast, feeding a little of it to his cat Thompson, then putting on his jacket, ready to embark on whatever task the children are to learn about that week.

The opening music faded out as Mr Wiggle closed his front door and looked up at the sky.

'You need to come in . . . around about . . . here,' said Dorothy. 'And the first narration should finish . . . there . . . just as he gets to the corner.'

I nodded. 'Got it. Do you want to run that back, Mick? I'll give it a go.' Mr Wiggle pixillated crazily as Mick returned him to the front door. Then we were ready.

'"It's a lovely spring day,"' I read, '"and Mr Wiggle is walking down the high street."' The sentence, of course, was said in an ordinary narrator's voice. This wasn't the bit I was worried about.

'Spot on,' said Dorothy. Mr Wiggle rounded the corner and the shot cut to a street sign with arrows pointing in three directions, one of them marked 'Post Office'. 'You'll need to be quick with this one, otherwise we'll crash the next shot of Mr Wiggle.'

'"This morning he's going to the post office,"' I read. '"Can you see which way he needs to go?"' Again, neutral voice. This still wasn't the bit I was worried about.

A shot of Mr Wiggle with his hand on his chin, looking thoughtful. Then another shot of the sign. Then Mr Wiggle looking inspired, and pointing to the correct arrow.

'OK,' said Dorothy. 'We go into Mr Wiggle's voice here.'

This was the bit I was worried about.

Mr Wiggle's voice, as invented by myself and Dorothy over the course of two auditions, is a curious voice. He's quite high-pitched and croaky, in a cute, James-Stewart-as-a-baby sort of way that makes him stretch out his vowel sounds. And he slurs his 's's, like Sean Connery. It's a voice perfectly suited to a cartoon aimed at four-year-old children. It's a voice you're more than happy to do in front of the producer who's paying you for it, and the engineer who's getting paid as well. It's just not a voice you want to do in front of two high-ranking American executives and a woman you've recently started sleeping with.

'Shall we run it a few times so you can get used to the lip-movements?' asked Dorothy.

'Yeah, that'd be good.' *How about a couple of thousand times, so the Yanks have to leave before I start?*

Mick ran the sequence three times. On the last one I sneaked a look at Walter, Mary and Elisabeth. Two of them were watching their monitor intently, clearly fascinated by the whole process. The other was trying not to laugh.

'Got that?' said Dorothy.

I nodded.

'Let's go for a take, then.'

The green light in front of me flashed on. And stayed on. And stayed on.

'Are you all right, Alex?'

I coughed. 'Yeah, sorry. Throat was just . . . thought I'd . . .'

'No problem. Have some water, we'll go again.'

I took a drink, wishing it was poison. The green light came on again.

I could feel myself sweating. Two, three, four seconds . . .

'Alex? Are you sure everything's all right?'

'Yeah, it's just . . . erm . . . I was . . . sorry, lost my place for a minute.'

'Bottom of the first page, "Wiggle line 1".'

'Yep, of course, sorry. Got it now.'

'Right, let's go again.'

The green light. The terror. The sweating. No way out. All I could do was go for it.

'"Aaahhh yesh, datsh de way to de Posht Offish."'

There was a pause. Then Dorothy said, 'Erm, yes . . . that was lovely, Alex . . . but maybe a bit louder? You were looking down at your script, I think. You need to project more.'

'Sorry . . . yes. Of course . . . OK . . . still rolling? Right . . . "Aaahhh *yesh*, *datsh* de way to de Posht Offish."' I paused. 'How was that?'

'Much better.'

Thank Christ for that.

'Hang on,' said Mick, 'I think you might have popped the "P" on "Post Office".' He played the line back. There was the faintest popping sound. 'Better do another one.'

Thanks, Mick. Thanks a bundle. 'OK. Ready? . . . "Aaahhh *yesh*, *datsh* de way to de Posht Offish."' I looked over Dorothy's shoulder again. Walter and Mary were looking determined and serious. Elisabeth had her hand over her mouth.

I tried to ignore her. 'Was that all right?'

Mick nodded.

'Next line, then?' said Dorothy.

The shot was of Mr Wiggle walking along, holding up an envelope. '"I'm go-o-ing to de Posht Offish becosh I want to posht thiiish. Itsh a ca-a-rd, for Thomshon. Itsh hish bi-i-rday on Shunday!"'

'Great, great . . . and the next one?'

Mr Wiggle arrived at the post office. '"Itsh not jusht lettersh and ca-a-rdsh dat the Posht Offish can he-elp you wid. Dey can give you p-a-a-shportsh here too!"' Cut to a young woman handing over an application form. '"Datsh a speshal book which letsh you go to diffrend c-o-o-ountreesh!"'

Elisabeth, who had moved right in line with Dorothy so I couldn't miss her, put on a look of surprise and mouthed, 'Oh really?' Under cover of scratching my head I gave her what's known in her country as 'the finger', but quickly had to abort when Walter looked up. He smiled at me. I smiled back, trying hard not to look like a man who had just said, 'datsh a speshal book'.

I heard Dorothy clearing her throat. 'Erm, Alex . . . the next line . . . it goes here?'

'Oh yeah. Sorry.' I looked up at the screen. The shot panned from the passport woman to a man being served at the next window. '"Shumfink elsh you can get at de Posht Offish ish inshurance. Dish ish money dat you gi-i-ve to the Posht Offish – only a shma-a-ll bid of money – and den if b-a-a-d fings habben to you, dey give you a b-i-i-g lod of money!"'

Mary caught my eye. 'You probably knew that,' I said. She smiled. So did Walter. His smile was what you might call 'sympathetic'.

At the next window was an old woman paying a gas bill. '"Alsho ad de Posht Offish you can pay b-i-i-lls. Deese are pieces of p-a-ay-per dat tell you how much money you musht give for fings you have b-o-u-u-ght." I've got to pick you up on your realism there Dorothy – if that was a genuine old woman she'd still be getting her purse out of her bag, even though she's had half an hour in the queue to do it.'

'Next line . . . Mr Wiggle's being served.'

'Yeah, right . . . "Hell-o-o-o. I'd like to buy a shtamp for dish ca-a-rd, pleash.'" He held it up to the window. The address read 'Thompson, Wiggle Cottage, Wiggle Lane, Wiggle-On-The-Marsh, Wiggleshire.' *Thanks Mr Wiggle. Did it not occur to you to just give the cat the fucking card? Then I could have taken the Americans down the pub instead, and had a shred of dignity left. Wanker.*

The man behind the counter nodded. '"Certainly, sir. Would you like it to go first class or second class?"' Mr Wiggle turned to the camera. '"Firsht clash meansh de card will get there quigly, shecond clash meansh it will take a bid lo-o-o-nger. Firsht clash coshts more money . . . bud Thomshon's bi-i-i-rday ish nod till Shunday, sho I can shend de card shecond clash."' *Cheapskate as well, I see.*

'That's all lovely,' said Dorothy. 'Just the song left now. Shall we crack straight on with it?'

Oh no. The song. The bloody song. I'd forgotten about the bloody song. 'Erm . . . actually . . . would you mind if we took a break first? I'd, er . . . a coffee. I'd really like a coffee.'

I could see Dorothy was surprised. 'Oh, OK . . . if you'd like . . . Yeah, we've got lots of time left . . . Why not?'

I went back through to the control room.

'That was . . . interesting,' said Walter.

'Yes,' nodded Mary. 'Very . . . interesting.'

Elisabeth was too busy fighting back her laughter to say anything.

I gave an 'it's nothing really' shrug. 'Well, it's something to do on a Wednesday afternoon . . .' *Make yourself look a complete tit, that is.*

Dorothy poured herself an apple juice. 'It's something to do on a Wednesday afternoon that helps educate the grown-ups of tomorrow.'

170

Ah, had to be careful here. Couldn't 'dis' the cartoon too much. Still three weeks until they started airing. Enough time for Dorothy to get someone else to voice them. 'Yes, of course . . . it's great to be doing something so educational. Normally when you do a cartoon character it's trying to sell margarine or something.' *What are you doing? Get OFF cartoon characters. Remind them that you occasionally get paid to talk like a grown-u— like an adult.*

'Tell me,' said Elisabeth, who'd finally controlled herself. 'How do you . . . find the motivation for a character like Mr Wiggle?'

'Oh, you just think "stupid voice" and see what comes out.' I caught Dorothy's eye. 'But that's only for the first attempt, of course. After that you work on it, refine it . . . With the producer's input, of course.' *She's the nutter here, not me. I'm just trying to keep her sweet, can't you see that? Walter, Mary – PLEASE tell me you see that.*

'Yes,' said Dorothy. 'Alex has been so good to work with on this. He's really . . . he's really got inside Mr Wiggle's mind.'

Yes, thank you, Dorothy. I clapped my hands together. 'Anyway, Walter, Mary, Elisabeth – thanks for coming. Hope it wasn't too much of a drag for you.'

'Not at all,' said Mary. 'I really enj—'

'We don't have to go yet,' interrupted Elisabeth. 'We're not seeing Miles until five. What d'you say, guys? Stay and watch some more? I'm sure we'd all like to.'

I went back into the studio. This wasn't an execution any more, it was a torture session. Execution would have been a relief. I put on the electrodes. I mean headphones.

'Ready?' said Dorothy.

I'll never talk, you can do what you like but I'll never talk. 'Yeah, fine.'

Mick positioned the cartoon at the point where Mr Wiggle had just got blocked in by a woman with a pram.

Look, can't you just ask her to move it? Tap her on the shoulder and say, "Excuse me, would you mind letting me out?", like any normal person would? Why do you have to sing this fucking song? If the kids grow up and do that in a real Post Office they'll get arrested. The jangly synthesizer came in with its first few notes. Mr Wiggle's face registered alarm at his predicament. I thought about running from the studio.

The synth held down a chord. 'Cue Alex.'

I gulped. Then started to sing. '"Oh dee-wer, oh dee-wer . . ."' The synth added another note, raising the kids' anticipation of the really good bit to come. '"Wot h-a-a-ve we hee-wer?"' Another note, together with a faint drum roll. '"Wot c-a-a-n I doo-ooo?"' A final note, and the drum roll building to a crescendo. '"I know – do yoo-ooo?"'

The chord held for about five seconds. This is where the children stand up, ready to do the Iggle Wiggle dance. On the screen Mr Wiggle himself assumes the same position. He keeps his arms straight and his hands down by his side, as though they're manacled to his feet. Then he tilts forward slightly from the waist. Finally, when he's decided which way he needs to go, he very rapidly shakes his backside, causing his hands to slide up and down his thighs, and "wiggles" his way out of trouble. He looks like a *Riverdance* performer having a fit.

The chord was still being held. Mr Wiggle had tilted forward. '"I-i-i've . . . g-o-o-t . . . t-o-o-o . . ."' *Please God, take me now. Bolt of lightning, spontaneous combustion, anything you want, just take me now . . .*

The drum roll broke into a beat. The synth started pounding out a boogie-shuffle rhythm. Mr Wiggle's arse started vibrating. '"Do an iggle wiggle!"' The synth repeated the six notes, dah-dee dah-dee dah-dee, encouraging the kids to echo Mr Wiggle's line. Then he (or rather I) sang the line again, half an octave lower, '"Do an iggle wiggle!"' The synth replayed these notes, to let the kids reply again. Then, back up at the first pitch, '"I've got to do an iggle wiggle!"' Dah-dee dah-dee dah-dee. '"Do an ig—"'

'Alex . . .'

I stopped. Dorothy was holding her hand up. 'Sorry, Alex, but er . . . I wonder if we could go again . . . ? It hasn't got quite the . . . quite the "ping" you seemed to be giving it last time.'

Ping? PING? Have a look behind you, Dorothy. Do they look like the sort of people you want to 'ping' in front of? Concentrate on the two older ones, by the way. The one who's shaking and pretending to blow her nose isn't worth the time of day. 'Really? Sorry, Dorothy. I don't know why . . . perhaps it was . . . er . . .'

'Do you know what? I think it could have been because you were doing the dance then. What if we tried that again?'

Oh shit. 'OK . . . if you insi— right. Right.' *Has Elisabeth bribed you?*

Has Elisabeth bribed you?'

I put my script on a stand. Then I placed my hands on my thighs. 'Ready.'

Mick started the cartoon. I took a breath. '"Do an iggle wiggle!"' As I said it I started to wiggle my backside. God knows how, but I did. The studio glass is, of course, sound-proof. So it must have been my imagination that made me think I heard a thirty-three-year-old American shrieking. '"Do an iggle wiggle!"' Dah-dee dah-dee dah-dee. '"Do an iggle wiggle!"' Still I shook. The only thing keeping me going was a desire to get it over with as soon as possible.

Stopping would mean going back to the beginning. '"Do an iggle wiggle!"' Then the synth cranked up, the drums really began to swing for the song's finale, which builds to a climax like a Broadway show-stopper. To get through it I had to persuade myself that Walter and Mary weren't there at all. I leaned forward even more so I couldn't see them. '"Iggle here, wiggle there, iggle wiggle everywhere . . . d-o-o an iggle w-i-i-ggle . . . and I'm F-W-E-E-E-E!!"'

The final cymbal died away. I stopped wiggling. But I didn't look up. I couldn't. I remembered that Walter and Mary really were there, that they'd just watched me demean myself, that their colleague, the one who'd put me through all this, was there too. I didn't know whether I wanted to kill her or myself.

'That was lovely, Alex. Really great.'

I looked at the floor. 'Thank you.'

'That's the whole episode done, then.'

'Yeah.'

'All finished.'

'Yeah.'

'Er . . . do you want to come back through, then?'

Not really. 'OK.'

Walter and Mary looked shell-shocked.

'That was . . . er,' Walter said, 'that was . . . really something different.'

I nodded and attempted a smile. But I couldn't speak. I felt like someone who'd just been caught having intimate relations with a vacuum cleaner.

'Yes,' said Mary, 'I certainly never realised how much work went into a cartoon like this.'

I gave another nod, another feeble smile.

'Tell me,' said Elisabeth. *Here we go.* 'Do you often copy

174

the character's actions when you're recording a voice-over? Or is that something you only do with Mr Wig—' But a sudden coughing fit stopped her.

'Are you OK?' asked Mary, putting a concerned hand on Elisabeth's arm.

'Yes . . . yes, I'm f— I'm fine,' came the spluttered response. 'Maybe . . . maybe some water . . .'

'Of course,' I said, pouring her a glass. *How would you like it – over the head or in the face?*

Walter turned to Dorothy. 'Mick was telling us you've sold the cartoon to lots of countries overseas?'

'Oh yes, we're up to seventeen now. In fact the last deal was with a cable channel in New York.'

'Really? Well, Alex, I'll have to look out for you!'

Are you taking the piss? 'Yes, you'll have to.'

'Or should I say "listen" out for you!'

'Ha-ha.'

Mary gathered up her belongings. 'We should be getting along, guys, don't you think? Listen, Alex – thank you so much for letting us come along today.'

'Don't mention it.'

'It was a real eye-opener.'

Now you're at it as well. 'We aim to please.'

'Yes, thank you, Alex,' said Elisabeth. 'I'm so glad we had a chance to watch you at work.' *Of course you are.* 'And now we know what to do if we ever find ourselves in a tight spot – we'll just "Do an igg—"'

'Glad you enjoyed yourself,' I said quickly.

As everyone made their way out, I muttered to her, 'You're going to suffer for this, you know.'

Her eyes sparkled. 'I do hope so.'

*

So that pretty well decided what we did when we got back to mine that night. At about ten we got up to have some supper. I put a dressing gown on, Elisabeth wore one of my old T-shirts.

She caught sight of herself in a mirror. 'Oh my God! Alex, why didn't you tell me how much of a mess my make-up was in?'

'Funnily enough that wasn't the main thing on my mind just then.'

She grinned. 'No, I guess not.'

'In fact the tousled look suits you. Adds to your vulnerability.'

'Don't get used to it, honey.' She picked up her make-up bag. 'Back in a minute.'

I waited in the kitchen. She was upstairs for ages. When she came down I found out why.

'Wouldn't have thought you needed this.' She was holding *The Road To Commitment*.

'You cheeky . . .'

'Oh come on, Alex, a girl earns snooping rights on her second day in a man's flat, has no one ever told you? And it wasn't as though I snooped very hard. The thing was on your desk.'

'Yeah, but . . .'

'But nothing,' she said, flicking through it. 'Is it any good?'

'Yeah, it's OK.' To my surprise I found I wasn't ashamed. 'Makes quite a bit of sense.'

She nodded.

I opened the fridge. 'I don't know what you want to eat . . .'

She came over and stood behind me, put her arms around me, kissed me on the neck. 'Oh, whatever. I'm not really that hungry. Shall we just have that salad?'

'Sure.' I emptied it into a bowl and added some dressing. We sat on either side of the table, picking at it with forks.

'Tell me about the book, then.'

'Friend of mine was reading it, said I should get a copy too. I did it to humour her, really.' OK, maybe I was a little ashamed. 'But the first chapter or two didn't seem too bad. Talks about us being the "change generation".'

'The what?'

'"Change generation." Things are way more difficult for us than our parents, because all their choices were made for them. More or less.'

'I don't follow you.'

'Everyone had the same lifestyles, did the same things. Wore the same things, ate the same things, watched the same things on TV.' I remembered the other weekend at Mum's. 'Like, over here in the seventies we had these two comedians called Morecambe and Wise. Everyone used to watch them. I mean *everyone*. The big thing used to be their Christmas special. It was the standard issue British Christmas – turkey, Queen's speech, Morecambe and Wise. One year twenty-eight million people watched it. Twenty-eight *million*. That was half the population. Literally. If you'd walked down the street the next day you could have pointed at every other person and gone, "They watched it, they watched it, they watched it . . ." But we only had three channels then. Now there are hundreds, everyone watches their own thing.' I picked up a lettuce leaf with my fingers. 'I mean, I got that figure from a Morecambe and Wise documentary. In the old days you used to watch television programmes. Now you watch television programmes about television programmes.'

'Lots of people watch *The Simpsons*.'

'Nah, it's not the same . . .' I tried to think of another way of putting it. 'I mean, in the old days there were really big events, weren't there? Like the moon landing. Our parents had the moon landing. That brought the whole world together. Our generation didn't have anything like that.'

'Live Aid.'

'Well, yeah . . . maybe . . . but—'

'I will *never* forget Simon Le Bon's voice giving out in the middle of that high note. We laughed so much.'

My favourite bit was Phil Collins getting Concorde so he could play at both gigs. The worst bit was when he came back. 'But Live Aid was twenty years ago. I mean now, the twenty-first century. There isn't anything now that brings everyone together.'

'Nine-eleven.'

'Well, OK, that, but . . .' I'd thought she'd get it more easily than this. 'It's . . . what I'm saying is . . .'

She patiently chewed a mouthful of salad.

'Forget important events. Think about the little things. Social things. In the old days everyone shopped at the same stores, didn't they? Over here it was Marks and Spencer, for example. It was almost like there was an Act of Parliament that said, "The only people allowed to sell clothes will be Marks and Spencer." Men wore suits, women wore dresses. End of story. Now it's all changed.'

'Everyone shops at Gap instead.'

Was she *trying* to be difficult? No, I didn't think she was. I had another go. 'All right, food – think of all the places you can go to eat and drink, all the variety there is. Now, our parents—'

'Starbucks,' said Elisabeth. 'The whole world goes to Starbucks.'

I gave up. She'd really disappointed me. Out of everyone I knew, I'd have said she'd be one of the first to understand. Strange, isn't it, how people can surprise you?

The real turning point, though, came the next day. Lunchtime. Elisabeth had reminded me of my promise to take her to Rossi's. We'd got a table by the window.

On the other side of the street a young woman was pushing a buggy laden with shopping and, somewhere in the middle of the supermarket bags, a sleeping baby. With her other hand she was dragging a toddler. And I mean dragging – the little so-and-so was in a major tantrum about something. Screaming at the top of his voice, and then, when that didn't get him whatever it was he wanted, crying. Or rather pretending to cry, in that way kids do, screwing their eyes up and making a screeching sound from the back of their throat in the hope you won't notice there aren't any tears. Top marks to the lad for effort – he screeched so loud he woke the baby up, who started to cry for real.

'Poor woman,' said Elisabeth.

'Yeah, because she can't have expected that when she decided to have them, can she? Children hardly ever cry, do they? She must have been really unlucky to get two bawlers.'

'Come on, have a little sympathy.'

The toddler had now moved on to footstamping. He forced a passer-by to step into the road, where she nearly got run over by a cab. The mother broke off from shouting at the toddler to apologise.

'No, I won't have a little sympathy,' I said. 'That's what kids do. They keep you up all night then embarrass you in public during the day. That's the deal. You sign up for it the day you get pregnant.' *Go on, push it a bit more. Find out where she stands.*

'Don't you also sign up for the good stuff?'

'Like?'

'I don't know – like the first painting they bring home from school.'

'If I want crap art I can go to Tate Modern.'

'So you're saying you'll never have kids?'

'I don't know about never . . . maybe never . . . Certainly not for a long time, that's for sure.' I left a pause. Elisabeth played with a sachet of ketchup. 'How about you?'

She kept her eyes on the ketchup, spoke very quietly, 'I'd love to have children . . .'

I waited, sensing there was something else to come. But it never got the chance. Because there was a very loud rap on the window that made us both jump.

I've done it! I've asked her! Elisabeth! And she said yes!

It was today. At lunchtime. I was on my way back to the office, going past this café, and there she was, sitting in the window! And Alex was with her! I stopped and stood there, expecting them to look up and see me, but Elisabeth was looking down at the table, and Alex wasn't saying anything either, maybe they were a bit bored, you know, couldn't think of things to talk about. Anyway, I knocked on the window, and they both turned and saw me, and Elisabeth smiled, and after a couple of seconds Alex did too, and I went into the café to see them. I said hello and they both said hello back. I said, 'Fancy seeing you here', and Elisabeth said, 'I know, fancy'. She explained that she'd bumped into Alex outside the office and they'd decided to have lunch together, which I suppose was nice of him, to be polite. Then none of us said anything, and I got the feeling things were a bit awkward, so I thought yeah, I was probably right about them not having much to say to each other.

I asked if they'd had a nice lunch, and Elisabeth said yes, her sandwich had been very good, and Alex said the same about his jacket potato. Then I said, 'How's it been, staying with your friend this week?', and Elisabeth said, 'Kinda boring, actually', but when she said it she looked across at

Alex and gave a funny little smile, I suppose she'd been telling him about her friend earlier on, making a joke of it. But I don't think he heard, because he was looking out of the window and didn't smile back at her. Perhaps he'd been distracted by something.

I said, 'Oh, that's a pity'. Then there was a little gap. Then Elisabeth asked if I wanted a coffee or anything with them, and I said no thanks, I'd just had one. Then there was another little gap, and Alex looked up and said well, he might as well go and pay, and Elisabeth reached for her purse but he said it was his treat, and he went off to the till.

Now, I hadn't had the idea until then, until me and Elisabeth were left on our own together, but the fact that it was just the two of us made me think of it. And also maybe because I was standing up and she was sitting down I felt a bit more confident as well, I don't know. Anyway, I found myself thinking, If you don't ask her now you're never going to ask her, you've got to take your chance. I took a deep breath and said, 'Elisabeth', and she said, 'Yes?' and I said, 'I was wondering if you'd like to have dinner with me tomorrow night?'

She looked surprised, which I can't say I wasn't expecting, and she thought for a moment, and said that her friend had something planned, and I said, 'But you just said you'd been bored with them, why don't you come and have dinner with me instead?' I hope I didn't sound too desperate when I said that, but I'd decided this was it, this was when I really had to make it happen. And Elisabeth said, 'Er, OK, sure, that'd be nice', you know, you could tell she was only saying yes because she couldn't think of an excuse quickly enough, but I didn't mind that, I'm not kidding myself that she'd leap at the chance to have dinner with me because she's mad about me, I know she's not. All I wanted was to get another chance to spend some time with her away from the office. And I've got it!

Alex came back and said right, were we all ready, and the three of us left. He said he was off to do some shopping, so he said goodbye to us, and Elisabeth said it was nice bumping into him, and maybe she'd see him again before she went back to America, and he nodded and said, 'Yeah', and then me and Elisabeth went back to the office and got on with the accounts. But after a bit I thought, I've got to get hold of Alex, to ask him his advice about the dinner, so I sent him a text and said was he still in town? and he replied and said yeah, he was in HMV on Oxford Street. So I said to Elisabeth that I had to pop out for a few minutes, she said fine, she had plenty to be getting on with. I sent Alex another text and told him to stay in HMV, I'd meet him in Soul.

When I got there he looked confused and asked what was going on, and I told him about Elisabeth coming over to my place. He looked surprised, just like Elisabeth had, but again I expected that. I told him she'd only said yes because she couldn't think of an excuse, and he nodded, I could tell he didn't want to make it too obvious he was thinking the same thing, but I bet he was. I didn't mind, I told him that, I said, 'Alex, I know the odds are against me here, but I really, really like Elisabeth, and if there's any chance I can make an impression on her, you know, get her to like me, then I'm determined to give it a go.'

He looked at me for a minute, I don't know, it was strange, it was like he was weighing something up in his mind . . . anyway, whatever it was, after a bit he smiled at me, a really friendly smile. That made me feel good, and he said, 'I think you should give it a go.' I was glad he said that, it gave me a lot of encouragement.

Then I asked if he could help me, give me some tips, because now I thought about it, about Elisabeth coming to my house, on the one hand it was good, like I said before, being on my own territory would help me feel confident. But on the other hand it was a bit of a challenge, because I realised I'd never actually had anyone round for dinner before, not a woman, not on my own. Anita and me had people round but that's different, isn't it? So I said to Alex could he talk me through it a bit, give me some pointers?

Once you've identified your Unique Staleness Point, you must have the courage to act on it. You must stop yourself falling into the same old behaviour patterns, ending up with the same sort of person you've always ended up with. This will often call for real strength of resolve. Have the determination to hang on in there, doing whatever you need to to 'force the change'.

Reading more of the book was one way I coped with what I was doing to Elisabeth. The other was talking it through with Rosie. I'd toyed with calling Amy because I valued her opinion but thought it might be a touch insensitive. So I was sitting with Rosie in the food court of a huge shopping complex about twenty minutes' drive from where I live. One of those temples to the great god Retail. She'd felt like doing some worshipping, and I met her for an early lunch, which had started with the obligatory ten minutes of giving verdicts on her purchases. I'd liked the dress, not liked the photo frame, been undecided about the perfume.

Then I told her about Tony. 'I know I should have told him about me and Elisabeth, but I didn't.'

'Meaning?' Rosie's expression showed she still wasn't convinced about my behaviour.

'Look, I know Elisabeth is the woman I'm sleeping with—'

'The woman who's come all the way across the Atlantic you're sleeping with.'

'Yeah, but she's not here just because of me, is she? She's on business.'

Rosie shifted her chair to let someone past. 'True. But she might have come across to see you anyway.'

'We don't know that. Anyway, that's not the point. What matters is I know she's not the right woman for me.'

'In which case why don't you tell her that, rather than trying to offload her on to your friend?'

'I'm not trying to "offload" her. Come on, be fair, Rosie. How often have you said to someone, "Right, it's not working, we're going to stop the relationship now, this minute"? You don't, do you? You let relationships fade away, die a gradual death. It's easier that way. More . . . I don't know, more polite.'

She snorted. '"Polite"? Alex, you're telling someone you don't want to sleep with them any more, not that you don't want to come to their drinks party.'

'So you've always told blokes it's over the minute the thought's entered your head, have you?'

'No . . . not always.' She paused. 'All right, maybe I'm being unfair. That's not the way it usually works. Elisabeth might well get back to New York and find she's not thinking of you as much as she expected to.'

'That's what I mean. There's no need to make a scene now, ruin things by getting all dramatic. We won't see each other again, and it'll be fine. A nice memory of a few good nights. Nothing more, nothing less.'

'Perhaps,' said Rosie. 'But what about Tony? Where does he come into it?'

'I don't know,' I replied. 'It's just, when he told me about it, about inviting Elisabeth over to his place, something told me it might not be such a lost cause after all.'

'Are you serious?'

'Yeah. I think I am.'

'From what I've seen, Tony's not exactly a ladykiller.'

'He's not. In fact I think he'd struggle to stun one.'

'So why do you think he's got a chance with Elisabeth?'

'Don't know. I really don't know. She likes working with him, she told me.'

'And what advice did you give him?'

'Basic stuff. You know, make the place look nice. Few candles here and there. Put a bit of effort into setting the table. Maybe some flowers. Think about what music he's going to put on.'

'I'm sure he felt honoured, being enrolled into the Richards Academy Of How To Seduce A Lay-Dee.'

'He only got the introductory course. If he'd signed up for the full Honours degree I'd have told him about wearing a cravat and taking her for a spin in his open-top sports car.'

'Pity he's only got until tonight – no time to grow a moustache he can twirl at her.'

'He did actually ask me about tricks like that,' I said, laughing at the memory. 'Not moustaches and sports cars, but he kept saying was there anything he could do to tip the balance, any little tactics I could recommend. I tried telling him he shouldn't think about it like that, he should just be himself and pay her lots of attention and see how it went, but he wouldn't listen. He kept going on about "tactics". In the end, just to shut him up, I told him about the clock trick.'

'The clock trick?'

'Don't worry, it's nothing I've ever done myself.'

'I should hope not. It sounds suspicious.'

'It isn't really. Just a bit naff. A guy I used to work with fancied himself as a bit of a ladies' man. Told me that whenever he had someone coming round for dinner he'd set all the clocks in his flat half an hour slow. That way, when it got to what he called the "action end" of the evening . . .' Rosie cringed, '. . . yes, I know, I know – when it got to that part of the evening, if the woman was umming and ahhing about whether to stay for another drink or not, her thinking it was thirty minutes earlier than it really was might make the difference. Assuming she was too well-mannered to look at her watch.'

'And that really worked?'

'I don't know. That guy probably talked more than he walked. Anyway, it doesn't matter – it was something to shut Tony up. Not that it's stopped him calling me three times this morning, asking whether he should buy a new shirt, what aftershave he should wear, God knows what else . . .'

'Poor thing.'

'Elisabeth's meeting Walter and Mary for an after-work drink while he goes home to get things ready. He's asked me if I'll nip round before she gets there, check everything's all right.'

'Are you going to?'

'Yeah, I said I would. I'm up in town anyway for a session.' The Rover ad I should have been doing on Wednesday, before Mr Wiggle stuck his nose in. 'Obviously nothing's going to happen tonight, but if Tony doesn't make too bad an impression he could put down a marker for the future. Elisabeth was on about trying to get out of it last night, but I talked her into going ahead. She'll leave Tony's quite early to go back to her "friend's" place. Get a cab to the station, as though she's going to take the train out of town. But I'm going to pick her up in the car. I'm driving in this afternoon.'

Rosie nodded. 'Busy day for you.'

'You could say that.'

We sensed people standing by our table, and looked up. It was a middle-aged woman and her teenage son. She'd noticed our empty plates. 'Excuse me, but I don't suppose . . . ?'

I looked around. Every table was taken.

'Of course,' I said, standing up and moving our tray.

The woman smiled. 'That's really kind of you . . . Sorry to . . . I mean, I don't want to . . .'

'It's fine,' said Rosie. 'I hadn't noticed how busy it had got.'

'I know . . . Thank you ever so much.' As Rosie and I moved off, the woman turned to her son. 'Now come on, you sit here. Wasn't that nice of the lady and gentleman?'

'"Gentleman"?' said Rosie. 'She's obviously no judge of character.'

But I didn't reply. Something about the boy had caught my attention. If 'boy' is the right word – what was he, fourteen, fifteen? When do you stop being a boy and become a man? I'm thirty-four and I still feel uncomfortable using the word 'man' about myself. What are you at fourteen? A youth? A kid? A lad? I tell you what you're not, though – and this is what made me turn to watch the son as we walked away – you're not the boy your mother still thinks you are. His body was moving out of childhood; he had the look of someone who's grown four inches in the last year, and his trousers (safe, old-fashioned – I bet she'd bought them for him) finished two inches above his shoes. His face was spotty, the hair on his top lip had gone from downy to 'needs shaving', his muscles were beginning to develop. He looked awkward, embarrassed, almost like a man being forced to play the part of a child.

His mother showed him something in a shopping catalogue, talking about it enthusiastically. He nodded, didn't say anything; you could tell he didn't want to be seen out with her. I'd guess he didn't have many friends at school, wasn't part of the gang that went out on their own, buying the clothes they wanted rather than the ones their mums bought for them. But he was still growing up, growing away from his mother. Not yet brave enough to tell her he didn't want to come shopping with her. But it wouldn't be long.

'Why do mothers never notice that their children aren't children any more?' It was a moment before I realised I'd asked the question out loud.

'Sorry?'

I stopped and pointed back at the table. 'Her. Look at her son. He doesn't want to be here, does he?' Rosie watched for a while as I carried on talking. 'He's not her little boy any more, but she hasn't noticed. She still thinks he's the four-year-old she had to dress and feed, who loved her for doing those things, cried when he had to leave her and go to school. But it's not leaving her he hates now, it's having to stay with her.' I paused, turned to Rosie, realised I'd started to get a bit worked up. 'Sorry.'

'It's all right,' she said. We resumed our journey. 'You don't have to apologise.'

She said it very gently, as though she'd understood what I'd meant. Gradually, so did I. Twenty years ago there'd been another teenager, not very different from that one in the shopping centre, in Suffolk. With a mum who hadn't noticed how her son was changing. Still hasn't noticed, in some ways. That's why I got so angry with her the other week. (I'd told Rosie about what happened, about my 'big world' theory.) I mean, it's not her fault, she probably only had a couple of boyfriends before my dad, if that. Settled down as soon as she could. Why should phrases like the 'change generation' mean anything to her? But they do to me, there's that world out there that I haven't finished discovering. I feel like that boy – lad, whatever you call him – today. I've broken free from my parents' life, I'm not stuck in a rut, I'm different from them. I'm not ready for the bloody *cosiness* of settling down, of having kids, of never changing. Yet all my relationships seem to have led in that direction. I needed to understand why that was.

Rosie stopped by some escalators. 'Right, shopping time again.'

'Have fun.'

'I will.' We hugged. 'Hope the dinner goes well. You're adviser to one of them, chauffeur to the other.'

'Yeah. Just got to get my own life sorted now. I think I'm getting there. Slowly.'

She smiled. 'Dr Susanna would be proud of you.'

'Maybe.'

'No,' said Rosie, 'I really think you are getting there.' She looked away, her smile a little fainter but still there. 'I think we both are.'

I don't really know what she meant by that – she'd told me over lunch that she still wasn't seeing anyone – but something in the way she said it told me I shouldn't quiz her. She was probably still working it out in her mind. That must have been what it was.

'Hi there, it's me.'

Ten minutes later, sitting in my car, still in the shopping centre's car park. On the way back to the car I'd thought about Amy again. Hadn't spoken to her since Mum's party, nearly two weeks ago. Now that I'd got this children thing sorted in my head, I felt I wanted to apologise.

'Hi.'

'You're not busy, are you?'

'No. I've got a client due in a quarter of an hour, but I'm OK till then.'

'Right. I was just ringing to say sorry. About the other day.'

'Mmm. Not the nicest car journey I've ever had.'

'No. I'm sorry, Amy. I was completely out of order. It was . . .' I stopped. Before making the call I hadn't intended to tell Amy everything. But my apology wouldn't make sense without it. She deserved an explanation. And besides, I found I wanted to tell her. 'Look, I've been reading this book. It's called *The Road To Commitment*. It's a self-help book. It's been making me think a lot. You . . . you got caught up in the crossfire, if you like.'

As explanations went, this wasn't great. In fact it was closer to an excuse than an explanation. Amy's silence told me she saw it that way too.

'I don't want to bore you with all the details, but essentially I think my problem's about children.' I could hear her tense at the mention of this old chestnut. 'Don't worry, I don't want another discussion about it all.'

'Good.'

'It's just that I hadn't realised until the other weekend how much of an issue it is for me. All that pettiness was me coming to terms with it, slowly understanding what my . . .' I stopped myself saying 'USP' '. . . what my problem is. My problem with commitment, I mean.'

'I'm glad you're thinking about it at last.' She paused, trying to decide how to play this. 'And do you think you're getting an answer?'

'About commitment, you mean?'

'About why you're scared of it, yeah.'

'I'm not sc—' I stopped myself. I didn't want another argument with Amy, not when I was trying to apologise for the last one. I took a breath, made sure I kept my voice calm. 'It's not a question of being scared of commitment, it's more a question of how you find it.'

'You commit to someone, Alex. That's how you find it.'

'But it has to be the *right* someone, doesn't it? The right sort of someone. And I think what I'm learning is that the right sort of someone for me is . . . someone who wants to do some more living.' I held my breath. This was a tricky job, explaining myself to Amy without implying criticism of her. I feared I wasn't doing very well at it.

'Some more "living"?' She gave a bitter laugh. 'What better way of "living" is there than creating another life?'

What the hell did that mean? I decided that Amy and I were never going to understand each other about this. Plus, I was determined that this call would not develop into another argument. 'Well, whatever, Amy. All I wanted to say was sorry.'

'OK. Thanks for that. Let's forget about it.' She sounded sad, disappointed in me.

It all started with the shirt. Maybe that should have been my clue. Maybe I should have taken one look at the shirt and said, 'Alex, this is a bad situation, remove yourself from it now.'

Tony was tucking it in when he opened his front door to me. He was smiling, an optimistic smile that said, 'Look what I've got to show you, I've put a lot of work into this and I'm sure I've got it right.' But it was mainly the shirt I noticed.

'Hi, Alex.'

'Hi.'

'Thanks for doing this.'

'It's all right.'

He made some final adjustments to the shirt, then looked up at me expectantly. 'What do you think?'

'That's new, isn't it, Tony?'

'Yeah. Told you I was thinking of buying one, didn't I?'

'Mmm. But even if you hadn't I'd know it was new.'

'Eh?'

'Go and have a look at yourself.' I indicated the mirror hanging in his hallway. He went and stood in front of it.

'Oh.'

'Yes,' I said, coming in and closing the door behind me. '"Oh."' Down both sides of the shirt's front, and horizontally across its middle, were three enormous creases. They were so prominent that an oblong piece of material was sticking out, as though Tony had a chopping board strapped to his chest.

'Time to get the iron out, don't you think?'

'Yeah. Good point.'

It was then I noticed the music coming from the main room.

'Tony.'

'Yeah?'

'You know yesterday, when we talked about the music you were going to play tonight?'

'Yeah.'

'And you know I said it should be the sort of music that would create a relaxed atmosphere without being overtly sexual?'

'Yeah.'

'Well, do you not think that if you were going to make a

list of records that you could say, without fear of contradiction, were overtly sexual, "Let's Get It On" by Marvin Gaye would be on that list? Somewhere quite near the top?'

He looked disappointed. 'Not a good choice then?'

I shook my head.

'Damn.'

'Is it a Marvin Gaye album?'

'No, it's a tape I made myself. Did it last night, spent bloody ages on it. I bought most of the CDs in HMV after you left.'

'Let's Get It On' was fading out. There was a second or two of tape hiss, and then the opening bars of the next song. 'Careless Whisper' by George Michael. I tried not to let Tony see me cringe, but I couldn't help it.

'I haven't got it quite right, have I?' he said miserably.

'What other songs have you used?'

'Erm . . . "Three Times A Lady" by The Commodores. "I'm Not In Love" by 10CC. A couple by Luther Vandro—'

'No, Tony, you haven't got it quite right.' I sighed. 'But that's what I'm here for, isn't it? To sort these little problems out. Now come on, let's get this tape off and I'll pick you some decent music.' I began to edge towards the door.

'No, no, hang on,' he said, blocking my way. 'You can't see in here until I've got it ready.'

'What do you mean? Isn't it ready now?'

'Yeah, nearly, but I've still got a few . . . I've done most of them . . . You can't see it till . . . Wait there.' He shot into the room and closed the door behind him. The music stopped. I waited. And waited. Every ten seconds or so I'd hear Tony's muffled voice: 'Wait there . . . nearly finished . . . won't be long . . .' He seemed to be moving around the room.

At last the door opened, and he stuck his head out. The

grin showed that his confidence was back. 'All done. Are you ready for this?'

'I don't know. Am I?'

'Close your eyes.'

'What?'

'Close your eyes.'

He was so excited I didn't have the heart to say no. I closed my eyes, then felt him gripping my arm and leading me into the room.

'Right, you can look now.'

I opened my eyes.

'What do you think?' he asked.

'It's incredible.'

'I thought you'd say that.'

It *was* incredible. Everywhere I looked, every surface – and I mean *every* surface: the coffee table, the mantlepiece, the television, the stereo, the big unit that took up most of one wall, various bits of the floor – every available square inch of space was covered with candles. Big candles, little candles, medium-sized candles. White candles, red candles, green candles, multi-coloured candles. Long thin candles, short round candles, cube-shaped candles, candles that tapered, candles that didn't. The curtains were drawn and all the lights were off. The only illumination in the room was coming from the dozens and dozens of candles. Their constant flickering sent sinister shadows darting across the walls.

'Tony, the last time I saw anything like this it was a Hammer House of Horror film.'

He didn't reply. I think he'd just twigged that my 'it's incredible' hadn't been intended as a compliment.

I turned towards the dining table. All the way round it

were tiny tea lights, apart from a gap at either end where the places had been set. 'What are you planning to do, Tony – serve Elisabeth dinner or sacrifice her?'

'But I thought you said candles were good?'

'Yes,' I snapped, 'candles *are* good. Candles are very good. In *moderation*. Used *properly*. Like music is good, when it's chosen *properly*. With the proper sort of music, and the proper number of candles, you can create a really nice, relaxing atmosphere that'll make the evening go as well as possible. That's what you get when you do things properly. When you don't do them properly you end up with something that looks like Julio Iglesias just got into black magic.'

He wouldn't look at me. I thought I saw his bottom lip tremble.

'I'm sorry,' I said. 'I didn't mean to shout.'

He looked up at me.

'It's just that . . . it's all a question of degree.'

He nodded. 'A question of degree.' He looked around the room. 'I'm not very good on questions of degree.'

'Come on,' I said, 'let's go and check the food, shall we?'

We went through to the kitchen. On the stove was a saucepan, its lid rattling slightly as steam escaped round the edges. There was a chopping board on the work surface, with stray bits of onion and garlic still sticking to it. Not, in itself, a bad sign. What was a bad sign was the unopened packet of spaghetti next to it. I began to fear the worst.

'Tony, are you, erm . . . are you cooking . . . ?' As I spoke I edged towards the saucepan, and lifted the lid.

'Spaghetti bolognese!' he announced proudly.

I peered inside the pan. 'So it is.'

'There were two reasons I decided on that. It's the one

thing I'm really good at cooking – Joe and Georgia love it, they're always asking me to do it when they come round. I don't always do it for them, you have to keep some things as a treat, don't you, otherwise you'd spoil them, but anyway, I know I do it really well. And the other thing was – Elisabeth used to live in Rome! In Italy! So I thought doing Italian food would be . . . you know . . . she'd like it.'

He paused. I carried on staring into the pan.

'I mean, obviously when I do it for Joe and Georgia I have to cut their spaghetti up for them. I won't have to do that for Elisabeth.'

I quietly put the lid back on the pan. I could feel him looking at me, waiting for me to say something. I didn't.

'And I've got some Parmesan in the fridge to go wi— I've buggered this up as well, haven't I, Alex?'

I nodded.

'Oh *shitting* hell,' he said. 'What's wrong with spag bol?'

'Nothing's wrong with spag bol, Tony. Spag bol is lovely. On a Wednesday night when you've been going out with each other for three months. But not when she's coming round to dinner for the first time and you're trying to impress her.'

'No?'

'No. What you want tonight is "lurve" food. Spag bol's comfort food.' I stopped myself. I'd had enough of that with Jill. 'Spag bol's . . . well, it's just not very . . . it's not very *different*.'

'I put oregano in it.'

I picked up a spoon and tasted a mouthful of the bolognese. 'And you know what, it's great. Joe and Georgia are right – their dad makes the best spag bol in the world. With or without oregano. But it's not quite what we want for tonight.' I turned the gas off. 'So I tell you what we're going to do, Tony, we're going to let that cool down and then you're going to freeze it.'

'Save it for the kids, you mean?'

'No, I mean save it for you and Elisabeth. For when you've been going out with each other for three months.' I gripped him by the shoulders. 'You can do this. I know you can. I really know you can do this, Tony.'

'Are you sure?'

'Of course I'm sure.' I turned him round and marched him back into the main room. 'Right, plan of action. You're going to get rid of,' I pointed, 'those candles there – and those – most of those there – you can leave those – lose half of those – and a couple of those. Then put a few of those little ones up on the mantlepiece. Then you turn on . . .' I looked around the room. 'Haven't you got any lamps?'

'Lamps?'

'Yeah, you know, little lights with shades on. Run off the electric.'

He shook his head. 'No. Not down here.' That sort of touch vanished the day Anita did, no doubt. 'There are some upstairs, though.'

'Right, fetch them down and plug them in. I'm going to drive to the shops, get you some proper food. OK?'

'OK.'

I was back in fifteen minutes. With no time left for culinary creation I'd chosen a bung-in-the-oven tarragon chicken from the supermarket's really expensive range, and a pack of smoked salmon for starters. I happened to know that Tony's guest was very partial to it. That reminder of what I was doing, or rather who I was doing it to, didn't feel very nice. I tried to ignore it.

I rang the doorbell, and Tony let me in.

'How's it going with the candles?'

'I think I've done it properly this time. Come and have a look.'

We went into the main room.

'Tony, what's that?'

'It's one of the lamps you told me to get down.'

He was right. It was a lamp. In the technical sense of the word. It was an anglepoise lamp, in black metal, about five feet long. It looked like the sort of thing they used in factories in the 1970s. Tony had fixed it to the dining table.

'I had to put it there. Nowhere else was strong enough to take the weight.'

'Right.'

'I used to have it in the garage, but then I put a strip light up so I didn't need it any more. It's been stored on top of the wardrobe since then.'

'Hefty wardrobe, is it?'

He looked at the lamp. 'Not really appropriate, you don't think?'

'Not really.'

'I'll get rid of it.' He started to unscrew the lamp from the edge of the table. 'The other one's the right size, though, isn't it?' He nodded towards the far end of the room.

I turned around. On a small table by the fireplace was a yellow lamp, about ten inches tall. 'Yeah, it's the right size, Tony.'

'Good.'

'But, er . . .'

He stopped what he was doing with the anglepoise. 'What? What is it?'

'How can I put this . . . ? It's, er . . . it's the shade.'

'The shade?'

'The shade.'

He came and stood next to me, and we both looked at the lamp.

'Imagine it,' I said, 'imagine the night's gone as well as you could have hoped. She's loved the food, she's enjoyed the conversation, the jokes, finding out about you, having an interesting time with you. You've retired to the sofa, the second bottle of Pinot Noir is slipping down very nicely thank you, the strains of Miles Davis floating seductively across the room. There's a pause in the conversation, she avoids meeting your eye, because – you sense – she's deciding whether her next move should be more talking or just leaning across to kiss you. She's weighing up the mood of the moment, wondering what she should do, when her gaze shifts slightly and into view comes . . . a *Lion King* lampshade.' I put a hand on his shoulder. 'Which way do you think that's going to tip the decision, Tony?'

'It's the only one I've got. It's from the kids' room. Georgia's mad about the film. I got her it on DVD for Christm—'

'Yes, all right, Tony, the history of the lampshade isn't important. What *is* important is that you can't have it in this room, tonight, with Elisabeth coming round for dinner.'

He went and unplugged it. 'What are we going to do, then? It's too dark with just the candles.'

I walked over to the switch for the main light and turned it on. It was unbelievably bright. 'Christ, Tony, where did you get that bulb? One of the advertising signs at Piccadilly Circus?' I turned it off again. 'What power's the one in that lamp?'

He peered at it. 'Forty watts.'

'Right, let's swap 'em.' I stood on a chair and did just that. 'Just remember to swap them back before Georgia comes to stay again. You'll give the poor kid nightmares. And probably blind her as well.' I got down from the chair and turned the light on again. 'Not brilliant, but as good as we can do, I think.' Then, remembering that I needed to keep his spirits up, 'Those flowers are good.' There was a vase in the middle of the table. 'You might have to move them to one side so you can see each other over dinner – but they're good.'

'Do you think so?'

'Yeah.'

'At least I got something right.'

'Tony, we're going to get it *all* right. Next up, you iron that shirt while I do the food.'

'Yes, boss.'

I went into the kitchen and turned the oven on. Its clock said seven-twenty; that was OK, Elisabeth wasn't due until eight. I opened the wine, then took two small plates from the cupboard ready for the salmon. Meanwhile Tony had fetched the ironing board from under the stairs, set it up in the corner of the kitchen, and gone back out for the iron.

'Hello, darling,' I said when he returned. 'Good day at the office?'

He started to undo his shirt. 'Some wife you are – I'm having to do my own ironing here.'

The packet of salmon was one of those with a piece of cellophane between every layer of fish. Making sure I'd got them all out was a very tricky job. I took a breather halfway through, and looked up. Tony was ironing round the buttons on his shirt, concentrating so intently that the tip of his tongue was poking out.

'Now just make sure you stay away from this salmon,' I said. 'Those chest hairs of yours are all very impressive, and I'm sure they could drive a woman mad, but not if she finds one of them in her starter.'

I arranged the salmon on the plates with a few lettuce leaves, and stored them in the fridge. Then I put the chicken in the oven. By this time Tony had his shirt back on.

'That looks much better,' I told him. 'Good choice, too.'

'Is it?'

'Yeah. Really good.' It was all right, I suppose. Plain blue, with the emphasis on plain. But I wanted to talk his confidence up.

He looked at his reflection in the window. 'Thanks.'

'Right, all we've got to do now is get you some music sorted. Then I'd better make myself scarce.'

'OK.'

We went into the main room and stood in front of his CD collection. There were some good ones in there: Eminem, Bob Marley, the first two Oasis albums. Good, but not suitable. There were some that were acceptable because Tony had bought them when he was seventeen and hadn't got round to throwing them out yet, like Simple Minds and Van Halen. And then there were the ones, like Michael Bolton and 'Candle In The Wind' (Princess Di version), which I hoped fell into the 'Anita's, but she forgot to take them with her' category. I hoped, but decided not to ask, just in case I didn't like the answer.

As I was trying to make a decision, Tony gave a little sniff. And then another.

'Can you smell something?' he said.

I gave a sniff of my own. 'Don't think so.'

'Oh. Thought I could.'

'Might be the food.'

'Yeah.'

But then, a minute or so later, 'Are you sure you can't smell anything?'

I sniffed again. 'Actually I think I can. *Is* it the food?' I stuck my head round the door. 'No, it's definitely stronger in here.'

We found ourselves edging towards the other end of the room, the one at the front of the house, where the sofa stood in front of the bay window.

'It's something round here,' said Tony. 'I'm sure it is.'

That was when I saw the smoke going up the curtain. I rushed round the end of the sofa, followed by Tony.

'FUCK!' he yelled. 'I'd forgotten about them!'

Along the floor, hidden from our view by the sofa, was a row of about a dozen candles. The bottoms of the curtains were only a few inches above the flames, and charred completely black. The smoke, which by now was pretty thick, billowed upwards.

'I put them there when I was moving them all around! To create space! I meant to move them!'

'Nice one, Tony.'

Suddenly there was an incredibly loud beeping sound.

'THE SMOKE ALARM!' he shouted, running back to the other end of the room.

'Good to know it's working,' I said, but the alarm was so loud he couldn't hear me.

Tony grabbed a chair and stood on it, reaching up to try and get the cover off the alarm. He couldn't.

'HURRY UP!' I screamed. 'I'M GETTING DEAFENED HERE!'

'WHAT?'

'I SAID HURRY UP!'

'EH?'

'HURRY—' I could see what was going to happen here, so just waved him to get on with it. I turned back to the curtains. At three separate points the black had turned an alarming shade of orange.

Very quietly, and very calmly, I said, 'Oh shit.'

Two of the three patches of orange burst into flames. They were only small flames, and I managed to stamp out the ones nearest me, but in doing so I made the curtains flap around, which breathed life into the other flames. At the same time the third patch of orange caught light as well. It was too far from the other fire for me to be able to stamp on both at the same time.

I looked round, and spotted the vase of flowers on the dining table. Rushing over to get it, I yelled up at Tony, 'FORGET THE ALARM, COME AND HELP ME WITH THIS!'

'WHAT?'

I pointed at the curtains. The second flame was now halfway to the ceiling, the other one just getting into its stride. Tony jumped off the chair and ran towards me as I pulled the flowers from the vase and threw them on the floor. If I'd known just how close he was I wouldn't have pulled my arm back quite as far when I went to throw the water. The vase caught him in the most painful place a vase can catch a man, and he fell to the floor, yelping in agony. What was worse, the unexpected contact completely messed up my throw, so that instead of emptying its contents all over the flames the vase slipped out of the side of my hand, smashing against the wall. The carpet got covered in broken china, the wallpaper got soaked and the flames raged on. As did the smoke alarm.

Tony uncurled himself from the foetal position and looked up. 'What did you do that for? I haven't got any other vases to put the flowers in!'

I couldn't believe I was hearing this. 'If we don't do something about this,' I shouted, pointing at the flames, 'you won't have a HOUSE to put them in!'

He struggled to his feet.

I indicated the smaller fire. 'Try and stamp this one out. I'll have a go at the other one.' By now its flames were beginning to lick at the curtain rail.

I ran into the kitchen, yanked open all the cupboards, found the biggest saucepan I could, put it in the sink and turned the tap on full. While the pan was filling it occurred to me that a bucket would be even better. I ran to the cupboard under the stairs and opened the door. Couldn't see one. But there was a broom. I grabbed it, ran back to the kitchen for the saucepan, then took them both into the main room.

Tony had all but got his fire under control – he was stamping out the last few embers – but the other one was looking seriously angry. I threw the water at it, which didn't do very much good, then started jabbing the broom at it. Fortunately this worked better, and within about thirty seconds I was in a winning position.

'Tony,' I yelled, 'will you PLEASE turn that fucking smoke alarm off? It's doing my HEAD in!'

He went to do that while I carried on battling with the curtains. After a minute the alarm still hadn't stopped. I turned round to see him abandoning his struggle to prise the cover off. He climbed down from the chair – I lip-read several 'f's and 'b's as he did so – picked it up, turned it upside down and jabbed one of the legs at the smoke alarm. At his third attempt he hit it, bringing it down, together with much of the surrounding plaster. As it hit the floor the battery bounced out, and the beeping stopped. The silence was beautiful.

Beautiful but brief. I'd managed to extinguish almost all the fire; there was just one bit left, at the very top of the curtain. I tried more jabs with my broom, but couldn't get the right angle. Jumping up and jabbing while I was in mid-air didn't produce enough force. So I moved back round in front of the sofa, stood on it (having taken my shoes off first), and tried attacking the fire from there. It was better, but the curtains were just that bit too far away to land a real killer blow. I suppose I could have taken the trouble to get off the sofa and push it nearer the window, then start again. But I didn't. I put my right foot up on the sofa's back, braced my left leg to keep everything steady, and gave the broom one final, decisive jab.

Not enough bracing with the left leg. I remember the thought going through my mind as the front of the sofa started to come away from the floor. But there was nothing I could do about it – the laws of physics had taken over. My weight carried me forward. It felt like surfing. By the time the broomhead connected with the curtain, the sofa was up at forty-five degrees. Which meant it had another forty-five to go. The broom smashed straight through the window, taking the curtain with it, which in turn ripped the curtain pole from the wall, so that as the back of the sofa (my right foot still balanced on it) hit the floor, the pole crashed down on my head. Instinctively I pushed the broom away from me, trying to get rid of the curtains that had draped themselves all over me. It worked – the curtains flew out into the front garden. As did the one remaining piece of glass that had clung stubbornly to the window frame. Cool night air wafted into the room.

My left foot was still on the front of the sofa, up in mid-air. I'd managed to keep my balance throughout the whole thing. Pretty scant consolation in the circumstances.

Tony certainly thought so. 'Oh well, that's just fucking TREMENDOUS!' he shouted. 'No front window! That's REALLY going to make tonight go with a swing, isn't it?'

'Don't fucking well blame me!' I shouted. Then, realising that having one foot in the air karate-style wasn't doing much for my authority, I stood up properly.

'What do you mean, don't blame you? You're the one who's just put a broom through my window!'

'Yes, and WHY was I doing that? Because someone had left this room looking like an arsonists' convention, THAT'S why!'

He didn't say anything.

'And if we're talking about structural damage to the room, Tony, I don't think you're entirely without blame, do you? EH?!'

I pointed to the ceiling above his head. But again, he wouldn't reply.

'And quite apart from all that, why am I round here in the first place, eh? I'm round here to try and help YOU get somewhere with ELISABETH! I'm doing you a favour because I want you to succeed with her. REMEMBER?!'

It was when he didn't respond to that that I knew something was up. He wasn't looking directly at me, but at something behind me. I noticed the clock on the mantelpiece. It said twenty to eight. I looked at my watch: ten past eight.

The clock trick.

I turned round.

Elisabeth.

She was standing on the garden path, looking in through the empty window frame. First at me, then at Tony. Then back at me.

When she spoke it was with total dignity. 'You want him to succeed with me? That's . . . that's nice. Thank you for letting me know where I stand, Alex.' Then she turned, walked to the end of the path, closed the gate behind her, and was gone.

'Elisabeth . . .' I called. Just the once, though. Even before the sound had died away I knew there was no point going after her. What else could I say? 'It's not what it looks like'? It was, and she knew it. 'Don't go'? Why should she stay? 'What I've done is totally unforgivable'? She knew that already.

Besides, I had another problem, closer to hand. I turned to look at Tony.

He pointed out of the window. 'You've . . . You and Elisabeth . . . You were . . . ?'

I nodded.

'She hasn't been staying with a friend, has she? She's been staying with you.'

I nodded again.

'So why . . . what were you . . . what are you doing here tonight?'

Even trying to explain would have made me sound like a snivelling creep. And I wanted to keep that fact covered up.

'Why did you want to help me with Elisabeth when you were seeing her yourself?' Tony wasn't angry any more, just confused. He was speaking very quietly. And I wasn't speaking at all. It was as though, after the bedlam of the last ten minutes, Elisabeth had walked in and restored peace with just one softly spoken remark. We were following her lead. That seemed kind of appropriate.

I decided I had to say something. 'I'm sorry, Tony.' Yep, pretty snivelling. Total creep. 'I think I'd better go.' I began heading for the door.

But Tony, who was staring into the fireplace, didn't seem to hear me. 'Why didn't you and Elisabeth tell me you were seeing each other?'

I stopped. He looked like a kid who's just been told that Santa Claus isn't real. 'We didn't tell anyone. You know, the merger and everything . . .'

Now he looked at me. 'Yeah, but Alex . . . You could have told *me*? You knew I liked her.'

'That was *why* I didn't tell you. I mean, you say "seeing each other", as though we were planning to get married or something. We slept together in New York, and then at mine . . . and that's it. I've got no reason to think Elisabeth's any more interested in carrying it on than I am.'

'Not now, she isn't.'

'No. That's true.'

He gave a disgruntled kick at the smoke alarm. 'Oh, why is life never simple?'

'Because it's life, that's why.'

'I never seem to understand it, though. Get on top of it.'

'What, and you think I do?'

He looked up at me. He seemed shocked.

I turned towards the door again. 'Well, I'll be off.'

'No,' he said quickly, 'don't go. Stay and have a drink.'

'Eh?'

'Stay and have a drink. If you want.'

I don't know why but I wanted to hug him. 'All right then, yeah.'

'Have a sit down,' he said. 'I'll get some glasses.'

I sat in one of the two armchairs that faced each other

across the coffee table. Tony went to the drinks cabinet and fetched two glasses and an unopened bottle of Glenfiddich.

'I'm having one of these,' he said. 'Fancy it?'

'Yeah, cheers.'

He broke open the cap and poured our drinks. They were on the generous side.

'I wouldn't have put you down as a whisky drinker.'

He handed me my glass. 'I am in front of Elisabeth. Cheers.'

We chinked our glasses together. 'Cheers. What do you mean, in front of Elisabeth?'

'New York, remember?'

'Oh yeah. You were drinking it at the Paramount. Why?'

'Because you did.'

'Tony, what are you talking about?'

'That first night we were at the hotel, with Walter and Mary and Elisabeth, and you were all being dead smart, I didn't know what to drink. You were all ordering smart drinks and I didn't think it'd go down that well if I asked for a pint of bitter. A pint of bitter isn't a smart drink. So I just had what you had.'

'Oh.'

'And then when I went out for a drink with Elisabeth, at Grand Central, I thought I'd better have the same again. I didn't want her thinking it wasn't my usual drink.'

'I see.' I didn't.

'Once I'd started on whisky I had to stay on whisky. So I got some in for tonight, in case it came to having a drink after dinner.' He lifted the glass to his lips, pausing just before he took a gulp. 'As if.'

'Tony, why do you have to copy me?'

''Cos you know what you're doing.'

'Do I?' I pointed at the broken window. 'Where's Elisabeth, then?'

'You know what I mean. I had whisky because it was a smart place and I didn't know what I was doing and you did and you had whisky so I had whisky.'

'You mean you had whisky to impress Elisabeth?'

'If you like, yeah.'

'Why couldn't you just be yourself to impress Elisabeth?'

'Alex, I thought we'd worked out that me being myself was a bad idea when it came to Elisabeth? The candles, remember? The music? The spag bol?'

'Yeah, but . . . I don't mean the little things.'

'The little things are important, though, aren't they?'

'Yeah, they're important. At the start. But not really. They're not *really* important.' I took a drink of my whisky, about half of it in one go. The burning in my mouth felt good. I drank some more.

'They may not be *really* important to you,' said Tony. 'But that's only 'cos you're good at them.'

'I'm not "good" at them,' I laughed.

'You're better than me. For what that's worth. Which isn't much.'

'Oh pack it in, Tony.' I wasn't laughing any more. 'What is it with this "I'm so crap" routine? It's like you think there's some secret you're missing out on, some proper way of doing things that no one's told you about. Some key to being successful, and you've got to keep on trying until you find it. But the only thing that stops you succeeding is that you're trying so hard all the time.' Now he was genuinely shocked. So was I, come to that. 'Sorry. Didn't mean to snap.' Why had I? I tried to take a drink, but found my glass was empty. Ah, that'd be it.

'It's all right,' he said after a moment. He lifted his glass up.

'I'm switching to vodka – do you want this?' As he handed it over, together with the bottle, he gave a little smile.

'Thanks,' I said, smiling back.

Tony fetched the Smirnoff bottle and a clean glass from the cabinet, as well as some Schweppes from the kitchen (where he also turned the oven off – we'd had enough fires for one night). He came back and sat down again. He poured some vodka into the glass, then some tonic, tasted it, then added another big dose of vodka. Meanwhile I half-filled my glass with whisky. A bit more than half, actually.

He took a swig of his drink. Then, 'Do you mind if I ask you something about Elisabeth?'

'Depends what it is.'

'Don't worry, it's nothing like that.'

'All right then.'

'Why don't you want to carry on with her?'

'I like her, but the spark isn't really there. I don't know, it doesn't feel right. Plus, this book told me not to.' *Why the hell did you say that?*

'What?'

I downed a load of my whisky. *In for a penny . . .* 'I've been reading this book. It's all about how to commit. To a girlfriend, like.'

'Really?'

'Really.'

'But I thought you'd be good with girlfriends. Haven't you had lots of them?'

'A few, yeah. That's the point, though. I haven't found the right one, have I?'

'Some people are so choosy.'

I nearly laughed, but realised just in time that he hadn't been joking.

He finished his drink, started to pour himself another. 'What's the answer, then?'

'Eh?'

'How do you commit to a girlfriend?'

'It's all to do with change.'

'What do you mean?'

'Change. You know, changing, not being the same . . . Being someone different.' Should I run him through what the book said? I leaned my head back, closed my eyes. This whisky was really good . . . Where was I? Oh yeah, the book. Nah, couldn't be bothered. I mean, it took me time to understand it; explaining it all to Tony in five minutes wasn't going to happen. But I did understand it . . . I was sure I did . . .

'I've spent my whole bloody life wanting to be someone different,' said Tony miserably. Then, after a pause, 'Ian Watson.'

'Eh?'

'Ian Watson. He was a lad at my school. He was in the top year when I was in the first. He'd passed his driving test. Had this Austin Allegro, used to drive it to school. I wanted to be him.'

'You wanted to be someone because they had an Austin Allegro?'

'I remember thinking I didn't want to get the bus to school, I wanted to be able to drive there like Ian Watson. I used to look at him every morning, parking his car next to the teachers' cars, and I'd think, Wouldn't it be great to be like him, to have a car?'

I lifted my glass to my lips, realised it was empty again. Still without lifting my head, or even opening my eyes, I felt for the whisky bottle. I unscrewed the bottle and took a swig from it. A bit of whisky dribbled down my chin, but I wasn't bothered.

'And then, years later, when I was in my twenties, and I'd got a car, I was driving along one day and I passed an Austin Allegro, and it reminded me of Ian Watson. And I thought, Once upon a time I thought getting a car would make me really happy. But it hasn't. I used to want to be like Ian Watson, now I want to be like . . . Well, I can't remember who it was at the time. It was someone, anyway. Whatever you get there's always something new you haven't got. God, life's shit.'

It struck me that up until the 'life's shit' part, everything Tony had said was what the book says, only put differently. Keep on changing, etc. That was supposed to be good. Why was he calling it shit? He'd made sense as well. I couldn't work out where I disagreed with him. But I knew I must do, because I agreed with the book . . .

I opened my eyes. It took a moment to get him in focus. He was staring at the table.

'You know what, Alex?'

'What?'

'I'm *bursting* for a piss.'

'Thanks for keeping me informed on that.'

He stood up, swaying a little. 'Back in a minute.' On the way out he caught the door frame with his shoulder. 'Ow, you bastard . . .'

I sat there, drinking my whisky. From the bottle. I'd started, I might as well carry on.

Tony stumbled back into the room. 'I've just had a thought,' he said, collapsing into his chair.

'Right.'

Silence.

'You going to tell me what it is?'

'Eh?'

'Your thought. Are you going to tell me what your thought is?'

'Oh yeah. It's about what you were saying, about me thinking there was a secret and all that.'

'All right, I said sorry, didn't I?'

'No, no, no, no, no – you don't understand. What I mean is, you and this book – it's the same, isn't it? You're looking for a secret too. In the book.'

That should sound like he's having a dig at me. I should feel offended. But I don't. Why not? 'Mmm. You could say that.'

We fell silent for a few minutes, both staring at the table, drinking.

Eventually Tony said, 'So how did the book tell you?'

'Mmm?'

'About Elisabeth. How did the book tell you you shouldn't be going out with her?'

'Oh, that.' I'd had my legs crossed for a while, and they'd started to feel uncomfortable. I uncrossed them, but managed to hit the table with my foot. It spilled Tony's vodka. 'Shit, sorry.'

"S'all right.'

We both looked at the pool of drink, its tiny bubbles popping themselves out of existence.

I went to get up. 'I'll fetch a cloth.'

'Ah, fuck it,' said Tony, pouring himself another glass. 'Carry on about Elisabeth.'

I settled back in my chair. 'It's to do with kids. Having them, I mean. I've tended to end up with women who are maternal. And I don't want that yet.'

'And Elisabeth does?'

'Yeah. So did Amy. And a few others. Maybe I attract them.'

'Opposites. You know, "opposites attract".'

'Could be. Mmm, maybe that's it.' I took a swig of whisky, found myself feeling angry, slamming the bottle down on the arm of the chair. 'It's all so fucking *sudden*, you know what I mean? Why can't you have a chance to live your life a bit? Last year, right, my dad died, and I realised when I thought about it that he'd never been to Africa. A whole continent, a huge part of the world, and he'd never set foot on it. Not one little bit of it, not in all the time he was alive. Never got round to it. Well, I'm not going to make that mistake. I'm going to *do stuff* before I settle down, before I have babies and all that crap. That's crap as in real crap, of course. Why does it have to happen so *soon*?'

Tony watched me, but didn't reply. I think he must have sensed it'd be a bad idea to interrupt.

'Do you know what it seems like?' I said. I was a bit calmer now. 'It seems like about ten minutes ago – if that – I was seven. And I was sitting at home with Mum, playing with my toys, not a care in the world, and I'd got a drink of orange squash, and everything was brilliant. Then I went for a wee-wee, and now I've got back they've nicked my orange and replaced it with whisky, and nicked my toys and replaced them with a job and a mortgage and a pension plan and lots of other things that are really shit. And they've nicked my mum as well, and instead of her there's this woman called my "girl-friend", and all she goes on about is having kids. Whatever they are.' I threw the whisky bottle's screw top at the fireplace in a 'there, I've finished now' kind of way. It bounced off the wall and landed near the defunct smoke alarm.

Tony wasn't watching, though. 'I wish I'd lived a bit more,' he said.

Now it was my turn to keep quiet.

'Done some things. Been some places. Grown up, I suppose.' There were tears in his eyes. I looked away. But he carried on, didn't seem at all embarrassed. 'It's like you said, it doesn't seem long enough since I was a kid for me to be a man. And I've got a job and a mortgage and a pension plan as well – bloody hell, Alex, I've got *three* pension plans – but I don't feel like any of them belong to me. Grown-ups have all that. I shouldn't. I'm not a grown-up. I don't feel like I've passed any of the exams.'

I felt tears welling in my own eyes. Don't get me wrong, neither of us was crying. Just teary, that's all.

It was weird, everything Tony was saying backed me up, made the same point I'd been making . . . so why did I feel like he was making the opposite point? I tried and tried and tried to get my head round it, but it was like the argument was a pinball and I couldn't get it in any of the right holes. It just kept dropping back down. I looked at the gap at the top of the whisky bottle. No chance.

And then Tony stared at the fireplace, and spoke. Not really to me, more to himself: 'But I wouldn't change Joe and Georgia for anything in the world. They're the best things that have ever happened to me.'

We sat there for ages, not saying anything, just drinking. The tears left our eyes. Tony began to nod off. I wasn't far behind him.

The next thing I knew it was a quarter to one. I had a crick in my neck, but luckily I was still drunk enough not to feel too bad.

I stood up and nudged Tony. 'Come on, mate.'

'Mmm? What?'

'We're going to feel bad enough in the morning as it is, without sleeping in these chairs.'

'Mmm. Right.' He struggled to his feet. 'Is that window gonna be OK?'

'Let's hope so. Not a lot we can do about it at this time of night, is there?'

'Suppose not.'

We made our way up the stairs, bouncing off the walls as we went. Tony opened one of the doors. 'You'll have to go in here. Is that all right?'

I went into the room. It was Joe and Georgia's. There were teddy bears everywhere, a huge cardboard box full of toys and games, piles of kids' books and posters of cartoon figures. Plus the *Lion King* lamp.

'Didn't they take all this with them when they left?' I asked.

'This is only the old stuff,' said Tony. 'They've got a load of new things at Anita's.'

In the corner was a bunk bed. The duvet on the bottom bunk had a *Star Wars Phantom Menace* cover. Ewan McGregor stared up at us.

Tony pointed at the bed. 'You'll be all right in there, won't you?'

'Haven't you got an original one?'

'Eh?'

'The original *Star Wars*. Haven't you got a duvet with that on? The proper Luke Skywalker. What was he called . . . ?'

We both tried to remember the actor's name, our mouths slightly open as we concentrated. Then, at precisely the same moment, we both said: 'Mark Hamill!' This is the sort of thing you can only remember when you're very drunk.

I bent down to see if I could fit in the bed. Unfortunately I was standing slightly too near the bed, and my head hit the top bunk. 'Ow, fuck.'

'You all right?'

219

I rubbed my forehead. 'Mmm, think so.' I tried again, and this time managed to squeeze my head in. Then I collapsed my legs so I could fall on to the bed. There was a horrible creaking sound, but it just managed to take the weight. With a lot of difficulty I managed to turn over so that I was facing outwards.

'How's that?' asked Tony.

I straightened my legs to their full length. Everything below the knees was hanging off the end of the bed. I pushed myself up until my feet were supported, but this meant I was sitting virtually upright. Or would have been if the top bunk wasn't in the way – I was hunched over. I lay back down, settling for keeping my legs bent so that only my feet were sticking over the end. 'I'll be OK.'

'Right. See you in the morning, then.'

'Mmm. Night.' Just before he closed the door, I said, 'Hang on.'

'What?'

'Can I have a drink? For the morning. We're gonna need one, you know.'

'Oh yeah – good thinking. What do you want?'

I thought about it. 'Have you got any orange squash?'

'Think I might have, yeah. Hang on.'

While he was gone I got undressed. This is always difficult when you're paralytic, but especially when you're trying to do it in a bunk bed (it had been difficult enough getting in the first time, I didn't fancy having to do it again). I banged a few elbows and knees in the process, but eventually got down to my underwear. I pulled the duvet over me.

Upside down I read the words 'Star Wars'. It was the first film I ever went to see at the cinema. The first proper film, that is. Mum took me to see it at Lowestoft.

I started to sing the theme tune. 'Dah-dah-dah DAAAH-DAAAH.' I closed my eyes, and saw that big writing sloping away into space: 'A long time ago in a galaxy far, far away . . .' 'Dah-dah-dah DAAAAAAAH-DAAAH, dah-dah-dah DAAAAAAAH-DAAAH, dah-dah-dah—'

'Here you are.' Tony was holding out a pint glass of orange squash.

I took it. 'Thanks.' I drank some, then put it on the floor.

As Tony got to the door he said, 'Do you want me to turn the light out?'

'Yeah, please.'

He flicked the switch. 'Night, then.'

'Night.'

As he was pulling the door shut he paused. 'Thanks, Alex.'

'What for?'

'For coming round tonight. Helping me.'

'Didn't do much good, did I?'

'No, but I mean, you tried, that's the thing. That's what counts, isn't it?'

'Suppose so.'

'Yeah.'

We both nodded wisely.

'Thanks for the squash,' I said.

'It's all right. See you tomorrow.'

'Yeah, sweet dreams.'

The door clicked shut.

'Dah-dah-dah daaah-daaah,' I hummed. 'Dah-dah-dah daaah-daaah . . .' But before I could get much further I felt myself drifting off. The whisky meant I slept very soundly. Like a baby, you might say.

*

221

'Fuck, my head hurts.'

It was the next morning. The whisky was having its revenge. As was Tony's vodka. Hence his comment. He was sitting at the kitchen table, wearing a dressing gown. I'd managed to get dressed. It had taken me a quarter of an hour, but I'd managed it. 'How are you feeling?' he continued as I sat down opposite him.

'As bad as you look. For the first few minutes after I woke up I thought I was dead. Now I just wish I was.'

'Do you want some coffee?'

I nodded. Then, because it hurt, I stopped. 'Please.'

He indicated the cafetière on the table between us. I picked it up. 'Tony, this is stone cold.'

'Is it?' He felt it himself. 'You're right. That's weird. I only made it just now.' He looked at the clock. 'Oh. Forty minutes ago.' Hangovers can do that to you.

'I'll make some more.' I stood up, looked at the kettle and the packet of coffee and the sink. 'Second thoughts, I'll just microwave this.' I poured us a mug each and reheated them, making sure I opened the door before the time was up. Didn't want any loud beeps.

'Not exactly what I was hoping for last night,' said Tony.

'Could have been worse.'

'How?'

I thought for a moment. 'You're right.'

'What are you going to say to Elisabeth?'

'I don't think there's a lot I can say. Apart from the obvious. And even if I said a million "sorry"s, it wouldn't be enough. I think the best thing I can do is leave the woman alone.'

'Right.'

'Plus I doubt Miles'd want me doing anything that might upset the deal.'

Tony winced.

'You OK?' I said. 'Shall I get some Nurofen?'

'No, no, it's not my hangover. It's . . .' He looked away. 'It's nothing.'

'What?'

He didn't say anything.

'Tony, what is it?'

'Honest, it's nothing.'

'Then why won't you look at me?'

He returned my gaze. 'It's . . . I promise you, Alex, it's nothing.'

I stared at him. 'It's something to do with the deal, isn't it?'

He looked away again. 'No.'

'Tony, stop lying to me.'

'I'm not.'

'You are.'

'I'm not.'

'Look, we can carry on being intellectual like this, or you can tell me what's wrong with this deal.'

He played with the handle of his mug. Eventually he said, 'I don't suppose you know what the term "off balance sheet" means, do you?'

'Not so I could pass an exam on it, no.'

'Miles does.'

'I see. And would I be right in guessing that "off balance sheet" isn't a good thing?'

'Yes. I mean, yes you'd be right, not yes it's a good thing.'

'Tony, what's going on?'

'It's very complicated.'

'All right, give me the layman's version.'

He gave a big sigh. 'Basically, what it means is that Miles owes lots of money. Or rather the business does.'

'Go on.'

'He borrowed a load two years ago, when things were looking a bit sticky.'

'I never knew about that.'

'No one did. They still don't. I didn't know about it until a few months ago.'

'How come? You're his accountant, aren't you?'

'This was borrowing that didn't go through the books. Not properly, anyway. Conrad was very, very clever.' Miles's last accountant.

'And very, very bent, by any chance?'

'His pay-off for keeping it all quiet was a villa in Portugal.'

'I always wondered why he retired at forty-eight.'

'Because he could afford to. Miles has said he'll look after me just as well if I can keep it all under wraps while the merger goes through. But I'm not sure if I want that.' He slurped miserably at his coffee. 'I can't even speak Portuguese.'

'What was all this borrowing for? I thought the business was a gold mine.'

'It is. It was just a loan to get him through a difficult patch. And it's all set up to pay itself off in eighteen months or so. If everything goes to plan the Americans'll never know there was a loan there in the first place. But it does mean that the business, right at this minute, is worth a lot less than Miles says it is.'

'Tony – two questions.'

'Yeah?'

'Number one, what the hell are you doing wrapped up in all this in the first place?'

'Like I said, Miles didn't tell me about it for ages. The merger was really advanced by then. And because of the way it's all structured, because Conrad was so devious, there's no way I can prove I didn't know about it from the start. People might believe me. Then again they might not.'

'And Miles knows that, of course.'

Tony nodded.

'The bastard. The absolute bastard.' There were stronger words I could have used. But words weren't really good enough here. I wanted Miles, in person. And a pool cue.

'I've just got to hope the scheme works itself out,' said Tony.

'He can't *do* this to you.'

'He already has.'

I remembered my other question. 'What happens if the scheme *doesn't* work itself out? If the Yanks discover they've been had? Is it . . . ? Would you . . . ?'

'About three years. What with it being my first offence.'

'Three *years*?'

'Probably. No more than four, anyway.'

'I don't believe this, I really don't. And meanwhile, no doubt, Miles'll have sentenced himself to life – on a beach somewhere that doesn't have an extradition treaty with Britain.'

Tony didn't say anything.

I slammed my fist into the side of the table, imagining it was Miles's mouth. It hurt, and made my head throb as well, but somehow that didn't seem as important now. 'Look, Tony – you can't go through with this.'

'I can't *not* go through with it.'

'But *prison*, Tony. Four years in prison. And a knackered career when you come out. You can't . . . you just can't.'

'I've already done enough to get me sent to prison. OK, not for four years, but even so. And if everything works out I won't go to prison at all.'

'I've heard some pretty big "if"s in my time, but that one takes the biscuit. Even if it does work out you've got loads of worry ahead of you. No, come on, Tony, you can't do this. You've got to tell someone.'

'Who?'

'The Americans. They're the ones you're trying to con. I mean the ones Miles is trying to con.'

'If they shop me, Alex . . .'

'Would they do that?'

'Who knows?'

I thought about it for a minute. 'Look – why don't you tell Elisabeth? Granted, you can't be sure what Walter and Mary would do, but—'

'I can't be sure what Elisabeth would do, either.'

'No, but she knows you better than they do, doesn't she? She's the one who's done all the work with you. Tony, she's going to realise you're not an international fraudster. She'll be on your side, I know she will.'

'What will Miles say?'

'*Fuck* Miles. What do you owe him?'

He didn't answer that one. He couldn't.

'Tony, if you don't tell Elisabeth, I will. And trust me, after last night she's going to be better disposed to hearing things from you than from me.'

He shifted in his seat. 'Well . . .'

'Look, I'm not going to sit here and say "you haven't got any alternative", because you have. And you know what it is – eighteen months of worry. Eighteen months of praying that Conrad's house of cards stands up. All I'm saying is that relying on Elisabeth trusting in you has got to be a better option.'

'You really think so?'

'Oh come on, it has to be it, doesn't it? She'll do her best for you, I know she will. Think back to last night, Tony. Someone acted badly, but it wasn't her.'

'Maybe you're right.'

'And you've got to do it today. She's flying home tomorrow. This isn't the sort of conversation you want to have on the phone.'

'No. I suppose not.'

'You'll do it then?'

He nodded.

'Promise me, Tony.'

'All right, I promise.'

I knew Alex was right. I'd been trying to put this merger thing to the back of my mind for ages, but it hadn't worked. So I rang Elisabeth up this morning to tell her that I had to see her – I didn't tell her about the thing itself on the phone, just that I had something to tell her, could she come round? I couldn't believe how nervous I was about telling her. The thought of it made coping with the fact that I was nervous about fancying her seem like a doddle. At least there was that to be said for the situation, I suppose.

What made it even worse was that I had the kids this afternoon. There was no way I could get out of it – Anita was going on a day trip with Shaun, they'd already booked it and everything – so what I decided I had to do was send them upstairs while I told Elisabeth about the accounts; there was no way I could break something like that to her with Georgia trying to show us her new toy pony. I told her and Joe that if they behaved themselves they could have spaghetti bolognese for dinner.

Anita had dropped them off at half-eleven, just after Alex left. I told her I'd had an accident with the curtains and the window, which was true, but I didn't give her the whole story. Everything was OK at first – Georgia kept combing her pony's mane again and again, and Joe was finishing off a colouring book with these crayons I gave him the other week, he loves them, according to Anita, uses them all the time. She's not bloody wrong either – that was the problem – I'd just gone out to the kitchen to get them a drink of squash, and when I came back he was standing there looking half-excited, half-scared. For a moment I couldn't work out why, but then I turned round and saw that he'd written on the wall – in red, the brightest red in the whole set of crayons, and the wall's painted cream – he'd written – in enormous letters, I mean, about a foot high, capitals – he'd written the word 'TITS'.

I didn't know if I wanted to burst into tears or go berserk. Not only did I have a room with no front window and burned curtains, now I also had 'TITS' written across one of the walls. What with everything else that's happened when Elisabeth's been around, I thought, I wouldn't be surprised if she tries to have me committed to some sort of institution. This really wasn't the setting I wanted for telling her what I had to tell her. There was about half a second when I felt the tears coming, but then suddenly I shouted at Joe louder than I've ever shouted at him before. 'What do you think you're doing?' I screamed. I only just managed to stop myself swearing, I try not to swear in front of him and Georgia, although in view of what he'd written I don't know why I bothered. He looked really scared and he said it was a new word he'd heard someone say at school. 'Well just because you hear other people saying things it doesn't mean you should say them, does it?' I shouted. 'And it certainly doesn't mean you should write them on the walls at your daddy's house. Or anyone's house, come to that. Writing on walls is very, very naughty. Isn't it?'

He nodded his head, and I realised I'd scared him a bit

too much, well, quite a lot too much actually, he was almost in tears himself. I stopped myself and thought, You shouldn't take it out on Joe, the only reason you're so angry is that Elisabeth's coming round, you shouldn't go over the top about this. He has to be told off, but you've got to keep it in proportion. So I stopped shouting, and I told him because he'd done that he couldn't have his spaghetti bolognese, and he looked upset but I think he knew that was fair. Then I went over to the wall and licked my finger and tried to wipe the crayon off, but I knew it wouldn't work, it just smudged it, and I thought, Christ, what am I going to do now? I thought about moving one of the pictures to cover it up, but none of them were big enough, and anyway, it was quite low down, it'd look stupid hanging a picture that low. In the end the best I could come up with was moving the sofa in front of it. That didn't cover it itself — the word was too high up — I had to pile all the cushions along the back of the sofa, two rows of them, it took ages to balance them so they wouldn't fall down. It all looked very strange, I've got to be honest, the sofa being in such a weird place and the cushions being stacked on top of it rather than where you should have them to sit on, but it was the only thing I could think of in the time I had before Elisabeth turned up. And I tried to tell myself it wasn't as strange as a curtain rail lying in the front garden (I'd brought it in by then, of course, but she'd seen it the night before). Or at least no stranger, put it that way.

So Elisabeth turned up, and she was wearing jeans and a jumper, really nice jeans and a really nice jumper, but still it was unusual to see her out of her smart work clothes. I said thanks for coming round, and I started to say especially after last night, but I didn't, I thought it was best not to refer to that. But then she made a joke about Alex, saying it had never been anything that serious, and that she'd been pleased I'd asked her to dinner, although the scene she'd arrived to hadn't quite been what she'd envisaged. Then I introduced her to Joe and Georgia, and as soon as she saw them she smiled, she looked really happy, and she said, 'Hello, I've seen your picture at your daddy's office.' They nodded but didn't say anything, so Elisabeth pointed to Georgia's pony and said, 'What a lovely pony, she's beautiful, isn't she?' and Georgia nodded but still didn't speak, and it was all a bit awkward. Elisabeth looked at me and smiled and said, 'Ah, I think they're a bit shy', and I said yes they were, and I was thinking, It's a pity Joe wasn't shy about writing "TITS" across my bloody wall twenty minutes ago.

Then I told them they had to go and play in their room now because I had to discuss something with Elisabeth. They went upstairs, and I made Elisabeth and me a cup of tea, and we went and sat in the main room, at the table. She gave the sofa a bit of a strange look as we went in, but thankfully she sat with her back to it, so I didn't have to worry, she wasn't going to spend the whole time wondering about it. Then she said, 'What did you want to talk to me about?' and I thought, This is it, this is the moment, Tony, say your prayers.

I'd worked out exactly how I was going to tell her, and I stuck to my plan. The first thing I said was, 'It's to do with the merger.' That made her go all formal, and she said, 'Right, I see', she'd obviously guessed it was going to be something serious. I said, 'I'm going to tell you the history of all this exactly as I found out about it' – I thought that was my safest bet, to go from the beginning when I didn't know about what Miles and Conrad had done, all through the bit where Miles told me, and then right up to date. If Elisabeth saw how it happened, I thought, she would be more likely to believe me.

So that's what I did. Like I say, it's very complicated, and it took me ages to tell her all the details, and all the time I was talking she kept very quiet and still and serious, she looked me straight in the eyes (that made me really nervous, I told myself that if I looked away it'd seem suspicious, so as much as I could I looked back at her, but it was really difficult), and she listened to everything I had to say. When I'd finished she took a deep breath, and blew it out again, and then she said, 'I see'. That was all. I thought about saying some more, telling her I really hadn't had anything to do with it, not in the beginning anyway, that I'd only gone along with it because Miles had made me, that I couldn't see any alternative. But I didn't say that, because I realised she was thinking, she was trying to work out what she made of it all. So I stayed quiet.

After a minute she said, 'Do you have anything on paper?' I said no, but I did have a laptop with it all on, I'd kept it in my cupboard, so I got that out and plugged it in and turned it on. It took a while to boot up, she still wasn't saying anything, and I felt really nervous now. I called up all the files I needed to talk her through it, and as we sat together looking at the screen I tried to watch her out of the corner of my eye to see how she was reacting. From what I could make out she was still looking very serious.

Then she said could she have some time to look through the files herself? and I said of course, I'd make us some more tea. I did that, and while the kettle boiled I said some more prayers. I took the tea back through, and hoped she wouldn't notice how much my hands were shaking, then sat opposite her again. I said, 'I know this must be a big shock to you, Elisabeth. It was a big shock to me too. Miles only told me a few months ago, and I didn't know what to do. I promise you, honestly, I had nothing to do with setting any of it up.' And she took a sip of her tea, and looked at me without speaking for a few seconds, she had this really serious look on her face, as though she was deciding what to say, God it made me scared. And then she said, very quietly, 'No, Tony, I don't think you did.'

I have never felt so relieved in my whole life. I said, 'Thank you for believing me.' Elisabeth laughed a little bit, and said, 'You don't have to thank me', but I couldn't think of anything else to say apart from thank you, so I just nodded. Then she got serious again and said, 'What I've got to decide now is how I'm going to handle this.' And I said, 'Yes', and she said, 'What do you suggest?' I hadn't thought that she might value my opinion. I really had to think on my feet, and I couldn't stop a few ums and ers slipping out, but eventually I got myself together.

The first thing I said was that strictly speaking, according to the letter of the law, we had to go and tell the authorities, even knowing what we did and not reporting it was an offence in itself. Elisabeth said of course, she knew that, but we could also 'think along different lines', that was the phrase she used, and then she talked for a little more, and although she didn't mention Miles by name, I got the feeling that she'd never really liked him very much. I thought, That makes two of us, and then I replied to what she'd said, added a couple of thoughts to it, and then she did the same, and gradually we came up with a plan.

We talked for ages. It was only after a while that I realised what had happened: I'd stopped feeling nervous. I'd

233

been so scared before, but now I saw that Elisabeth believed me, and not only that, she was taking me seriously, listening to my suggestions, and I felt good. I really did feel like her equal, like we were both adults. But also I sort of still had my feeling from before, like I was a child. I know that's silly, I mean obviously you can't be an adult and a child at the same time, but that was what I felt. I suppose all the pressure must have got to me or something.

When we'd finished, Elisabeth sat back in her chair and did that breathing in and blowing out thing again, and said, 'Well, that certainly came as a surprise.' I said I bet it did, and then she said, 'This house seems to have a habit of giving me surprises', and for a moment I felt a bit awkward, but then she burst out laughing, and I thought, sod it, if she's laughing about last night then it shouldn't bother me either, so I laughed as well. She finished her tea (I'd made a third pot), and she said thanks for that, and stood up, and it was obvious she was going. I felt sad about that.

She said, 'I must say goodbye to Joe and Georgia', so I called them down and said Elisabeth was going. This time they managed to speak. All Georgia said was 'bye bye', and Elisabeth kissed her and said 'bye bye' as well, but before she could kiss Joe he looked at her very seriously and said, 'Are you a real American?' That made Elisabeth laugh, and she said, 'Yes, I'm afraid I am.' Joe looked at me like he still couldn't really believe it, and then he looked back at her and he said, 'Honestly?' and Elisabeth laughed again and nodded. Joe stood there, taking it in for a moment, and then he said, 'Wow'.

Elisabeth and I looked at each other and smiled. Joe said, 'What's it like being an American?' and Elisabeth said, 'Just the same as being an English person', and Joe said, 'Don't be silly, it can't be, tell me, really, what's it like?' Elisabeth said, 'OK then, let me think . . . it means you don't have pavements.' Joe said, 'How do you get anywhere, then?' and Elisabeth said, 'We go on the sidewalk.' Joe said, 'What's a sidewalk?' and Elisabeth said, 'It's a pavement.' Joe looked confused, so Elisabeth said, 'A sidewalk is what we call a pavement', and he said, 'Oh, I see. Wow.' Then Elisabeth started to tell him about crossroads being intersections, and lifts being elevators, and ground floor being the first floor — that one really fascinated him, he asked about that a lot.

While she was talking, Elisabeth took a step back, and knocked her leg against the sofa. The first cushion began to wobble, and then it fell off the back of the sofa, and you could see the letter 'T'. She'd turned round to steady herself, and saw it, and stopped talking, and all four of us watched the other cushions fall off. The last one took a bit of time, it sort of slid off, but then it went and you could see the whole word 'TITS'.

I didn't know what to say. I looked down at Joe. He was looking really scared, he probably thought I was going to shout again and Elisabeth would go and he wouldn't be able to ask her any more questions about America. But when I looked at her I realised she was trying not to smile. I said, 'That was courtesy of Joe, earlier', and she nodded, and bit her lip, but it was no good, she couldn't stop herself giggling. Then Georgia giggled too, and that was it, I burst out laughing. Joe looked relieved he wasn't going to be told off again, and he started laughing as well. Elisabeth said to him, 'That's a word we *do* have in America', and that set us all off, none of us could stop laughing for ages after that. Elisabeth was almost crying at one point.

Eventually we calmed down, and she said she'd be going now, and Joe and Georgia looked disappointed (I felt it, but I tried not to look it). Georgia said, 'I'm having my dinner now', and Elisabeth said, 'Are you? What are you having?' Georgia said, 'Spaghetti bolognese'. Elisabeth said, 'I *love* spaghetti bolognese.'

So I asked her if she'd like to stay and have some with us.

She looked at me, and then at the kids. Then she smiled, and said she'd love to. She helped Joe and Georgia lay the table while I cooked the spaghetti (I decided to forget about telling Joe he couldn't have any), and then we all sat down and had dinner together.

We had a really nice time.

I guess I always knew Jill would only ever make one telephone call to me. That there'd be only one thing she would ring to say.

Never actually thought it through in those terms, not consciously. But I did when it happened. And I do mean that: I had the thought before she said what she had to say. In the gap she left just before she said it. I was in the kitchen (I'd just put the washing machine on – I wonder how often people get news like that at such an ordinary moment?), and the phone rang. I went through and answered it, and a voice said, 'Hello, Alex?' I said, 'Yes', and she said, 'Hello, it's Jill'. Right then, that's when I had the thought. It felt so strange, Jill ringing me, because she'd never rung me before. Why would she? I was June's little boy, I was young Alex, it was as though I only existed when I went back home. The rest of my life, moving to London and getting jobs and flats and girlfriends, that never really happened as far as Jill was concerned. It was completely outside her world. All that was (to use the phrase I'd become so fond of) the big world. She'd never had any reason to phone me when I was out in the big world. But now she did. There could only be one reason.

So before she told me, I knew. And I actually felt sorry for her, having to tell me, having to find the words to say it. I suppose she'd spent ages before she picked up the phone trying to think how she was going to phrase it. Whether she'd got anything ready or not I don't know, but if she had it went out the window. I can't remember now what she did say, I was too busy feeling sorry for her and wondering how it was going to hit me. The call went on for a while, with Jill saying 'I'm so sorry' a lot, and telling me what had happened, in a pretty roundabout way. In her sleep, apparently. Sudden heart attack. Big one. The doctor said she wouldn't have suffered too much. Jill latched on to that, kept mentioning it, I think to try and comfort herself as much as me.

But there's not much you can say, not really, when you've just told someone something like that. I thanked Jill for calling, and said I'd get some things together and get up there straightaway. She said she'd wait up for me. Then we said goodbye.

I put the phone down and sat there, waiting. Waiting to see what I'd feel. But I didn't seem to feel anything. All I remember thinking is, The washing machine's going round. A moment like that, and all I could think of was which cycle the washing machine was on. I began to feel guilty, worried that Mum would resent me for not bursting into tears. But that's how I was. Shock, I guess. Didn't feel like that, though. It felt like I was waiting for something else, some other news, some other . . . *thing* to come along and make sense of it all, make me feel something.

I thought back to our last conversation on the phone, a couple of days before. I wanted to remember the last thing we'd ever said to each other. But I couldn't. Not exactly. I wanted to know *exactly* what it had been: 'bye' or 'goodbye' or 'see you' or 'lots of love'? That was the first bit of hurt I felt, the realisation that I'd never know what my last words to Mum had been, or hers to me.

Before I knew it, I heard the washing machine slowing down after its final spin. I looked at my watch. I'd been sitting there for nearly an hour. An hour of feeling numb, wondering why I couldn't feel anything except numb. I went into the kitchen, turned the machine off, waited for it to let me open the door. Then I hung the washing up to dry in the bathroom. It was such a mundane thing, but I thought, It's stupid not to hang it up, if I leave it in the machine while I'm away it'll get damp and smell. Normal life carrying on. I'd noticed that when Dad died. At first it feels disrespectful, but you soon accept that that's the way it is. It can't be any other way. That's how it was for my parents when their parents died. And their parents before them, all the way back. Death's part of life. For a while I thought, This time it should be different, though, I knew Dad was dying but this is a shock, I should go to pieces now. But I didn't. I hung up the washing. Packed a bag. Put the bag in the car.

And then the next thing I did felt just as natural. I took out my mobile and dialled. I wanted her to come with me. It seemed right that she should. And when she answered, and she'd got over the shock of the news, she seemed to think it was right and natural too. She said, 'Pick me up, come now, I'll have my stuff ready by the time you get here.'

When we got to . . . I was going to say Mum's, but . . . well, you know . . . when we got there things started to feel less normal. For a start there was the fact that she wasn't there. She was at the undertaker's. Jill explained how it had all happened: they'd been due to go shopping, she'd called Mum first thing to see what time she wanted to go, there was no reply. Probably in the bath, thought Jill, I'll give it half an hour then try again. Half an hour later, still no reply. Jill started to worry, came round, rang the bell, nothing. Went back home for her spare key (Mum had one to Jill's house too), let herself in . . . found Mum in bed. Jill began to cry when she got to that bit, but she soon recovered herself. Once she got on to the practical stuff – how she'd called the doctor, the undertaker – she was fine. Jill's good with practical.

She said how strange it had felt, going through Mum's handbag to find my number (another 'not normal' moment). She could only find the book with my home number in. I'd been out all day, so it was the evening before she could get hold of me. Hadn't wanted to leave a message.

Jill told us all this as soon as we got there, the three of us standing in the hallway. When she reached the end she paused, then said, 'Anyway, come in, sit down. I haven't even offered you a cup of tea yet.'

'It's all right,' said Amy, 'I'll do it. You sit down. You've done more than enough for one day.'

'Thanks, love,' said Jill, smiling at her.

We went through to the kitchen. Jill and I sat at the table, Amy started on the tea.

'I'm just glad she didn't suffer too much,' said Jill.

'A heart attack,' I said. 'I'd never have thought of Mum having a heart attack.'

Jill looked at me as though she wanted to say something but wasn't sure if she should.

'Are you all right?' I said.

She looked relieved I'd given her a cue to tell me what was on her mind. 'It wasn't so much a heart attack as a . . .' She paused. 'As a broken heart. She missed your dad, you know. Really missed him. She wanted to be back with him.'

Amy, waiting for the kettle to boil, stood quietly, just listening to us.

'Do you think so?' I said.

Jill nodded. 'It's what the doctor said as well. It happens a lot, doesn't it? Couples dying within a few months of each other.'

'Yeah, but she didn't seem broken-hearted to me.' I thought back to her birthday. Well, OK, maybe a bit out of sorts, forgetful sometimes. But nothing serious.

Jill smiled, as if I was being stupid about something. She exchanged a look with Amy. Yes, I was definitely being stupid about something.

'Well of course she was happy when you were here,' said Jill, in a gentle, let's-explain-it-to-the-stupid-one voice.

'Having you here was like having your dad back for a couple of days,' said Amy, in a voice that wasn't too different.

Was it?

The kettle boiled. Amy turned round to get on with the tea.

Over the next few days there were plenty of 'not normal' moments.

Going to the undertaker's to 'pay my last respects', that phrase that really means 'seeing the dead person's body', but no one wants to say that. Amy came with me. We were quiet on the way there and on the way back. She cried. So did I. Not as much as her, but I cried. Felt better for that.

Organising the funeral. Jill knew the phone numbers of everyone locally, I did the relatives. That helped as well, in its way; telling them all the news, one after the other, sort of anaesthetised me to it, made it seem less horrible. By the end I'd even got a bit of a routine going, lines about sorry they had to get the black ties out again so soon, stuff like that.

Tidying up. They were some of the weirdest moments. Like picking up Mum's latest puzzle book from where she'd left it in the main room, on the footstool that she never used as a footstool but as somewhere to keep her puzzle books. It was open at a word search. Most of the words were circled, but there were half a dozen she hadn't found yet. I couldn't bring myself to close the book, let alone throw it away. Didn't want to admit that she was never going to find those words.

I was sitting looking at it, two days after we'd got there, when Amy came into the room.

'Listen, Alex . . .' She seemed uncomfortable. 'About work . . .' She'd called in sick that morning and the morning before. 'I've got some meetings in the next couple of days . . . they're quite important . . . I mean, I could get out of them . . .'

'Oh damn, I'm sorry, Amy – I should have thought – sorry . . .'

'No, I wanted to be here. But . . .'

'Of course, you've got to go back. I'll run you to the station . . .' I stood up, felt for my car keys.

'It's only for these meetings – I'll come back after that. For the funeral, I mean. If you want me to, that is . . .'

'Why wouldn't I?'

She smiled.

'Besides, Mum would have wanted you there.'

She nodded.

Then something occurred to me. 'Only come if . . . if it's easy for you,' I said. 'If it won't cause you any problems.'

'What do you mean?'

'With . . . what's his name . . . David. You know, I'd understand, if he wasn't happy.'

242

'Oh, I see. No, that's . . . that won't . . . We're not seeing each other any more.'

'Oh. I'm sorry.'

'Don't be. I'm not.'

'Didn't work out then?'

She snarled. It was meant to make me laugh, and it worked. She laughed as well. I felt even closer to her.

'Look, if you're going to be coming back, why don't you just take the car?'

'Are you sure?'

'Of course.' I gave her the keys.

'It'll be nice to drive your car without you being there to criticise me.'

'Don't worry, I'll send you texts along the way. "Stop hogging the middle lane", that sort of thing.'

'Right, I'll remember to turn my phone off.' She looked at her watch. 'If I'm going to miss the worst of the traffic I should set out now.'

'OK.'

She fetched her stuff from upstairs and we walked out to the car.

'Thanks for coming,' I said. 'It's been a real help.'

She unlocked the car, put her bag on the back seat. 'I'll give you a call when I get home.'

'Right.'

We hugged, kissed each other on the cheek. I could smell her perfume. It reminded me of being with her.

'I'll call you when I get home,' she repeated.

'Yeah. Speak to you then.'

'Bye.'

'Bye.'

I watched her drive off, then went back inside. The house

was quiet, empty. So empty I almost felt scared. The house still had all Mum's stuff in it, of course. But without her there it didn't seem real. It was like a museum to her.

I picked up the puzzle book. I began looking for the words Mum hadn't found. Got most of them straightaway, but there was one that took me ages. 'Fly', it was (the wordsearch was themed around travel). I remembered how Mum used to say there was always one it took a long time to get, and nine times out of ten it'd be a short one. In the end I got it, tucked away in the top right corner. I picked up Mum's pen, drew circles round all the words I'd found, crossed them off the list. I left 'fly' until last. Then I closed the book and put it back on the footstool.

I said, 'Finished it for you, Mum.'

The funeral went well, if you can say something like that about a funeral. Amy drove back from London on the morning itself. She had a bath and got changed. When she came downstairs again the sight of her in her black dress made me catch my breath. I instantly felt guilty, hated myself for having such a thought in those circumstances. I made myself busy helping Jill with some flowers.

Most people came back to the house afterwards. Jill and a couple of Mum's other friends had, inevitably, made enough food for a small army. They also took it in turns to operate the kettle, producing a never-ending supply of tea so that everyone had a cup in their hand at all times, whether they wanted it or not. Amy helped out, carrying trays round, telling people which cups had sugar in and which didn't. Seeing her do that surprised me, this woman who, if she was back in London and you asked her to 'make me a cup of tea, love', would punch you. But here she fitted in. Here it seemed normal for her to behave like that. She was like . . . well, she was like my mum.

'All right, Alex, lad?'

I turned round. 'Oh, hi, Norman. How are you?'

'Not bad, not bad.' He looked uncomfortable in his suit and too-tight collar.

'Thanks for coming today.'

He gave a grunt of acknowledgment. Then, 'Got here three-quarters of an hour early, we did. I allowed a bit more time for the journey, see. Bit of work on the motor yesterday. Changed the front diff, wasn't sure how she was going to settle down. But she were no bother in the end.'

'Right. That's good.'

'Aye.' He concentrated, obviously feeling that some comment about his sister-in-law was called for. Eventually he settled on: 'She were a good woman, your mum.'

'Yeah. She was.'

We both nodded.

'Aye,' he said once more, and moved away.

The next day I was sitting at the kitchen table, going through the cardboard box where Mum and Dad always kept their important documents. I'd fixed up a meeting with the solicitor and wanted to have everything ready. Jill was on the last leg of the morning's marathon washing-up session. Amy had gone to the supermarket to get us some proper food for dinner. After the day before we couldn't face another mini pork pie.

I'd sorted all the documents into piles: house, life insurance, pensions, wills. I was familiar with most of them after sorting things out when Dad died. At the bottom of the box was a miscellaneous pile: stray bank statements, a few

Premium Bonds, ancient Christmas cards that had got in there by mistake. And, right at the bottom, a dusty piece of paper folded into three. I opened it out. It was my parents' marriage certificate.

I couldn't remember ever seeing it before. It probably hadn't been out of that box more than a handful of times in the last three decades; the ink had hardly faded at all. It looked for all the world as though my parents had got married yesterday. The registrar's handwriting was very neat, almost beautiful. Strange to think that such an important document depends on who you happen to get on the day. If your registrar has bad handwriting, or if he's in a rush, or if he's got the shakes from a heavy session the night before, the record of probably the biggest event in your life is going to look a mess. They should all be done professionally, by the sort of people who used to do that writing in Bibles, where the first letter is as big as the rest of the paragraph.

I read the date, laughed at the memory that Dad usually had to ask me when his wedding anniversary was. If it got to the day before and he'd forgotten to ask, I'd ring him up, tell him to get down the corner shop for the box of Milk Tray. Then I looked at his name: Brian Philip Richards. Occupation: engineer. What will I put when I get married? You can't have the words 'voice-over artist' on a marriage certificate. It doesn't seem right.

Then I looked at the box containing Mum's name. I knew right away there was something wrong, but my brain froze, couldn't work it out. All I could manage was staring at the words. Understanding what they meant was beyond me. 'June Patricia Clarke, née Brailsford.' I kept looking at the word 'Clarke'. What was 'Clarke'? Who was 'Clarke'? Mum's maiden name was Brailsford. I knew that: it's a password on my bank account. And her married name was Richards, because that was Dad's name, that was my name. So what was this 'Clarke' all about?

My mind began to grab at explanations. But it was like watching an Agatha Christie film; I'd get part way through a theory and find it didn't match all the facts. I kept coming back to the thought that I might be adopted, although God knows why I thought that would mean Mum changing her surname.

In the end I said, 'Jill?'

'Mmm?'

'What's this?'

'What's what, love?' she said, drying her hands on a towel.

'This bit on Mum's marriage certificate. It says "June Clarke, née Brailsford".'

A look of horror crossed her face. She put the towel down, took the certificate from me, stared at it. It was obvious she knew exactly what it was all about, but didn't want to tell me. She sat down, still looking at the certificate to avoid looking at me.

'Jill, what is it?'

She gave up trying to think of a cover story. 'Alex, love, it's . . . I know your mum never told you, but . . . she was married before she met your dad.'

What?

Jill put the certificate on the table, tried to place her hand on mine. But I pulled away. I didn't mean to be rude, I just wanted to get this straightened out. I wanted information, not sympathy.

'What do you mean, she was married before?'

'Your dad was her second husband. She married another man when she was younger. His surname was Clarke.'

I shook my head. 'She can't have done.'

Jill said nothing. What I'd just said was clearly untrue, and saying nothing was the kindest way of pointing that out.

'Someone else?' I said. 'My mum was married to someone else?'

Jill nodded. 'I'm sorry, Alex, love.' What was she apologising for? For Mum getting married, or for me finding out like this?

I felt angry. With Mum for never having told me, with Jill for knowing something about Mum that I didn't. 'Why didn't she *fucking* tell me?'

The last time I'd sworn in front of Jill must have been nearly twenty years ago, when I was an objectionable teenager trying to shock her. It hadn't worked, of course, and I didn't shock her now either. She obviously understood what a state I must be in. It felt like she was in charge, calm. I was glad one of us was. 'It just never happened,' she said quietly. 'There never came a time it felt right for her.' She paused, as if to let her words sink in phrase by phrase. 'She couldn't tell you when you were a toddler, could she? Maybe she should have mentioned it when you were . . . I don't know, seven or eight . . . but it's hard, isn't it? To find a way of slipping something like that into the conversation.'

Suppose so.

'We talked about it once, you know, your mum and me. About her telling you.'

'When?'

'Oh, I don't know . . . when you were about twelve, I think. She said it got more and more difficult the longer she left it.'

I could see that.

'And I don't think she thought about it that much, you know. Your dad was the one she loved.'

248

'So who was this other bloke?' I asked. I still couldn't believe he'd really existed, this man called Clarke. A man who was married to my mum that wasn't my dad? It didn't make sense.

Jill gave a little laugh, as though to signal he'd never been that important. 'Someone your mum knew when she was seventeen—'

'*Seventeen?*'

'Yes. She only got married to spite your grandad.'

My mum? Did something like that? *She* was a rebellious kid? She couldn't have been. Rebellious kids weren't invented when she was young. They hadn't come along until . . . *What? Until you were a kid?* 'Who was he?'

'Someone she knew from work. He was a nice enough chap, from what she told me. Bit older than her. Twenty-three, I think. Just as immature as your mum, though. They thought they were in love. Their parents told them they weren't, but you know what youngsters are like. They got a little place of their own, and your mum said after the first week she knew she'd made a mistake. Stuck it out for four months, she did, then crawled back home with her tail between her legs.'

'And they got divorced?'

'After a while. It was all very friendly. Your mum kept his name.' Jill indicated the certificate.

I'd stopped feeling angry now, could see why Mum would have found it difficult to tell me. No need to, really. It didn't affect things with her and Dad and me, and that was her world. But I did feel cheated at not having the chance to talk to her about it. There was a bit of her life I was never going to understand. A bit of her.

There was the sound of the front door opening, then Amy

came into the kitchen, laden with shopping bags. 'You should have seen that supermarket. Jam-packed it was.' She plonked the bags down on the side, turned to us. 'The queues were backing up the aisles, and then the guy in front of me . . .' She stopped. 'What's wrong?'

Jill looked at me. This was my call.

'I've just had a bit of a surprise.'

'What do you mean?'

'Mum was married to someone else. Before she met Dad.'

I watched for her reaction. Maybe it'd give me a clue to what mine should be. She looked shocked. 'Really?' she said. There wasn't much surprise in her voice. There was a bit, obviously, but her tone was less 'that's a real shock to me' than 'that must be a real shock to you, Alex, I'm worried about you'.

'Yeah. Someone she worked with, apparently.' I looked at Jill. She told Amy exactly what she'd just told me. Hearing the story again was like seeing a movie for the second time, getting the chance to decide whether you like it or not. I decided that I quite liked this one. Well, not liked it, but I didn't dislike it. I was glad this Clarke guy hadn't done anything to hurt Mum. He sounded all right. I could imagine going down the pub with him. With the twenty-three-year-old him, I mean, the one that was married to Mum, not the . . . what would he be now? . . . seventy-odd-year-old him, wherever he was, if he was anywhere.

'Well,' said Amy when Jill had finished. 'I see what you mean, "bit of a surprise".'

Jill got to her feet, obviously sensing that the right thing to do was leave me and Amy alone. 'I'd better be off,' she said. 'Malcolm'll be wondering where his lunch is.'

We both thanked her for all her help with the funeral. She

took as many of her Tupperware containers as she could carry, saying she'd pop round for the others later.

Amy and I went into the main room, sat on the sofa.

'You all right?' she said.

I nodded. 'Think so.'

'Your mum must have forgotten about the marriage certificate.'

'Mmm.'

Silence.

'It was good that Jill was with you – to talk you through it.'

'Yeah.'

It felt like Amy was some sort of therapist, trying to get responses from me. She already knew what she thought about the news, had everything sorted in her own mind. Her comments weren't to help her come to terms with it, they were to help me. I resented this, as though she knew something I didn't, but at the same time I felt comforted by it too.

I traced my finger over a square in the sofa's pattern, kept tracing it as I spoke. 'What I can't believe is . . . well, *it*. Mum being married to someone else. She was Mum. She was married to Dad. That was it. She can't have been married to someone else first. Not back then.'

Although I wasn't looking at her, I could feel Amy smiling. 'What, you think people getting married more than once is a modern invention?'

'Well, no, obviously. I mean, look at Henry the eighth. But not *Mum*.'

'Why not?'

'She wasn't like that.'

'Like what? Like someone who made mistakes, who had emotions?'

251

'Of course she had emotions. And made mistakes. But not big mistakes, not messing-up-relationship mistakes. They're what I do.'

I sensed a strain between us when I said that. I'd thought Amy and I were both reconciled to things being over between us, that it was a given, that we were bouncing along just being friends. But now I wasn't so sure. And I got the feeling she wasn't either.

'You think you're so different from your mum?'

Yeah, that's exactly what I think. Bang on. That's the whole point. 'I suppose so.'

'How can you be that different from her? She was your mum, Alex.'

'But I *am* different from her. If I was the same as her I'd have stayed out here, wouldn't I, in the country? Not moved to London.'

'You've moved out of London again.'

'Yeah, but . . .' *But what?* 'Not back here.'

'Where you are isn't that different from here.'

'It's not the country, though, is it?'

'All but.'

'No, it's the edge of a small town, it's not a village.' *Anyone got any more straws I can clutch at?*

Amy went quiet. There could have been an air of bickering, of niggly points-scoring about everything we'd just said. But I knew there wasn't. Amy was trying to get something across to me. I remembered that night with Elisabeth, when she found the book and I told her about the 'change' theory and she couldn't get it. I'd thought she was in the wrong. But now I had my doubts. Was it me who had something wrong? The something that Amy was trying to get across? She was being very patient about it, like a governess helping her

252

pupil. No, it was more than that. It was like a mother helping her child.

'All right,' I said, 'forget the geography, what I really mean is . . . ambition. Doing something with your life. Changing. All Mum ever wanted was to settle down. Have kids, just like her mum had done.' After the drive home from Mum's birthday you'd have thought I was mad to mention that again. But I felt safe talking to Amy about it now. I suppose deep down I'd begun to realise what this was all about. 'And I'm not like that.' *Sure?* 'I don't want to do that.' *Really?*

'I seem to remember you pointing that out once or twice before, Alex.' She said it with a smile, not nastily. Someone who knew . . . not that she was winning an argument . . . but that the other person was coming over to her side and she was waiting for him.

She only had to wait until the next night. We'd had dinner at the Swan, a pub a few miles away. Amy drove back. I was feeling tired, the last few days had started to get to me. I sat in the passenger seat, slumped down, my head resting against the window. I watched the headlights reflecting off the hedges, off each familiar twist of the lane. And I thought of Mum driving me along that lane when I was a kid, when I'd been to play with Paul Tunnicliffe who lived over towards the Swan. My head would be pressed against the window then too, because I was small rather than because I was slumped, but still, I remembered watching the headlights' beam travelling along the hedge.

My 'big world' spiel – what was it all about? What was it going to mean for my life? Jetting around the place, meeting new people, doing new things. Yeah, great. But that had all started to sound hollow. It had dawned on me that the world's round. It might be big, but it's round. If you travel all the way across it, where do you get to? Back to where you started. It's like that thing they used to say during the Cold War: if you looked at the map, at the very top right bit of the Soviet Union and the very top left bit of America, they seemed as far apart as you could get. But in reality they met round the back. There was only a couple of hundred miles between them. Go as far as you possibly can in this 'big' world and you end up back at the beginning.

I pressed my face against the glass, looking out, transfixed by the headlights dancing. What had changed, *really* changed, since I used to do this as a kid? Nothing. Nothing could ever really change about me. I was always going to be my mum's son. I started off as part of her, literally, and I was always going to be part of her, even though she wasn't here any more. *Especially* now she wasn't here any more. None of us ever really grow up. Not me, not Tony, not Amy, not even my mum. We're all kids, and the only truly big or clever thing you can ever do is admit that. Go back to the beginning. That's what having kids is – going back to the beginning. Having kids isn't the end of change in your life, it's the start of it.

And who do you do it with? Well, odds are, you spend a decade or two congratulating yourself on how different you are from your parents, how much you've progressed from the start they gave you, how you eat comfort food but they just eat sausage and mash, and then you realise that actually you're not that different from them after all, and you never really have been, and you notice that the person you're with is like them too. I thought of all the time Mum and Amy had spent together. They were the same as each other. Yeah, Mum liked Cliff Richard and Amy didn't, Amy could send an e-mail and Mum couldn't . . . but what does that amount

to? That's nothing more than the fact that one of them happened to be born thirty years before the other. If you'd ever
seen my mum and Amy fussing a dog someone had left tied
up outside a supermarket, if you'd ever heard them dis-
cussing Princess Di's dresses – then you'd know how similar
they were. Same as if you'd ever watched either of them
cooking me sausage and mash because I'd had a bad day.
One of them was less ready to oblige if I actually requested
it, and has been known to say, 'What did your last slave die
of? Make your own sodding dinner.' But even there, not
always.

Amy slowed down for the pothole in the lane just before
the big oak tree outside Mrs Bryant's. I've always wondered
if the council are going to fix it, but they never have. You can
miss it by swerving, but then you catch another one on the
opposite side of the lane. Mum used to take the left one as
well.

I reached out with my hand. Stayed slumped in the seat,
face against the glass, but I reached out. Amy took my hand,
held on to it until she had to change down into first to pull
into the drive at home. We didn't say anything, just held
hands. And that was it. That was when I knew. It was going
to be another ten days before we went out for a drink, back
in Kent, and another week after that before Amy came back
to mine and stayed the night, and three or four days after
that before either of us actually mentioned out loud the idea
that, yeah, maybe we should get back together.

But that was when I knew.

We did it! We sorted the deal out! Yesterday. Me and
Elisabeth. And then . . . oh, I still can't believe this.

She's over in London with Walter and Mary again, this is
the trip to finally sign the contract. She'd told them about
everything, and suggested what we thought the best thing to
do was, and they thought about it and said OK, you two
know the details, we'll let you handle it.

We all met in Miles's office – him, me, Elisabeth, Walter
and Mary. He sat on his side of the desk, and the Americans
sat on the other side. The logical place for me to sit would
have been next to Miles, but I didn't want to, I sat at one
end of the desk. He'd got a bottle of champagne ready, one
of those big bottles, a magnum. All the papers that needed
signing were laid out in front of everyone.

Once we'd sat down and finished doing all the small talk
(I let the others do that, as I was so nervous), Miles said,
'Welcome, everyone, what a pleasure it is to be doing business with you.' No one said anything, we all just smiled and
nodded a bit, and Miles said, 'Right, let's get this paperwork
out of the way, there's champagne that needs drinking.'
Walter said, 'Yes, indeed, let's get the paperwork done,' and
he nodded to Elisabeth.

She passed Miles the first few documents to sign, the

boring, run-of-the-mill ones that were necessary but didn't have any figures on them. I passed the equivalent ones to Walter and Mary, and they signed them and Miles signed his. Then they swapped, and signed each other's, and while this was happening Elisabeth looked across at me and gave a little wink. She knew I was nervous. It was nice of her to do something like that, I thought.

Then it was time for the big document, the important one, the one that had the amount on it, the price we'd agreed for the business. Elisabeth picked up the first copy, and turned to the page that had the figure on it (a big figure, with lots of noughts at the end), and she folded it open and put it in front of Miles. She didn't say anything, and I didn't either, and Walter and Mary stayed quiet as well, and I think it was then that Miles started to worry. I watched him as it all happened, he'd started to sweat a bit. And do you know what? I was glad. I looked at that document too, and that was when I stopped feeling nervous and I started feeling angry, because it made me realise that if I hadn't told Elisabeth what was going on, and we'd got to this stage and the Americans didn't know about the loan, Miles would have signed the document and got his money and then run off, leaving me right in the shit. With all that worry to face, and maybe even prison too. I thought, yeah, what you're about to get serves you right, you bastard, I'm going to enjoy this.

He looked at the figure on the piece of paper, and you could tell it was like he could see all the money just in front of him, and he wanted to reach out and take it, but he wasn't allowed to just yet. Elisabeth said, 'As you know, Miles, this is the amount that we had negotiated as your price for selling us the agency.' It was the way she said 'had' that made him sweat a bit more. She didn't actually put any emphasis on it, but if everything had been all right she wouldn't have said 'had' at all, would she? Miles looked at her. She said, 'But I'm afraid that those negotiations took place without both sides being in full possession of the facts.'

You could really see him panicking now. He looked at me. I nearly looked away, it was very hard not to look away, but I was determined that I wouldn't, he wasn't going to make me do that. I stared back at him, and I concentrated on not blinking, and I knew that he knew what I must have done. I was glad about that.

Then he looked back at Elisabeth, and he said, 'I'm sorry?' He was trying to smile when he said it, you know, hoping he could bluff his way through it, but he must have known by now that he couldn't. She said, 'Forget it, Miles, we know about the loan.' He stared at her for a moment, and then he looked back at me, and he said, 'You—', but Elisabeth interrupted him. She said, 'Save your breath, Miles, I think you should concentrate on what's going to happen next.' I stared him out again – this time I even managed to give a little smile – and then he turned back to Elisabeth and he said, 'OK, what *is* going to happen next?' He knew we'd got him.

Elisabeth said, 'We're going to have a small renegotiation.' Miles looked a bit relieved at that – just a little bit, mind you – because he must have twigged we weren't going straight to the authorities to grass him up. But mainly he still looked worried, and to be honest he had every reason to be. Elisabeth picked up her pen, and leaned across the desk, and she didn't turn the piece of paper around, she left it facing Miles so he could see exactly what she was doing, and she crossed out the last zero at the end of the figure.

Then she took her hand away so that Miles could see the new amount, and she said, 'We thought we'd open negotiations like this.'

Miles stared at the paper, and his mouth dropped open a bit, but he was so shocked he couldn't actually speak. I mean, he said 'but' and then he paused and said 'what' and then he paused again and then he said 'you', but he couldn't actually make a sentence. This was good, because it meant we could get on to my part of the plan without any distractions. Elisabeth handed me the pen, and I reached over, and I left the paper exactly where it was too, and I said my line, I'd rehearsed it and rehearsed it and I delivered it brilliantly, even if I say so myself, I said, 'And then, Miles, we thought we'd end negotiations like this', and I crossed out the second-last zero as well.

He was really stuck for words now. It was *bloody* fantastic. He kept staring at the new figure, and none of us were saying anything, we wanted to watch him suffer. In the end, after his mouth had opened and closed for a bit, he said, 'You are joking, of course?' None of us said anything to this either.

You could see Miles trying to get his act together, trying to tough it out. He said, 'You're clearly not going to take my business off me for that amount of money.' Elisabeth said, 'I think you'll find we are.' He said, 'Oh *do* fuck off, darling, you can't even buy a decent Bentley with that.' That made me angry, him talking to her like that. She said, 'If you want to consult an independent arbiter before going ahead, Miles, I'm sure there are some gentlemen from the Serious Fraud Office who'd be interested.'

And this was where I said my thing. Miles obviously knew this was the best figure he was going to get, and it was better than going to prison, and we knew we were safe because the only person who knew what we'd done was Miles and he couldn't land us in it without landing himself in it too. Anyway, he's all right, he's got loads of bank accounts and shares and all that sort of stuff, he's not exactly going to starve. But he was obviously furious at losing out on his really, *really* big payday, and he pointed at the contract and he said, 'You can't knock me down THAT much, it's . . . it's . . .' He couldn't think what to say, so I looked at him and said, 'What, Miles – you mean it's criminal?'

Everyone looked at me, I think they were surprised I'd made a joke. I can't blame them, I mean, *I* was surprised I'd made a joke. I didn't know how I'd thought of it. It was like, I hadn't tried to think of something to say, I'd just been feeling angry, about what Miles had tried to do to me, and how he'd spoken to Elisabeth, and the words just sort of came out. And I remembered what I'd thought that day I spoke to the woman at the cinema: maybe that's the trick, maybe when you try too hard things don't happen. You could tell Miles was really surprised, because that shut him up completely, he didn't even try to say anything else, he just picked up the pen and signed the contract. Well, he hesitated a bit when the pen was touching the paper, before he actually wrote his signature. But he knew we had him where we wanted him.

While he was signing his name, I looked across at Elisabeth. She was still looking at me from my 'criminal' thing, and I could see it had surprised her. When she smiled at me, and tilted her head a bit, I realised she'd liked the surprise, it had . . . well, I guess it had impressed her. But not in a way that she thought I was super-funny or super-clever, like Eddie Murphy or someone, but just that me standing up to Miles, and saying something that had made him go quiet, was what she'd liked. And I got a definite feeling she was looking at me in a way she hadn't looked at me before. I liked it. It was scary, but the good sort of scary, you know, the sort of scary you like.

Miles had one or two more places where he had to sign, and Elisabeth pointed them out and he did it. While that was happening I went over to the side-table where his computer is, and I opened up his e-mail and started typing. This wasn't in the plan, it had only occurred to me just then, and Elisabeth watched me do it; she was obviously curious what I was up to. Miles finished signing, then he put his pen down, and said, 'Is that it, or would you like the shirt off my back as well?' Elisabeth said, 'No thanks, Miles, I think we can live without that sight.'

I finished my typing, put the cursor over 'send', kept my finger on the mouse and said, 'Actually, Miles, there is one more thing', and they all looked at me. I said, 'Perhaps you should come and read this', and Miles came and stood next to me, and Elisabeth stood on my other side, and Walter and Mary stood behind us, and they read the e-mail, which was to Miles's 'Circular: All Staff' group, and it said:

Dear Everyone,

This is to let you know I have now signed the contract to sell the agency, so I am no longer your boss. But I have remembered my promise about taking you all to Paris for the weekend, and I'll be getting that organised very soon.

Best wishes,

Miles.

I gave Miles just long enough to read it, then I clicked 'send'. I turned to him, and he was doing his mouth-opening-and-closing thing again. Then he said, 'But that's going to cost . . .' and he started to do some sums in his head, and I said, 'Yes, Miles, it's going to cost almost exactly the figure on that piece of paper you've just signed.' He began to say something — I think he was going to call me a rude word again — but he stopped because someone in one of the offices shouted 'Hooray!' at the top of their voice. Then another person yelled out as well, and then another, and soon you could hear the whole firm cheering and clapping. Then the door flew open and Hazel ran in, and she shouted 'ooh la la' and gave Miles a big hug, and he looked at me over her shoulder and he had a face like thunder, but obviously he couldn't say anything, especially when loads of the others began piling into the room as well. All he could do was pretend to look happy. It was ace.

Kathy opened the champagne, and someone else started handing the glasses out, and Kathy was nearest to me and Elisabeth, so she poured us both some champagne, and said, 'This calls for a celebration, don't you think?' and smiled at us and then went off to fill some other people's glasses. Elisabeth turned to me, and tapped her glass against mine and said, 'Yes, I think it does', and then she carried on looking at me, and she had that smile again, the one with her head tilted a bit to one side. And I got that scary feeling again.

I didn't lose it till . . . well, to tell you the truth I still haven't lost it. But I don't mind that, because like I say, it's a good sort of scary. What happened was a load of us went out celebrating (Miles came too, I mean he couldn't not come, could he, but I've never seen anyone have to work so hard at smiling), and we stayed out well into the night, and eventually people started to go home, but I didn't really notice who or when, because I was talking to Elisabeth most of the time. We talked about lots of things, but I can't remember any of them. Which is great. The only time I can remember what's happened is when everything's gone wrong, like that bloody night in the bar at Grand Central. But last night I forgot what we were talking about almost before we'd finished talking about it.

Except for one thing. Joe and Georgia. Elisabeth asked me about them, you know, what they were like and what games we played and all that sort of stuff, and I told her, and we talked about them for ages. And the funny thing was, if that had happened a few weeks ago I'd have hated it, I'd have thought, I don't want to talk about being a dad, I don't want Elisabeth to think of me as a dad, I want her to think of me as young and attractive. But I don't seem to see it like that any more. That day she stayed for dinner, when we had the spag bol, she was great with the kids, joining in their silly jokes and playing their games, being just like a kid herself. And that gave me the confidence to do the same. It made me think, Feeling like you're still a kid, like you've never really grown up, maybe that's not so uncool after all.

We ended up in this bar just off Beak Street. There weren't many of us left, and most of the others were completely slaughtered, but me and Elisabeth weren't, I mean, we were tipsy but we weren't slaughtered. And I looked at my watch and said, 'I should be off home, I suppose', but as soon as I'd said it I knew I didn't want to leave her, and without thinking (like I said before, I think that's the trick, not thinking) I said, 'Do you want to come back for a drink?' and Elisabeth smiled and said, 'Sure'. And it was only then I realised that I'd done it; I'd asked her back to mine and I hadn't panicked about it. Don't get me wrong, I was quite panicky in the taxi on the way back, and when I was unlocking the front door, and when I was pouring us a glass of wine each. And I felt panicky when she made a point of sitting on the sofa with me, you know, not in a separate chair, but then as we talked some more I calmed down, and it felt OK to be sitting there with her like that.

Actually, there was one more panicky moment. I said thanks for all her help with the Miles thing, and she said, 'Thanks for everything you did, you were great', and I said, 'Was I?' She said, 'Yeah, you were really impressive.' I said, 'Thanks, you were really impressive too', and she laughed and said, 'Well, I guess that makes us a really impressive couple', and I laughed as well, and looked at her, and she didn't look away. That was probably the most panicky moment of all. I leaned over to her, it was a bit awkward, she was sitting just that bit too far away, but she edged up the sofa towards me, which didn't stop me panicking but at least it told me she was thinking the same as me, and then we leaned together, and I tried to concentrate on not panicking . . . and we kissed. It was only a little kiss to start with, because we were both still holding our glasses of wine and we had to be careful about spilling them, but after a few seconds, when we'd stopped, I put my glass on the table and took Elisabeth's from her and put that on the table too, and then we leaned together again and we kissed again. Except it wasn't such a little kiss this time.

'I'm sorry about . . . what happened.'

'So you should be.'

Elisabeth wasn't going to make this easy for me. Couldn't blame her for that. We'd met in a pub near the office, three days after the merger had been sorted. I'd heard the official version of that from Kathy, who rang me the next morning with a hangover so bad she dropped the phone twice. Then I rang Tony and got the real version. I was so proud of him. Miles hasn't shown (and probably won't show) his face again, which is a pity, because I'd quite like to punch it. And while Tony was on the phone he gave me his other, not entirely unrelated, piece of news. Seemed I'd been right about him and Elisabeth being suited.

'I was . . . You see, the thing was . . .' What could I say? Tell Elisabeth how *The Road To Commitment* had affected my thinking? Don't be daft. Bit over the top for a relationship that never made it to half a dozen nights. That was what I wanted her to say, that she wasn't bothered about it, she'd never had any hopes pinned to it either. 'Well, anyway, what I did was outrageous. I'm sorry. Really.'

'I've had guys help fix me up with their friends before, but that was a little different.' There was just enough humour in her voice to convince me I wasn't number one on her Shit List. I might be in the top ten, but I wasn't number one.

'Yeah, well. At least I was pushing at an open door.'

She smiled. 'At the time I hadn't considered whether that particular door was open or not. But yes, I take your point.'

'Not a bad bloke, Tony, is he?'

Her smile got a little warmer. 'No, he's not bad at all.' She looked away from me, but didn't stop smiling.

'He tells me you're moving over for a while.'

She nodded. 'That was always going to happen. They wanted someone here for a few months to smooth the transition, and Walter and Mary have both got family, so Miss Free And Single here volunteered.'

'Miss Free And Single As Was.'

She smiled again. The warm one.

I checked my watch. 'What time's Tony getting here?'

'He shouldn't be long. He only had a few e-mails to send.'

'Are you off somewhere for dinner?'

'No, we're going back to his. Joe and Georgia are coming round. Which means I'll be saying "elevator" all night.'

'Hmm?'

'Joe. He likes me saying "elevator". Or rather,' she put on an ultra-strong Bronx accent, '"elevator". He still can't get over the fact that his dad's new friend is a real-life American.'

'Ahh. They're a good couple of kids. And Tony's been a good dad. Well, he still is. And you never know, he might be again.' *Oh dear.* 'Not that I meant . . . you know, I wasn't assuming anythi—'

She smiled. 'Tony won't be a dad again because of me.'

'No, I'm sorry, like I say, I wasn't assuming—'

She shook her head. 'I didn't mean that. Whatever happens, Tony won't be a dad again because of me.'

266

Oh. Shit. So that's what you were going to say that day in Rossi's. 'I'd love to have children but . . .' 'Elisabeth, I'm sorry.'

'You don't have to say sorry. It's not your fault.' She said it in a way that signified not so much 'I've come to terms with the fact' as 'it's OK, you don't need to make any great display of sympathy about it'.

'No. I see.'

'But there is that other thing that *was* your fault, which you *do* have to say sorry for. Lots of times. So far I'd estimate you've said approximately one-fifth of the "sorry"s you have to say for that.'

I took a deep breath. 'I'm sorry, I'm sorry, I'm sorry, I'm sorry—'

Elisabeth held up a hand. 'Maximum batch size – four.'

'Right. Another batch along in a while.'

'I'll be waiting.'

I could imagine Elisabeth saying 'elevator', watching *Lion King* videos, pushing swings in the park. And I thought I could imagine, although I probably couldn't, how much it hurt not to have children of her own to do those things with. But if she had to have an alternative, then with Joe and Georgia she'd got two of the best.

Tony showed up. Although it had been all of forty minutes since he'd last seen Elisabeth he'd obviously been missing her like mad. She stood up and hugged him. He grinned stupidly.

Actually, I thought, make that three of the best.

A week or so later. Sitting with Rosie in the café at Harvey Nichols. I was taking a break between voice-over sessions, she was taking a break between spending sprees.

'Special occasion?' I asked, eyeing her collection of designer bags.

'You could say that.' Her tone was unmistakable.

'Oh, *that* sort of special. What's his name?'

'Gavin.'

'*Gavin?*'

'I know, I've told him he should sue his parents. Trust me, he may be a Gavin, but he's not a Gavin.'

'And you're dressing to impress?'

'Darling, I don't need to dress to impress Gavin. I have already impressed Gavin. I impressed Gavin in combats and a T-shirt. At the checkout in Waitrose, as it happens.'

'But now you want to impress him that little bit more?'

'Alex, I've already impressed him as much as I need to. I've already impressed him . . . how can I put this . . . as much as a girl can impress a guy.'

I raised my eyebrows. 'You mean . . . ?'

'Yes, I mean . . .' She stirred her latte. 'And, as it happens, he's impressed me. A lot. Which was nice.'

'Not straight from Waitrose?'

'What kind of a girl do you take me for?' she laughed. 'We did have a couple of dates first. But tomorrow's our first posh night out.'

'Sounds serious.'

'Yeah, well, you're not the only one who's sorted themselves out lately.' I'd told her about Amy.

I waited. Then, 'Gonna tell me about it then?'

She began stirring her coffee again. 'The thing I've been getting wrong all these years is that I was waiting for a man.'

'I thought that was the idea.'

'No, I mean one particular man. I was waiting for him, and that stopped me ever making a real go of it with anyone else.'

'Are you serious?'

'Yup.'

She'd never told me about this. 'Who?'

No reply. Just the sound of her spoon tapping against the cup. She wouldn't even look at me. *Oh. That's who.*

She stopped stirring, and looked up at me. 'You never realised, did you?'

I shook my head.

'Don't think I realised myself for years. You were seeing Rebecca when we met, and then by the time you'd split up with her I was seeing Will, so it wasn't as if it was on the agenda. And even when we were single at the same time we'd got so used to being friends that I couldn't really admit what I was feeling. Admit it to myself, I mean, never mind to you.'

'Rosie, I don't know what to say . . .'

'There isn't anything *to* say. There never was, that's the point. I wasn't really in love with you, I was in love with the thought of being in love with you. You were an ideal, I suppose. Whenever I was seeing a guy and there was something about the relationship that was – shock, horror – less than a hundred per cent perfect, I'd think, Oh, if I was with Alex then it wouldn't be like this. But that wasn't true.'

'Of course not. I'm not perfect.'

'No.'

'I'm damn close, but I'm not perfect.'

'So the change I had to make was accepting that all relationships have their little niggles, and that you and I were friends, good friends, but that friends is all we were ever meant to be. Now I've done that, everything else is a lot easier.'

'Well, that's all very well, Rosie, but I'm not sure I can be friends with someone who's got a boyfriend called Gavin.'

'Oh damn, I'd forgotten that. Of course. It'd be terribly difficult for you. Shall we just call it a day?'

'Yeah, I think we should. Bye then.'

'See you.'

We lapsed into silence, nursing our drinks.

'We can put our copies of the book away now,' she said after a while.

'Suppose we can.'

'For what good they did. Did most of the work ourselves in the end.'

'No, that's not fair. It pointed us in the right direction, didn't it? That's all advice can do. Like you always said, in the end it comes down to you. Maybe there's a time in life when you're meant to understand these things, and whatever you do before that, however hard you think, you're not going to get it.'

'Maybe.'

'I mean, I wish I'd got my head round the kids thing while Mum was still here. She'd have been a fantastic grandma. But I didn't. Perhaps I wasn't meant to.'

Rosie smiled at me, and squeezed my arm.

We got the bill, then she hit the shops again, and I set off for my session. When that was finished I wandered over to Le Caprice to book a table for me and Amy on Saturday night.

I think I'll have the sausage and mash.

This is the best holiday I've ever had. Me and Joe and Georgia have come to New York to see Elisabeth. She moves over to England in four days, and I've timed it so that we fly back together. Joe wanted her to come and live with me, but I told him it was best she had her own flat. For now, anyway.

The four of us are having a brilliant time. We've done the Empire State Building, and the Staten Island Ferry, and Central Park, and loads of things. Joe's decided he likes the way Americans say 'to go' instead of 'to take away', and he's got this routine worked out with Elisabeth where when we order a coffee or a sandwich or something, she tells the person behind the counter what we want, and then she picks Joe up so the person can see him and he says 'to go, please'. In fact yesterday we had some sandwiches and wanted to eat them in the diner, but Joe was so desperate to say his line that we had to take them away.

The absolute best thing we've done, though, was today. We went to Grand Central. We looked all round the main bit of the station (I remembered that horrible time I had at the bar there with Elisabeth – seems so long ago now), and the kids loved it, and Elisabeth was telling them where all the trains go to, like she'd say she had a cousin who lived in one of the places, and a friend from college who lived in another, and they listened to her for ages, I've never seen them so quiet.

Then she said did we want to go to the Oyster Bar, and we said OK, so we all went down there. We got a table by the window where we could watch everyone rushing by (I managed to persuade Joe that we should sit down, just this once), and me and Elisabeth had beers and Joe and Georgia had Cokes.

Then I remembered the Whispering Gallery, standing there that morning when I couldn't sleep, not having anyone to do the whispering with. I asked Elisabeth if she'd come and do it with me, and she said of course, so we left Joe and Georgia talking to the waitress, and we went out into the passageway. It works because of the way the roof curves at that particular bit. Elisabeth told me to stand facing one of the pillars, which I did, and then she went over to the other pillar that was opposite, diagonally opposite, and I listened. I thought, there's no way I'll hear anything, not with all these people rushing past. But then I heard her voice saying 'hello', she was only whispering but because of the way it echoed you could hear it really clearly. And I said (well, whispered) 'hello' back to her, and then I said, 'this is great' and she said, 'yeah'.

Then I got her to keep speaking for a while, you know, just saying 'hello' over and over again, because I wanted to test something. I took a step back, and when you do that you can't hear the whispers any more, you have to stand in exactly the right place. No one around you can hear what you're saying to each other. You're in your own private little world, right in the middle of hundreds of people.

Elisabeth stopped talking. I turned round, but she was

272

still facing her pillar, waiting for me to say something. I knew what I wanted to say, but I was afraid, well, not afraid, nervous, I mean. But the fact that we couldn't see each other, only hear each other, made it slightly easier. I thought, Come on, Tony, just say it to her. So I said, 'Elisabeth?' and she said, 'Yeah?' and I said, 'Would you mind if I said something?' and she said, 'Of course not', and I said, 'The thing is – I think I'm a little bit in love with you'. There was a pause, and I was worried I might have ruined it all. But then she said, 'That's good, because I think I'm a little bit in love with you.' And there was another pause, and then we both turned round, and she came over to me – she had to work her way through all the commuters – and she smiled at me, and we hugged each other.

After that we went back into the bar and got Joe and Georgia, and they had a go at the Whispering Gallery and they thought it was brilliant too. Then Elisabeth said what did we all want to do next, and the children said they were a bit hungry, could we go for dinner somewhere, and Elisabeth said, 'Sure', and she thought for a minute about where we should go.

Then she got it. She said, 'Come on – I know a place near here that does the best spaghetti bolognese.'

Acknowledgements

Neither of my previous novels contained acknowledgements. I wasn't sure how to do them. At one extreme lay the risk of curt formality, at the other that of sounding like Gwyneth Paltrow at the Oscars. But after three books my admiration of, and gratitude to, everyone at Time Warner has grown so much that it has to be expressed. Thank you to Tamsin Barrack, Richard Beswick, Debbie Clement, Jo Coen, Andy Coles, Donna Coonan, Barry Gray, Nicola Hill, Terry Jackson, Sheena-Margot Lavelle, Alison Lindsay, Robert Manser, Nathalie Morse, Miles Poynton, Viv Redman, Simon Sheffield and Jennifer Richards. You are brilliant at your jobs and a real pleasure to work with.

Thanks are also long overdue to the team at Conville and Walsh. Kevin Conroy Scott, Jo Cooke, Ed Jaspers, Sam North, Sara Rance, Peter Tallack and Patrick Walsh – you are an elite squadron.

But the biggest thank you must go to Clare Conville. The phrase 'the best agent I could wish for' is a cliché. In Clare's case, it happens to be the literal truth. I wouldn't change a single thing about her, be it the way she improves a manuscript, the way she scans a contract, or the way she gets drunk with me and talks about films.

WHAT MEN THINK ABOUT SEX

Mark Mason

What? Men think about sex?
Er, yes. All the time. Once every six . . . sorry.
Where was I?

What *men* think about sex?
All men think about sex. Even John Betjeman
spent his twilight years musing 'I wish I'd had more sex'.
Twentysomethings Tim and Rob are determined
not to end up thinking the same.

What men *think*? About Sex?
They think it's more Gary Lineker than Desmond Morris.
It's all about scoring. And for Tim and Rob, it's all about
scoring with gorgeous new-girl-at-work Clare Jordan.

What men think *about*? Sex.
The Clare Jordan Five and Three-Quarter Feet
Handicap Stakes works as follows: Tim has to seduce
five women whose names start with C, L, A, R and E.
Rob's quintet has to be bedded in places beginning
with the same letters. He who bares wins . . .

What Men Think About Sex
is the male *Sex in the City* – the outrageously
funny novel that puts the man
back into romantic comedy.

THE CATCH

Mark Mason

Kirsty is everything Sam has ever
wanted in a woman – gorgeous, funny, bright,
brilliant company. But when he asks her to marry him,
he doesn't reckon on her response.

The catch

For Kirsty to accept him, he's going to have to
prove he's marital material. Over the next twelve weeks,
she's going to give his behaviour points (though she
won't explain how he scores them). If his total
hits 1000, then she'll be his bride.

However much Sam does the ironing or
puts the loo seat down, his tally resembles Norway's
in the Eurovision Song Contest. Where's he going wrong?
Assembling a sex war cabinet of best mates George
and Pete, Sam is no closer to an answer . . .
until the addition of work colleague Amanda
opens his eyes to the surprising truth about
what really winds women up . . .

Other bestselling Time Warner Books titles available by mail:

☐ What Men Think About Sex   Mark Mason   £5.99
☐ The Catch   Mark Mason   £6.99

The prices shown above are correct at time of going to press. However, the publishers reserve the right to increase prices on covers from those previously advertised without further notice.

TIME WARNER
BOOKS

TIME WARNER BOOKS
PO Box 121, Kettering, Northants NN14 4ZQ
Tel: 01832 737525, Fax: 01832 733076
Email: aspenhouse@FSBDial.co.uk

POST AND PACKING:
Payments can be made as follows: cheque, postal order (payable to Time Warner Books), credit card or Switch Card. Do not send cash or currency.
All UK Orders   **FREE OF CHARGE**
EC & Overseas   25% of order value

Name (BLOCK LETTERS) . . . .

Address . . . .

. . . .

Post/zip code: . . . .

☐ Please keep me in touch with future Time Warner publications

☐ I enclose my remittance £ . . . .

☐ I wish to pay by Visa/Access/Mastercard/Eurocard/Switch Card

Card Expiry Date | | | | | Switch Issue No. | | |